STRIP GIRL

'Yes!' he grunted. 'That's you, Sarah, my dirty little tart . . . my filthy dirty fat little tart.'

She was in orgasm, his words burning in her head, her resistance gone, and she was babbling, the awful words breaking through a final pang of despair.

'Spank me, Giles . . . spank my bottom . . . spank me, punish me . . . oh shit!'

Her orgasm exploded in her head, the awful admission only making it stronger, and she was still rubbing at herself and sobbing in ecstasy as he pulled his cock from her vagina and finished himself off all over her upturned bottom cheeks and in the crease between. As she sank slowly down onto the bed she could feel his spunk trickling down into the tight dimple of her bottom hole, for the second time. He spoke.

'You are such a trollop, Sarah. I think I'm falling in love with you.'

STRIP GIRL

Aishling Morgan

First published in 2006 by
Nexus
Thames Wharf Studios
Rainville Rd
London W6 9HA

www.nexus-books.co.uk

A catalogue record for this book is available from the British Library.

Typeset by TW Typesetting, Plymouth, Devon
Printed and bound by Clays Ltd, St Ives PLC

ISBN 0 352 34077 0
ISBN 978 0 352 34077 1

One

Sarah Shelley made a final set of marks with her brush, setting the number 302 on the heavy paper. Céleste du Musigny was nearing perfection: her face was a poem in confidence and poise, her hair a cascade of utter black, her body lean and taut and strong, her breasts high and firm, her hips in exact proportion, her legs pure grace. No, Céleste was perfect, projecting so strong a character from the page that Sarah found herself blushing for having drawn her heroine naked, and was immediately amused by her own reaction.

'I apologise, Mademoiselle du Musigny,' she said, once more dipping her brush into the Indian ink. 'I shall correct my error at once.'

She was smiling to herself as she began to paint on an elegant black cocktail dress. Naturally it was unthinkable that Céleste should be nude, even in the presence of her creator. Céleste was dignified. Céleste was refined. Céleste would have absolute confidence in her body, but would go naked only in the presence of some favoured lover, strictly off the page. Sarah, on the other hand, might very well go naked in the presence of Céleste. In fact it would be appropriate, save that to paint naked would have felt foolish.

A few practised strokes and Céleste was decent; more than decent in fact, she was exquisite. Sarah paused, wondering if it was possible to make Céleste anything other than exquisite. Perhaps drawing 303 should show Céleste in sloppy jeans and an ink-stained top, more like her creator? No; while Sarah felt a complete ragamuffin in her day-to-day work clothes, Céleste would come out as the darling of Montmartre and the *Rive Gauche*. Besides, it would be an unthinkable liberty to attempt to spoil Céleste's poise.

Smiling for her own fanciful imagination, Sarah sat back, sucking her brush and immediately regretting it as she realised it was still full of ink. A moment with tissues and water, and she returned to her thoughts. Yes, Céleste was perfect, at last. All Céleste needed was a buyer.

As always, the thought of her efforts to make her art work commercially broke Sarah's mood. Rising, she went to the kitchen and began to make coffee. Mak had left everything out before going to work, including the milk, which she returned to the fridge after just a moment's hesitation. Refusing to play mother to her flatmate was all very well, but sour milk was vile. It looked like being another hot day too, with the sky pure blue save for a pair of vapour trails and the air hazy above the rooftops of Stepney.

Céleste, Sarah reflected, would never have lived in an attic flat in Stepney, except possibly while working undercover as the moll of some dangerous East End gangster. If Céleste condescended to live in London at all, she would choose Chelsea, or somewhere equally expensive and fashionable, not Stepney. Céleste would have money, and accept it as her natural due, while Sarah had nothing, less than nothing when her student loan was considered.

The faint clack of the letterbox broke into what was threatening to become a depressing train of

2

thought. Sarah continued to make her coffee, telling herself she was not going to rush downstairs and see if it was the post, a resolve that lasted only as long as it took to scatter a spoonful of granules onto the milk. Knowing full well that she was almost certain to find nothing more interesting than a pizza menu, and that if it was post it would more than likely be a bill, she hurried down.

It was the post, mostly for the other flats, but two for her, one announcing that she might be the winner of an improbably large sum of money, the other a large brown envelope in her own handwriting. Unable to wait, she tore the flap open, as hopeful as ever despite knowing full well it was likely to be yet another rejection. The heading immediately caught her eye: Ehrmann and Black, the parent company for the *Daily Watch* and a host of other publications. Below was a brief note, from a Mr Bowle, the arts editor, asking her to come in for an interview.

Settling herself against her pillows, Sarah waited until the bang of the flat door signalled the departure of Mak. There was no hurry at all, with the interview at twelve o'clock and the Ehrmann and Black building just a ten-minute train journey away, yet she was already full of nervous tension. Everything was ready, her portfolio laid out the night before, along with the blue summer dress she had decided to wear. Looks shouldn't count, but they did, and Mr Bowle would undoubtedly spend his days surrounded by smart fashionable young women, women who didn't have awkwardly large breasts and the sort of bottom that had earned her the nickname 'medicine ball' at school. The blue dress made her look rustic, but that was an improvement on bulbous.

Not that she was actually fat, but if anything her slim waist only served to make her bust and bottom look bigger still, a source of constant embarrassment since puberty. Where most women could maintain as much or as little sexual display as they pleased by adjusting clothes and make-up, for her there was little option but to show off, and with a figure about as unfashionable as it was possible to imagine.

She gave a low sigh as she pushed the bedclothes down. The top she'd worn to bed had ridden up around her waist, leaving her hips and belly bare, with just plain white panties to cover the bulge of her sex. She was certainly feminine, that much was undeniable, as was her response to her own body, a blend of embarrassment and arousal. On impulse she pulled her top higher still, up over her breasts as she turned to see how they looked in the mirror. Big.

Actually, 'big' didn't really do her justice. Her breasts were absurdly large, two great heavy balls of female flesh, like something from the most primitive forms of male-oriented pornographic art, or some of the Japanese Manga she had seen at college, in which every woman had huge pneumatic breasts. Yes, she could very well be a Manga girl, holding her top up for the inspection of some eager Japanese boy with floppy black hair and a huge straining erection.

It was rather a nice thought, although not one she'd have admitted to, even to Mak, for all that he was forever trying to persuade her to be more adventurous. That was all very well for him. He was gay, and highly attractive, which allowed him to go through multiple partners the way she went through cups of coffee. Even had she wanted to, that sort of behaviour was impossible for a woman, and yet ...

... and yet it would be nice, even if only as a fantasy. It seemed to be a standard of Hentai Manga that the girls needed to be coerced in some way, or to display themselves by accident and have the boys take advantage. That would be good, because it would take the choice out of her hands. Perhaps she would tear her dress on the way to the station, right off, so that she'd be left standing in the street in her panties and bra? It would be unbearably embarrassing, unthinkable in real life, but as a fantasy, rather nice.

Sarah closed her eyes, wondering if she should masturbate, and telling herself that it was a good way to make herself feel less tense. Not that there was any real choice, as she was already stroking her breasts as she imagined going bare in public. Her bra would have to come off, obviously, and her panties, because naked was best, naked in the street as she made a pathetic and futile effort to cover herself, with just two hands and her pussy, boobs and bottom to conceal, leaving her no choice but to have something showing.

Another image came to her, a common one from the coy US girlie art of the 'fifties; a pretty girl, exposed in public, trying in vain to cover the V between her legs and a pair of large breasts. It was just the sort of image that had always fascinated her, as did any erotic art that focused on female embarrassment. Usually the girls' sexual characteristics were exaggerated, but with her body it really would be impossible to cover herself, her hands hopelessly inadequate to the task.

Feeling a little silly but strongly aroused, Sarah got up, peeled off her top, pushed her panties down to the level of her thighs and struck the same pose in front of the mirror. It was hopeless. She could cover her sex, but the bare spread of her hips and her lowered panties made her look both lewd and vulnerable. Her breasts were barely hidden at all, even the outer curves of her big areolae showing a little.

It felt right though, for her, stripped of her dignity in public, maybe even as a punishment, so that men could enjoy the view, maybe women too, maybe Céleste du Musigny. After a while – but only when everybody had enjoyed a good stare – somebody would give her a coat, not out of gallantry, but so he could get the introduction he needed to seduce her. He'd take her back to his flat, give her a large glass of whisky, and ... and talk her into showing her breasts again, into taking his cock out, into sucking it, into letting him rub it in her cleavage.

Sarah lay back on the bed, her eyes closed, her fingers busy on her nipples and between her thighs. Her panties were in the way and she pushed them further down, to her ankles, but not off. They felt better down, keeping her exposure constantly in her head as she masturbated. Maybe he would be Japanese, some firm confident young businessman from the city. Oh yes, he'd soon have her panties down and his cock between her breasts, just like in the cartoons, fucking her cleavage and coming all over her face.

She cried out, wriggling her body into the bed as her pleasure rose towards orgasm. Her legs came up and her ankles came wide, deliberately rolling herself up with her panties stretched as taut as they would go, imagining them pulled down to show her off the way she was, her huge breasts flaunted, her thighs spread to display her sex as her fingers worked in the slippery folds, even her bottom open to expose the rude pink anal star between her cheeks.

All it needed was a man, a man obsessed with her body, so urgent for her he couldn't control himself as he worked her over with his cock. He'd put it in her mouth, between her breasts, between her bottom cheeks, rubbing on the slippery little hole between, definitely in her pussy. She'd beg him not to do it inside her, and in return he'd whip it out at the last moment, to pull himself off all over her face and in her mouth.

At the thought of having a man come in her face Sarah's body arched in orgasm. Her mouth came wide in a wordless cry of ecstasy as she imagined gout after gout of sperm erupting into it and over her chin and neck and cheeks, and she was rubbing hard at her sex and clutching her breasts as shock after shock ran through her, until at last it was over. She subsided, to lie shivering on the bed, her eyes still shut, her mouth curved up in a contented smile. It had been good, one of her best, and if there was a trace of disappointment that it had been alone, again, then she knew full well she would have done it anyway, partner or no partner. Masturbation was nice, harmless and free and deliciously naughty.

Sarah took her time in the shower, then drank a leisurely coffee as she dried herself and brushed her hair. After twice changing her mind, she settled on the simple blue dress she'd chosen before, pulled on over a brand new lacy set of bra and knickers, chosen simply because they made her feel good, and to be dressed as well as possible went some tiny way to calming her nerves.

She found if hard not to fidget on the train, and it was worse still as she waited in the marble reception hall of the Ehrmann and Black building. Everybody looked exactly as she had feared, brisk yet relaxed, casual and confident. Even the receptionist looked as if she had stepped straight out of an expensive public school, svelte and impossibly neat, with her blonde hair up and her chic black skirt suit a perfect fit.

Every time the lift doors opened Sarah found herself looking around with a nervous smile, but none of the people who emerged took the slightest notice of her, until two men stepped out and stopped, glancing around. One was perhaps fifty, bald, with a thick brown moustache, his shirt front pushed out by a substantial paunch, his suit expensive but crumpled. The other was much younger, and taller, with untidy straw-coloured hair and an amused expression on his rather bony face. He was in shirt sleeves.

Sarah stood up, promptly dropped her portfolio but managed to catch it before the contents could spill out, and turned her smile to the two men. The older one noticed, his eyes flicking from her face to her chest and back in a manner with which she had become all too familiar. And it seemed to her that his smile held more than a little of the lecherous as he stepped towards her.

'Sarah Shelley?' he asked, extending a hand. 'Hugh Bowle. Pleased to meet you.'

She took it, a somewhat clammy grip, but a strong one. The other man had also approached and his eyes had also moved to her breasts, but with frank appreciation rather than the shifty manner of his companion. He favoured her with a wolf-like grin.

'Giles Compton-Bassett,' he said, his voice exactly the upper class drawl she had expected. 'I'm your writer.'

'My writer?' Sarah queried. 'But I haven't been interviewed yet, and –'

'No need for that,' Bowle interrupted her, starting for the main doors. 'Come and have some lunch.'

Sarah hesitated, wondering what she should do with her portfolio, but Hugh Bowle's hand was already on her hip, just high enough not to be actively objectionable, and she was being steered across the foyer. Giles Compton-Bassett fell into step on the other side of her, speaking as they stepped out into the plaza, with the towers of Canary Wharf rising up on three sides.

'I'm hoping you'll work with me anyway, but your art's great, so unless you turn out to be a complete flake, you're in.'

'Um . . . thank you, I think,' Sarah managed, 'but I thought my story . . .'

'No good, doll,' Bowle cut her off. 'All this feisty woman spy stuff is out. Too 'nineties. Anyway, who's to spy on, except the towel heads, and they'd spot her in a minute. We need something classic, something the boys'll get off on.'

'Have you read the old Wicked Wanda cartoons?' Giles asked.

'By Ron Embleton, yes, I know his work,' Sarah admitted, 'but wasn't that a bit – a bit –'

She wanted to say 'dirty', but she knew it would be the wrong word. It seemed that she had the job, or at least a job, a job as an artist. Something she had been working towards for years now seemed to have dropped in her lap. Everything was happening too fast for her to take in, but she finally managed to find the right words.

'– a bit too strong for the *Watch*?'

Bowle laughed.

'It's not for the *Watch*, darling. I'm arts editor for the adult division of our magazines group.'

'You know,' Giles put in unnecessarily, '*Hot Gun*, *Slap and Tickle*, *Lusty Legs*, *Black Booty*, *Boobie Babes* . . .'

'You'd be great for *Boobie Babes*,' Bowle cut in. 'I'll introduce you to Sid if you like? Earn a bit extra, you know?'

He nudged her and winked, but she was too confused to respond in any way at all. They were heading towards a pub on the far side of the plaza, the Wharfingers, a building of dirty yellow brick completely out of keeping with the steel and concrete all around them but presumably there long before any of it had been built. Bowle continued as they walked, either unaware of her embarrassment and confusion or indifferent to it.

9

'We're launching Giles' strip in *Hot Gun*, that's our lead title, with a circulation just under a hundred thou, which puts us number two in the market. Your girlie character is just perfect, smart, sassy and sex on legs. We pay twelve hundred a page, split sixty/forty, fixed rate, so I can't go higher, but it's a double-page spread.'

Sarah had been bracing herself to tell them there had been an awful mistake, but stopped. Forty percent of two thousand four hundred pounds made nearly a thousand pounds, and if *Hot Gun* was monthly it would be enough to live on. She would be more than just a paid artist, but a full-time professional artist, her dream since childhood, and the magazine sounded masculine and crude, but not actually pornographic.

'So that's forty percent of two thousand four hundred, and that's monthly?' she asked cautiously, sure there would be a catch.

'Sixty percent, darling,' Bowle corrected her.

'The artist gets the lion's share,' Giles added. 'Takes so much longer, you see.'

Sarah responded with a weak nod, although she was making frantic calculations in her head. By the time they reached the door of the pub she had realised she would be on around three hundred and fifty pounds a week, more than she had dared to dream she could earn for anything, let alone to draw. She was in a daze as the men led her inside, their words barely penetrating, so that when they reached the bar Bowle had to repeat himself.

'I said what's yours, darling? Oi, earth to Sarah, what are you drinking?'

'Sorry,' she said quickly, 'I was miles away. May I have a glass of white wine, please, if that's okay?'

'Have a bottle if you want, doll,' he offered, patting his pocket. 'It's all on expenses.'

'Thank you,' she answered, and found herself face to face with Giles Compton-Bassett as Bowle pushed in to get to the bar.

Somebody pushed against her back, making her stumble forward so that her breasts squashed against him, bringing the blood to her cheeks and a flood of stammered apologies to her lips.

'Any time,' he answered her, 'any time at all. Shall we go outside?'

'Yes, why not?' Sarah answered, and allowed herself to be shepherded through the throng.

A single table remained empty and they took it, Sarah speaking as soon as she had sat down.

'Could you tell me how this works, and exactly what you want me to draw? I'm new to this, and I thought I'd be doing my own strip, you see.'

'I write the story and you illustrate it,' he answered her, 'but I promise not to be a pain about it. Your character will make a great heroine and I don't want you to change her at all.'

'Thanks. How about her name? I'd like to keep her as Céleste du Musigny if that's okay?'

'Fine. I see her as a New York . . .'

'Paris.'

'Paris then. Yes, Paris is good, too many things are set in New York. She's a Parisienne socialite, from one of the old aristocratic families, single, independent, maybe a trifle bored by fashionable life.'

'Exactly,' Sarah agreed, now warming to Giles despite what seemed to be entirely unconscious arrogance and his habit of talking either to her breasts or over the top of her head, 'which is why I wanted her to be a spy.'

'A detective is just as good,' he went on, 'but she only takes on the really top-flight cases.'

'Fair enough,' Sarah answered, 'I can cope with that. Um . . . how sexual does it have to be?'

11

'Enough to keep Hugh happy,' he told her. 'I'm more in it for the story, but she needs to end up at least half naked in every issue, preferably tits out, because that's what Hugh likes. Do you know what they used to call him when he was deputy photographic editor? Boobman Bowle. We need a bit of bum too, and the odd flash of pussy.'

'Oh,' Sarah responded, colouring slightly, but more at the thought of drawing Céleste bare for public consumption than at Giles' language.

Bowle had come out, carrying a tray with a pint of dark ale, a bottle of white wine frosted with condensation, two glasses and a large cigar. He put the tray down and began to set things out on the table. Sarah poured herself a glass of wine, immediately taking a badly needed swallow. She had expected a formal interview, with one or more intimidating men or women examining her work and asking difficult questions. Instead, both Hugh Bowle and Giles Compton-Bassett could hardly have been more casual, and simply assumed she was competent from the samples she'd originally sent in. It was hard to take in, and yet as she began to study the menu, the men had already begun to talk cricket, Giles with his glass lifted halfway to his mouth and Bowle waving his cigar to illustrate his remarks, as if the vast change they'd brought to her life was completely ordinary.

Three hours and two bottles of wine later, they were still talking, although Sarah had contributed only the occasional word to the conversation. For the rest of the time she had concentrated on the food and let herself dream, imagining all the situations she would create for Céleste and how it would feel to be able to call herself an artist and not immediately feel it was a mere pretence. She was drunk, having taken more than her fair share of the wine, and already feeling sleepy when Bowle finally pulled himself to his feet.

'Better get back, I suppose,' he yawned. 'Do you two want me to put another bottle on the tab?'

'Why not?' Giles answered before Sarah could decline the offer. 'A nice meaty Aussie Grenache this time, I think.'

Bowle made a vague gesture of acceptance and moved off towards the pub door.

'I really should be getting back,' Sarah said, knowing that another couple of glasses of wine would put her to sleep.

'Oh,' Giles answered. 'Where are you headed?'

'Stepney,' Sarah told him.

'I'll walk with you if you like,' he offered. 'Maybe we can go over the story?'

She nodded as she got to her feet, wishing she didn't feel quite so unsteady, but enjoying the warmth of the alcohol. Halfway through the meal Hugh Bowle had produced a contract from his pocket, a scruffy thing she had merely glanced at before signing, not really caring what it said as long as she had the job. That had been the final stamp on her happiness, which had been growing ever since, along with alcohol-fuelled confidence. She could do the job, she was sure of that, and Céleste would just have to put up with going naked now and then. After all, she had created Céleste, so the bossy cow could jolly well do as she was told.

'I've got plenty of plots,' Giles was saying as they started across the plaza, he swinging the open bottle of red wine in one hand, 'but we need to kick off with something special. We need cars, we need guns, we need sex, lots and lots of sex.'

'It's the first issue that's really going to matter,' Sarah responded.

'Exactly,' he agreed. 'We get one chance to grab their attention. Lose that, and we're fucked. Now this is how I see it. The last two frames we have Céleste taking off her bra, then a rear view with her thumbs in her knickers, like she's about to take them down. That's the sort of thing *Hot Gun* readers will love.'

'I've never read it, I'm afraid,' Sarah admitted, with the image of Céleste doing what was effectively a striptease hot in her mind.

'Take it from me,' Giles assured her. 'They love that stuff. Tease 'em, that's the knack, but you've got to give it all up in the end, or they feel cheated. So what do you reckon?'

'I'm sure you're right about what they like,' Sarah answered him, 'but shouldn't we start at the beginning? What's the story about? Why is Céleste undressing?'

'Who cares? No, really, I've got a great plot.'

'Hang on a second,' she broke in. 'I've got an even better idea. Céleste is rich and bored, so we know she's only really playing at being a detective, and she only works for her own sort of people, and they like to employ her because she's one of them.'

'Yes.'

'So what if she does the crimes herself, then sets somebody else up to take the blame? That way we can make her wicked instead of good, which is much more fun!'

Sarah knew it was the wine talking. Sober, she would never have dared make such a suggestion, but where Céleste represented everything she looked up to normally, a few glasses of wine and she always found herself resenting her creation. Now was no different, and Céleste had grown as much in her mind during the last few hours as since she'd first put a 4B to paper with nothing more than a vague idea of how the ideal woman should look.

For a moment she thought Giles didn't like the idea, as he had walked on in absolute silence, but when he did speak there was a trace of awe in his voice.

'Brilliant! You are brilliant, Sarah! Yes, we can make her a villainess. She should be a villainess, shouldn't she, with that sultry look. Hang on, are you after my job?'

'No,' Sarah promised, flushing with pride at his words.

'Just joking,' he assured her, and as they left the plaza he put an arm around her shoulders.

Sarah felt herself start to melt. She was drunk, she had the job she'd wanted since childhood, and a tall handsome man was walking her up the street, just the sort of man she always assumed could not possibly be interested in her. Giles was obviously interested, and not just in her bust either. He appreciated her talent as an artist, her imagination too. When he bent to kiss her there was no resistance, her mouth opening to his just as eagerly as his to hers. Only when his fingers began to inch up the back of her dress did she gently push him away, thrilled by the prospect of being exposed in the street but completely unable to go through with it, drink or no drink.

Giles merely laughed and put his arm around her again as they walked on. Sarah snuggled into his side, blissfully happy, and in no doubt at all about what was going to happen once they reached her flat. He was no different, if anything more urgent still, hailing the first cab they saw. Ten minutes later they were in her room, kissing as his fingers found the zip to her dress, and this time she didn't stop him.

A shiver ran through her as the zip was eased down, and again as the dress was pushed gently off her shoulders. She wriggled her arms free and it fell

15

loose at the front, exposing the cups of her bra. A trace of embarrassment hit her for her sheer size, sure he would think her clumsy, inelegant, overweight, but the expression of rapture on his face told a very different story.

'Christ, you're big!' he breathed, and he buried his face in her cleavage, his hands already fumbling at her bra catch.

It came loose, her cups fell free as he pulled at them and her chest was bare in his face. She closed her eyes as he took hold of her breasts, squashing them around his face, his tongue flicking out to lap at her cleavage, groping and kissing at her in a reverent ecstasy. Her hands met in his hair, holding his head to her chest, even as she was eased gently back onto the bed with him on top of her. She let her thighs come open, accepting him between them, only for him to stand back, take hold of her dress and pull it up off her hips and legs with one smooth motion.

He stood looking down at her, his face flushed with arousal, the tip of his tongue flicking out briefly to moisten his lips as he shook. Sarah found herself giggling, flattered and surprised by the sheer intensity of his lust for her. Taking her breasts in her hands, she gave them a meaningful squeeze, deliberately showing off as she spoke.

'I thought you said Hugh was the one who liked big breasts.'

'He is,' Giles answered, and reached down to take a grip on her hips.

Sarah gave a squeak of surprise as she was turned over, face down on the bed and bottom up to Giles. For a second time she felt a flush of embarrassment for the sheer expanse of lace-covered bottom she was showing to him, and for the second time his reaction was not at all what she would have expected. He gave a low moan and his hands were in the waistband of her panties, pulling them slowly down, to expose her bottom inch by inch, until the whole plump globe was naked to him and Sarah was shivering hard for her exposure.

'Beautiful,' he sighed, 'so beautiful. God, I love a juicy fat-bottomed girl.'

Sarah opened her mouth to say something, despite feeling more flattered than offended, but all that came out was a squeak of shock as Giles abruptly buried his face between her bottom cheeks, and a second as his tongue found the hole between them, not her sex, but her anus. She began to protest, but all that came out was a sigh. It felt too good, far too good, and before she could stop herself she was pushing her bottom out to let him get his tongue deeper still.

He obliged, lapping between her cheeks and burrowing his tongue in up the tiny hole, until Sarah was gasping and clutching at the bed. Part of her wanted to tell him to stop, that it was too dirty, and she was scared he might try and bugger her. Still no words would come as she was licked and fondled, his hands now on her bottom cheeks, squeezing and pulling them wide to make them spread in his face.

When he did finally stop, Sarah wriggled around to find him standing over her, a long pale cock protruding from his fly into one grasping hand. He looked ready to come, and she reached out, her mouth open to take him in, wanting to suck and not wanting it to be over too quickly.

'Let me,' she offered as she took his cock, moving to sit on the edge of the bed.

His erection felt hot and hard, and it was good to be sitting in front of him in nothing but shoes and half-pulled-down panties, tugging his cock towards her naked breasts. He watched, letting her pleasure

17

him, but only for a moment. Then he had taken her breasts in hand, moving forward to straddle her and squeezing both fat globes around his straining erection.

'Christ, you're big,' he muttered as he began to fuck her breasts, 'so big, so fucking big. I want to spunk all over your fat tits, Sarah, I . . . no, I have to do your bum. Roll over, Sarah, you fat little tart, show me that gorgeous big bum . . . let me spunk over your cheeks . . . I'm going to spunk, Sarah, do it . . . roll over!'

'Look, I . . .' Sarah managed, but he'd already pushed her down on the bed and was tugging at her body.

With more than a touch of chagrin she let him do it, rolling her over onto her belly and humping her bottom up as he straddled her legs. She felt used, and yet it was good, to be manipulated so rudely, lying face down on the bed, her panties around her thighs, her bare bottom stuck up for a man to come over, his cock jerking in his hand as he masturbated over her.

'You – you can have me, Giles,' she managed. 'Go on.'

His answer was a grunt as he pressed the head of his cock down between her bottom cheeks. Sarah pushed her hips up, her mouth wide in ecstasy as she savoured the exquisite moment before she was penetrated, something she hadn't had for so long, and wanted so badly. His cock pressed down, the head firm and rubbery between her cheeks, too high, pressing not to her sex, but to her spit-wet anus.

'No!' she squealed, her ecstasy breaking as she realised she was going to be sodomised. 'No, Giles, not up my bum, you dirty pig!'

'Oh go on,' he answered her, still pressing down, with her bumhole spread out to his helmet. 'Go on,

Sarah, please . . . I want to fuck your big bottom . . . please?'

'No,' Sarah protested, trying to wriggle away, 'I'm too tight, I've never . . .'

'Oh you're virgin,' he sighed, 'a virgin bumhole, and such a big fat bottom, a fat girlie bottom . . .'

'Giles, look, I don't . . .'

'Oh Sarah, please. You need it . . . you need your bottom fucked, you really do, oh shit!'

As he'd been speaking he'd been pulling at his cock, with the head still pressed between her bottom cheeks. Now he'd come, filling her gaping anus with spunk, and more splattered between her cheeks as he began to fuck in her bottom slit, grunting and gasping, calling her a tart and a slut as he finished himself off in his own mess.

'You dirty pig!' Sarah managed as he finally stopped rutting her bottom.

'Yes, I know,' he sighed, his weight slowly settling on her body as he went limp. 'Good, isn't it?'

'Could you get off, please?' she asked, not wanting to admit how nice what he had done to her had felt.

'Sure,' he answered, and rolled off to lie spread-eagled on the bed with his slowly deflating cock sticking up from his trousers, the pale skin slippery with come.

Sarah ignored the urge to go down on him and suck him clean, making for the bathroom instead. His come felt sticky between her cheeks, a sensation at once disgusting and compelling. In the bathroom she locked the door, telling herself she wasn't going to do it, but knowing she was. Sure enough, as she pushed a double piece of loo paper between her cheeks to wipe herself it took a single touch to her slippery half-open anus and she had given in.

Her leg came up, cocked over the loo with her bottom stuck out in a thoroughly rude position that felt just right. She dropped the paper and began to tease the slippery little hole, her eyes already closed in bliss. He really had used her, fucking her breasts and licking her bottom hole, so uninhibited and so dirty, licking it to get her ready for a buggering. It didn't bear thinking about, and yet her finger was up that same rude hole, made slippery with come.

A soft choking cry escaped her mouth as she began to finger her anus, pushing deep and imagining his cock in the same tight dirty hole as her resistance snapped completely. Her other hand went to her sex, clutching herself back and front as she masturbated, with her breasts bouncing to the urgent rhythm as she thought of what he'd done to her, and what he might have done.

He'd stripped her to her panties and pulled those down too. He'd licked her bottom hole and fucked her cleavage. He'd called her a tart, a fat tart, so insulting and yet so arousing. He was right anyway. She was a tart, a fat little tart, exactly what he'd called her, a dirty description for a dirty girl, a girl who liked to be stripped and used, a girl who enjoyed the feel of a man's spunk between her bottom cheeks as she masturbated with one finger up the tight little hole he'd threatened to invade.

She cried out in ecstasy, pushing a second finger in, to hold herself open as she clutched at her sex. Why did she have to be so prissy? Why had she refused? It felt so good, and it would have felt so much better to get herself nice and juicy and let him push the full length of his cock deep up her bottom, to bugger her, to sodomise her, to fuck her fat girlie bottom.

Sarah bit her lip hard to stop herself screaming, determined that he wouldn't hear and realise how badly she had disgraced herself. Yet, even as she came slowly down from orgasm without having given herself away, there was regret mingled with her relief.

Two

A week after having sex with Giles Compton-Bassett, Sarah discovered that he had a girlfriend called Rebecca who rode horses and lived in the country. It came as no great surprise, being more or less what she would have expected of him, and her disappointment was tempered by more than a little relief. She knew full well that if the encounter had blossomed into a relationship she would have ended up with his penis up her bottom.

The information came from Hugh Bowle, dropped casually into a telephone conversation when she rang to thank him for lunch and check the details of the work she was supposed to do. In the excitement of sex, she and Giles had got no further with the plot, and when a letter arrived from him she had no idea whether or not he had taken up her suggestion, or if his apparent enthusiasm had merely been a device to get her into bed.

As she walked to her art desk with the unopened letter she was telling herself that whatever it said, she would take a professional attitude, turning in her best possible work well before the deadline in two weeks. Picture 305 lay on the desk, Céleste du Musigny in a fox-fur wrap and a long black coat, walking down an imaginary promenade beside the Seine.

'Are you ready for your public, Mademoiselle du Musigny?' Sarah asked as she pushed a thumb into the flap of the envelope.

Céleste's haughty stare made it quite clear that not only was she ready, but that it was the height of impudence for Sarah to even ask. With a wry smile on her face, Sarah tore the envelope wide and peered inside. There were four pieces of paper, neatly folded, which she opened: a plot outline, that and nothing more, no mention of their brief but dirty escapade, not so much as a thank you. Sarah drew a sigh as she began to read.

The story was entitled 'The Versailles Resurrectionists', and was a bizarre mixture of the Gothic and the macho, involving Céleste's attempts to divert money stolen from a South American drugs cartel to her personal use. The plot was weak in places, but Sarah quickly found herself drawn in, both intrigued and somewhat repulsed by Giles' imagination, which seemed to feed the male schoolboy fantasies of war, and horror, and sex.

For all her qualms, she could see that the story would be popular with the readers of *Hot Gun*, and also that it suited Céleste, or at least, the wicked sexually provocative Céleste she had described to Giles while she was drunk and horny. The original Céleste was rather a different matter, as she certainly would never have behaved as she was supposed to for the opening of the story, stripping to bribe a man in some imaginary French records office.

It was frankly sordid, and yet it not only provided a lot of artistic scope but fitted in with what she'd agreed with Giles. The first page would be a single frame, showing Céleste in all her perfection, about to cross a street in Paris towards an official-looking building, along with the title and a box of script to explain what was happening. Sarah knew it would be easy, and a scene she might very well have drawn herself.

The second page was to be more elaborate, showing Céleste entering the office of a man Giles described as 'a really greasy frog-eater, a bit like Hercule Poirot but gone to seed'. Céleste's request, to access the files of a wealthy South American businessman who had died in a car crash, was obviously outrageous, and as she made it she was supposed to lock the door, open her jacket, lift her bra, tug up her skirt, and start to take down her panties.

Céleste would never, ever have done anything of the sort, let alone for some greasy middle-aged civil servant, and yet despite her horror, Sarah could already see the frames in her mind. The first would show the official beyond Céleste's shoulder, seated behind a desk, a florid balding man with a nasty little moustache and a triple chin, a single bead of sweat trickling down the side of his face as he dabbed at his forehead with a monogrammed handkerchief. The second would show Céleste as the man would see her, cool and poised and beautiful, her mouth set in a small knowing smile, one hand to the middle button of her immaculately tailored jacket. She would already be speaking, making her proposal, the text of which would continue for the remaining frames, showing four close-up details in sequence: Céleste opening her jacket, pulling up her bra, lifting her skirt, and finally, drawn from behind, with her thumbs in the waistband of a pair of lacy black panties already half down as she prepared to expose her sex to the official, and her bottom . . .

. . . to one hundred thousand dirty-minded British boys; plumbers and builders, lorry drivers and cabbies, IT specialists, city-types, dirty old men, smug little perverts like Giles himself, all of them staring at Céleste's tiny perfect buttocks. It was impossible. Céleste wouldn't do it, couldn't do it. Never would she even think of giving such a display to a man, any man, to do a rude little striptease, like something out of the cheapest sort of peep show. Sarah might, it would be such a turn-on, but not Céleste, not ever.

Sarah had put the paper down on her art desk, Céleste now staring at her in haughty accusation from drawing 305. There was no mistaking the meaning in those hard French eyes. Sarah was about to prostitute her art and, frankly, it was just what Céleste might have expected of the fat little English tart with her oversized breasts and her big wobbly bottom. Céleste was right too.

'Sorry, Céleste,' Sarah muttered, turning drawing 305 face down on the desk.

Telling herself to stop being silly, Sarah selected a fresh piece of paper and set it in front of her. Choosing her preferred 4B pencil, she began to sketch, first picking out the lines of the street and Céleste for the first frame in rough, and writing the title in, splashed across the top in a bold curve. With the drawing begun, and fully formed in her mind, it seemed to flow from her fingers. The building took shape, a fine piece of the Parisian architecture she spent so long practising, complete with crossed *tricolores* just to make sure the readers knew exactly where they were. Céleste took shape, stepping out into the road with one perfectly shaped leg extended, her face a little turned, as if she was checking the traffic but really to get a better angle.

Only when it came to the second page did Sarah pause, reluctant to draw the lines that showed Céleste opening her jacket, from which there would be no going back. Again she told herself not to be silly, that

24

she had drawn Céleste naked over three hundred times, always beginning with a pencilled nude before adding clothes, a technique she'd used since college. Yet her hand seemed to have frozen, and she knew full well it was not the same. Céleste's naked body was a thing of beauty, something Sarah was privileged to see, had to see, but only as an old-fashioned lady's maid had to see her mistress. To draw Céleste naked in front of a particularly greasy civil servant and for the readership of *Hot Gun* was another matter entirely, rather as if that same lady's maid were to pull her mistress' knickers down in public.

There was only one thing for it. Putting aside her pencil, Sarah left the flat and made her way to the local off-licence. The owner greeted her with a friendly nod and she crossed to the fridge, opening it to take a bottle of the cheap Italian white she usually drank, then changing her mind. She was now earning money, and could afford better. After rejecting Champagne because Céleste drank it and red because Giles Compton-Bassett did, she bought the most expensive bottle of Australian Chardonnay they had cold and returned to her flat.

Just two glasses of the rich heady wine and she was ready to face her task. Taking up her pencil once again, she began to add detail to the outlines she had drawn, first Céleste, one hand on the button of her perfect little jacket. Now it was easy, but she left the face blank, sure Céleste's expression would still come out as haughty distaste instead of the wanton look Giles expected. Instead she started on the official, and as her pencil flickered over the page he grew quickly, his face sleazier even than she had imagined, his bulging chins more corpulent, his moustache more distasteful. By the time she'd finished he was far and away the most sexually repulsive man she had ever drawn, yet without an obvious deformity or anything to suggest that he might not be real.

Sarah was smiling as she sat back to reach for the bottle, placed safely out of the way of her art desk. With her chair pushed clear she poured herself another glass, filling it to the brim and sipping at the cool wine as she admired her half-finished drawing. It was going to be good. No, it was going to be great. It would drive men to distraction, and leave them desperate for next month's issue and the full exposure of Céleste's bottom. Certainly it would drive Giles to distraction. He would probably be straight round, begging to fuck between her tits and rub his cock in her bottom slit, and to sodomise her . . .

No, that was wrong. He was with Rebecca and probably loved her, despite what had happened. They'd just got drunk together, that was all. Besides, Rebecca would certainly be far more attractive, probably a natural blonde, wholesome and athletic from all the horse riding, with perfect skin and a full yet well-proportioned body. Sarah drew a heavy sigh and took another swallow of wine. It really wasn't fair. Why did she have to be so unreasonably voluptuous, so inelegant?

As she returned to work, the last of her qualms were gone. She sketched in the remaining outlines and began to add detail: the folds of Céleste's open jacket, the lacy borders to her bra, the contours of her high upturned breasts, the tight neatly formed bottom cheeks. All of it flowed from Sarah's pencil, until only Céleste's face remained. One more glass of wine and Sarah had completed that too, achieving a look so suggestive, so lewd and yet so fine and strong that had the official been real he would either have fled or come in his pants.

Sarah found herself giggling at the thought. Maybe that was what had happened, and Céleste would find that she'd let her panties down for nothing? The idea appealed to her sense of humour, just to imagine Céleste's consternation when she found she'd gone further than she had to for such a horrid man. Having come, he probably wouldn't give in to her demands either, which would be funnier still.

He had to give in, of course, or the story would be over before it had started. Maybe the greasy official wouldn't be so easy? Maybe he had a wife at home who sucked his morning erection for him, a duty one of Sarah's past boyfriends had demanded of her? If so, then Céleste might have to go a lot further. He'd make her strip nude. He'd make her get into naughty provocative poses, undignified poses, cupping her breasts in her hands and sticking her bum out to show her sex from the rear, and her anus.

Sarah's hand had gone between her thighs almost without realising it. Her pussy felt soft and sensitive beneath her jeans, with the material pulled tight against her sex lips. The temptation to rub herself off was overwhelming, and she decided to do it before common sense could get the better of her. A last swallow of wine and she had pushed her jeans and panties into a tangle around her legs, opening her knees to let her fingers touch her bare sex. Another quick adjustment and her top and bra were up, spilling out her big breasts into her hands.

She closed her eyes, toying with her nipples as she decided what she should come over. It had to be Céleste, no question, Céleste stripping for the greasy French official, Céleste with her precious silk panties held down for his inspection, Céleste nude and posing for him as if she were no better than some girl in a peep-show, a cheap peep-show.

One hand went to her sex, rubbing between her lips. She was wet, soaking, ready for penetration and ready for orgasm. A sigh of pure pleasure escaped her lips as she began to masturbate more firmly, bringing herself up towards climax as she imagined the scene. Maybe just posing wouldn't be enough for the Frenchman? Maybe he'd make her go down on her knees for him? She'd protest, oh how she'd protest, but she'd do it. She'd have to, because Sarah was going to draw her like that, stark naked under the Frenchman's desk, with her bare bottom sticking out behind as she sucked on his big dirty cock . . . as he made her take his enormous balls in her mouth . . . as he spunked in her open mouth and forced her to swallow what he'd done . . .

Sarah came to climax, long and hard, her body tense beneath her fingers as she pinched at her straining nipples and snatched at her clitoris. It lasted as long as she held the image of Céleste's beautiful face, open mouth full of spunk and more dribbling down her nose and cheeks and eyes to ruin her immaculate make-up, a perfect vision that broke only with the faint bang of the front door.

Worried that Mak might be back from work, Sarah quickly adjusted herself, pushing her sticky fingers into her mouth before struggling her clothes up her legs. Gay he might be, open-minded he might be, but to have him catch her with her top up and her panties around her ankles while she masturbated over her own creation would still be deeply embarrassing.

The distinctive creak of the stairs confirmed her suspicions as she was still struggling to do up her bra catch. She felt a twinge of panic as the door opened and Mak's voice called out, and she left the last two hooks undone as she quickly pulled her top down. Jerking her chair forward, she had just picked up her pencil and turned to greet him as he entered the room.

'You're off early,' she said.

'No,' he answered, 'just my normal shift time. Now that is good!'

'Thank you,' Sarah answered him, glancing at the clock to discover that she had been drawing for nearly four hours without a pause, completely lost in her work.

Mak leant closer, shaking his head in admiration as he took in Sarah's finished pencil sketch, then smiling.

'That guy looks like one major creep,' he said. 'Don't tell me your Céleste is going to blow him?'

'No,' Sarah answered. 'I think she's just going to give him a flash, but it's not really up to me. It's the writer's job to decide what happens.'

'This Giles guy, Mr Poshboy?'

'That's the one.'

'So he's into gross guys getting it with cute girls, huh?'

'Mr Bowle says the readers prefer the men not to be too attractive. They've done a survey apparently.'

'That sounds like straight guys all right, but Giles is public school, yeah? You'd think he'd like a nice young man, with smooth, smooth skin and arse cheeks so tight he could crack nuts between them.'

'I think that's just you, Mak.'

'Me and a lot of other guys, hon, and take if from me, if this Giles was at public school he either likes to take it up the arse or he'd like to take you up the arse.'

'That's just your wishful thinking,' Sarah replied, forcing a laugh and looking the other way to hide her blushes.

'That's how it is,' he assured her. 'So what, how long did this take you? You hadn't started this morning.'

'I didn't even have the story this morning,' she answered. 'Four hours, maybe a bit less.'

'And all you've got to do is ink it in?'

'That takes just as long, maybe longer, and I'll probably add some more detail as well.'

'So what, two to three days' work and that's you done for a month. I wish I had your talent, that's all!'

'I suppose I'm just lucky,' she said, 'and it's not easy to find work.'

'Maybe,' he answered, 'but while you're in the money you're doing well. You know you can claim all this stuff on expenses, yeah?'

'Reasonable expenses, yes,' she began, but he cut her off.

'Expenses like research. What you ought to do, honey, is go to Paris.'

As she stepped onto the platform of the Gare du Nord, Sarah was still having difficulty taking everything in. She had been to Paris twice before, as a child and while at college, but never alone and free to do as she pleased. There was still a dream-like quality to her new life, and it had been growing stronger every moment she was in France, so much so that as she began to walk down the Rue La Fayette she was expecting to pass Céleste du Musigny at any moment.

There were plenty of dark elegant women about, although none quite so perfect, and yet before she had gone too far she had seen three men who might have passed for the greasy official, and several others who were likely to provide future inspiration. Occasionally she would stop to sketch; a likely looking face, a detail of architecture, or a prospect down one of the long straight avenues. As she worked she was constantly hoping that somebody would ask her what she was doing, preferably a handsome and quintessentially French young man, so that she could explain that she was no mere tourist, but a professional artist. Ideally he would then offer to be her guide, take her to dinner at some little-known but fine restaurant, and come back to her hotel for a night of thoroughly rude sex.

Nobody approached her, but her good mood held as she walked. Hugh Bowle had been delighted with her artwork, and also the story. His only criticism had been the title, which he felt was too obscure for the readership. Giles had attempted to stand his ground, but after a few minutes' debate they had agreed to call it 'The Graverobbers' instead.

The change had meant Sarah had to rework the entire first page but, as she spent so much of her time drawing by choice that was no real hardship. Her second effort had been accepted without need for further change, which had left her with more than a fortnight free for her planned trip. Now she was here, and so pleased to have arrived that she continued to walk despite the weight of her bag, putting it down only when she stopped to draw.

She knew exactly where she was going; first to the Latin Quarter, where she would choose a hotel, then to the Île St. Louis, where she would fulfil one of her ambitions by drinking a glass of wine in a café beside the Seine. She had always pictured Céleste living there, in a beautifully appointed flat overlooking the river, directly across from Notre Dame.

Entranced, she walked across the Pont du Carrousel, stopping again and again to sketch. Not feeling financially secure enough to afford one of the grand hotels along the river, she selected a family establishment among the smaller streets behind the great Quais, secured a room, showered, and changed into a light dress more suitable for the weather than the jeans and top she had worn on the train. Despite being tired, she went out again immediately, walking along the Seine in a dream.

After crossing to the island she selected her café immediately. It was perfect, exactly as she had pictured it, and more. The round wooden tables were set out on a broad pavement, each with two chairs of a quality unthinkable in any British outdoor café. There was even a waiter in a white apron, whose nod carried exactly the amount of arrogance she would have expected as he took her order, while a young man was selling paintings by the road just a few yards away.

The waiter brought a half-carafe of white wine and a glass, again exactly as Sarah had pictured. She poured the wine and took her first sip in reverent ecstasy, absolutely content with her circumstances, which might well have been from one of her own drawings. Even her fellow customers were just as they should have been: a middle-aged couple as alike as twins, small and fussy and prim; a haughty *grande dame*, eighty if she was a day yet perfectly straight and composed as she sipped from a tiny glass; and three students in berets deep in discussion over the worth of Émile Bernard and drinking what appeared to be absinthe. There was even an immaculate young woman walking with purposeful grace along the pavement, a woman who looked exactly like Céleste du Musigny.

Sarah smiled for her own overactive imagination, and yet the woman was like Céleste, extraordinarily like Céleste, tall, beautiful, immaculately dressed, and with a manner of absolute confidence and unquestioning self-belief that would have shamed a Roman emperor. She was also heading directly for Sarah's table, and her expression was anything but friendly.

Alarmed and confused, Sarah began to rise, only to sit down again as the woman reached her, speaking immediately, in English, perfectly clear yet with an unmistakable French intonation, exactly as she imagined Céleste's voice.

'There you are, you little brat. You have a lesson coming to you.'

'I – I'm sorry, I think . . .' Sarah stammered, and stopped as the woman reached down to take a firm grip on her wrist. 'Hey!'

'Get up!' the woman snapped, and pulled hard, jogging Sarah's table and upsetting the carafe.

Sarah rose, still babbling questions and apologies, but unable to resist the woman's tone of command. Some of her wine had splashed her dress, the rest pouring onto the pavement, but she didn't protest, too shocked and astonished to react. The woman sat down on Sarah's vacated chair, her grip so hard it hurt.

'Across my knee with you, you dirty little monkey,' the woman ordered.

Sarah found herself drawn forward, unable to find the will to resist as she was put into the threatened position, laid across the woman's lap with her bottom lifted towards the other customers.

'What – what are you doing?' she wailed

'What am I doing?' the woman retorted. 'I am preparing you for a spanking, that is what I am doing. Is that not how one deals with a mischievous child, with a spanking?'

'A spanking?' Sarah gasped as her arm was twisted high and tight into the small of her back. 'You can't do that! You can't spank me!'

The woman didn't answer, but lifted one knee, bringing Sarah's bottom up into full prominence.

'You cannot do this!' Sarah squealed, wriggling in the woman's grip as panic took hold. 'You just can't!'

33

'I can, and I will,' the woman said, and Sarah's dress was being lifted.

'No!' Sarah screamed as the seat of her big white panties was revealed. 'You can't do this to me, you just can't! You can't!'

'I rather think I can,' the woman answered, perfectly calm, and with just a trace of amusement mixed in with the authority of her voice as she tucked Sarah's dress up. 'How typically English, no taste at all in lingerie. Still, I think we had better have these down, don't you?'

This time Sarah's scream was wordless. She tried to snatch at her panties, determined to keep them up, but she couldn't get her hand past the woman's body. A thumb had already been pushed into her waistband, and it was being done. She went wild, kicking her legs in every direction and thrashing her body, full of rage and frustration, threats and pleas and denials spilling from her lips. It was impossible, outrageous, unthinkable, that she should have her panties pulled down for punishment at all, never mind in a public place. Yet that was exactly what was happening, the taut elastic of her waistband moving inexorably down across her bulging cheeks, showing more and more chubby pink flesh, until it was all out, the full spread of her bare bottom on show to the other customers, the artist selling paintings, a dozen passers-by, the waiter.

'So I cannot take down your knickers?' the woman remarked, her voice as calm as ever and now openly amused. 'Yet they are down, no? And your naughty bottom is showing to the world. I suppose you think I cannot spank you either?'

'No, please,' Sarah sobbed. 'You can, but don't . . . please don't . . . please?'

'You are to be spanked,' the woman responded, 'and that is that. For what you have done, how could it be otherwise?'

34

'What have I done!?' Sarah begged.

'Ho, ho, she asks what has she done?' the woman answered. 'She knows what she has done, but perhaps she does not think it is wrong, yes? Perhaps she thinks it is *amusant, oui?*'

The tone of the woman's voice had changed, showing anger for the first time, and as she spoke she began to lever Sarah's panties further down.

'Look, no . . . you don't need to take them off! No!' Sarah babbled, but they were already around her knees, then her ankles, then free, hanging from one leg.

'Ah but I do,' the woman was saying, 'they must be off, I think, for you to feel proper shame, for you to understand, maybe, how I felt in front of the disgusting Monsieur d'Orsay! There, how does it feel, with your cunt on show to the crowd?'

As she spoke, the woman had hooked her leg around Sarah's and pushed her knee up, spreading the helpless girl's thighs and exposing everything between. Sarah gave a scream of raw agonising shame as the most bitter sense of frustration she had ever known hit her. She began to fight, writhing on the woman's lap, striking out with her single free fist, screaming incontinently, and yet nobody took any notice, least of all the woman, though there was a rising note of anger in her voice as she continued to speak.

'Not that you could know how it is for a lady, you, who are so common, such a – a whore!'

The first smack landed on Sarah's bottom, adding a squeak of pain to her clamours of protest and misery. Now it was done, her bottom not merely bare but being smacked, spanked in public, and as her cheeks began to bounce her raging frustration and self-pity redoubled. The woman talked as she spanked, her voice now loud and thick with anger as she belaboured Sarah's wobbling bottom and pumping thighs.

'You, you dare, to sell your art, to sell me! To make me bare for Monsieur d'Orsay! Never will you do this, never, do you understand me, you little whore, you filthy thing, you *salope . . . cocotte . . . branleuse . . . maquerelle! Putain de merde!*'

The spanking had become furiously hard, reducing Sarah to a wriggling squirming mess, her trapped arm and leg jerking helplessly, the free ones flailing wildly, with her lowered panties waving from her ankle like a flag. Her tears had come, spattering the pavement beneath her with every smack to her bottom, along with mucus from her nose and spittle from her mouth, while her attempts to speak had broken to a desperate pig-like squealing punctuated with yelps of pain.

'Be quiet!' the woman snapped, calmer now that she had expended some of her fury on Sarah's still dancing bottom. 'And will you hold still? This is just, as you must know, so at least try to take it like a lady. Now listen, *petite salope*, you will not draw me bare for your dirty English boys to make *branlette*, not again, not ever, and if you show me so in front of that foul *roué* d'Orsay, I swear I will have you make a pipe for him, you know, you understand? To suck his dirty penis! So, do you understand, Sarah?'

The spanking had become a little less hard as the woman spoke, allowing Sarah enough control over herself to gasp out a reply despite her pain and bewilderment.

'Yes . . . anything, anything you say . . . please just stop!? Please?'

She was whimpering, her entire body now prickled with sweat and aching, her bottom a glowing ball

36

behind her, hot and nude and fat, spanked, a word she couldn't get out of her head, that came back again and again as she lay sobbing across the lap of the woman who was punishing her, spanking her, spanking her in public. A choking cry escaped her lips at the sheer shame of it, then a gasp and a fresh squeal as the smacks grew firmer, this time delivered as glancing blows across the meat of her buttocks, to make them wobble and part, adding the exposure of her anus to her woes.

'Do you mean it?' the woman asked. 'I wonder. Perhaps you think you do, but perhaps you will change your mind later, yes? Understand this then, Sarah, that if you ever disobey me, if you ever insult me so again, this will happen again, and more. Am I understood?'

'Yes!' Sarah wailed. 'Yes, yes, yes, now stop spanking me, please!'

'A few more, I think,' the woman answered, 'just so, to be sure you do not forget.'

As she spoke she began to spank as hard as she could once more, full across Sarah's already blazing bottom. Yet it no longer hurt; the pain was gone, her cheeks were now warm and receptive, and with a stab of humiliation stronger even that what had gone before Sarah realised that the spanking was making her aroused. A fresh scream erupted from her mouth at the horror of what was happening to her, and another as a smack caught her low and she felt the air cool on the wetness of her sex.

They could see, a dozen or more people, not only her bare red bottom, but that the spanking had made her wet. It was worse even than the hideous shame of being given a spanking in front of them, to have them know that she was more than simply the victim of the awful woman's retribution, but that she found having it done to her exciting. She screamed again, unable to bear her own emotions, and again as a voice sounded from behind her, in French, cool and imperious.

'*Ça suffit, Céleste. Elle est si turbulente.*'

Sarah gave a heartfelt gasp as the spanking stopped. The elderly lady had spoken, a trace of irritation in her voice, indifferent to the bare-bottom punishment but annoyed by the victim's squeals, which added yet more outrage to Sarah's boiling feelings. A last gentle pat was applied to her bottom and her wrist was released, so suddenly that she tumbled off her persecutor's lap, to sit her hot bottom down in the puddle of spilt wine on the pavement, where she stayed, too dazed even to pull up her panties.

Three

Sarah fled Paris that same afternoon, pausing only to collect her things from the hotel before she took a taxi to the Gare du Nord. Only on the train did she begin to calm down, with the emotional reaction of what had been done to her slowly giving way to the reality, which made no sense. She had been spanked, with her bottom bare and in a public place, yet not one of the numerous bystanders had reacted, save to watch, and in the case of the elderly woman to complain about the fuss she was making.

It was not normal behaviour, not for the French, nor anybody else, of that she was sure. Somebody, surely, would have stepped in to rescue her, or at least made some sort of protest. Nobody had and, as she had run off, clutching her smacked bottom with her panties still hanging from her foot, the only reaction had been a quip from one of the students, who seemed merely to be amused by her fate.

Only one explanation seemed to fit: that the entire episode had been set up, and that she had been spanked as some sort of horrible joke, although that raised as many questions as it seemed to answer. One thing at least was obvious. She had not in fact been spanked by Céleste du Musigny. However real Céleste seemed at times, she had no existence outside

39

Sarah's head. Yet the woman had been so like Céleste that Sarah might have drawn her, not only in appearance but in personality too. Therefore whoever was responsible had to know about Céleste, which narrowed the possibilities down to only a handful of people.

Her parents, her college friends and her brothers could be discounted immediately. None of them would have dreamt of playing such a degrading joke on her, and nor could they possibly have known enough about the plot, nor to coach 'Céleste' on what to say during the spanking. It had to be somebody who had seen the cartoon, which meant Mak, Giles Compton-Bassett and any number of people at *Hot Gun*, or maybe even the whole Ehrmann and Black organisation.

Mak had a wicked sense of humour, and had occasionally shocked Sarah with the things he did with his gay partners, such as making them gag on his erection, but she couldn't imagine him setting her up to be spanked and humiliated in public, let also in Paris and by a Céleste du Musigny look-alike. Hugh Bowle was far more likely, and just possibly could have done it, yet the joke seemed far too abstract for his sense of humour. If photographs had been taken of the punishment, then maybe, but she was fairly sure they hadn't.

That left Giles Compton-Bassett as by far the most likely candidate, and she could just imagine him enjoying the joke, even if he didn't get to see. Or maybe he had seen? Maybe he'd watched the whole thing? He could easily have been observing her from a distance, or maybe even from a seat inside the café. She would never have noticed, especially once her panties had been pulled down, after which she'd been in far too much of a state to realise even if he'd been right behind her.

Yes, it really had to be Giles, although it was hard to see how he'd have set it up. Not that it mattered how. What mattered was that he had. Yet what could she do? If she accused him to his face or complained to Hugh Bowle, he only had to deny it, and no doubt he would find it extremely funny to hear her explain what had happened.

One point jarred, which was that throughout the punishment 'Céleste' had repeatedly told Sarah not to do exactly the drawings Giles wanted. Possibly he might find some perverse amusement in having the woman give the orders when he knew that Sarah had no choice but to follow his script or lose the job, yet he didn't even know she had any qualms about showing Céleste nude. Possibly he wanted her out of the job and might have guessed her weakness, but if so he had chosen a highly bizarre way to go about it, while his attitude suggested the exact opposite.

No better solution presented itself, and Sarah arrived back in London still puzzled, but also determined, not only to find out what was going on, but not to be a victim. There would be no visits to therapists, no allowing some psychologist to delve into the intimacies of her mind until she felt worse than she had done in the first place. Definitely there would be no admission of the darkest and most shameful secret of all, that towards the end of the spanking she had been highly aroused.

It wasn't something she wanted to think about, but it was very hard not to – the way her entire bottom had seemed to glow; the way her whole being had seemed to focus on her smacked cheeks and embarrassingly wet sex; the way it had felt to be held helpless across the woman's knee with her bottom exposed to others. All of it was so shameful it hurt to think about, but also so arousing it made her want to

41

get on her knees in something close to the same rude position she'd been punished in and bring herself off under busy fingers.

To do so, she knew, would be the final admission that she was exactly what the woman had called her, a slut and worse, and yet every time she let the words slip into her mind it sent a little shiver through her body. Common sense told her that no woman could possible enjoy the utter degradation of being spanked, let alone in public, and yet common sense had never really had very much to do with her sexual needs.

A week passed during which Sarah was left to herself. Most of the people she knew thought she was in Paris, Mak excepted, and she had found herself unable to tell him the truth, making up an excuse about feeling ill instead. Knowing, and dreading, that left alone she was all too likely to end up with her bottom in the air and her fingers down her panties, Sarah spent her time out sketching, shopping, or just walking, anything to keep her mind off how she had felt across the woman's knee.

Not to think about it at all was impossible, but the best distraction was to try and work out what had really happened. Her mind invariably ended up running in circles, with Giles Compton-Bassett at the centre. The more she thought about it, the more she was certain he had to be involved, save only for the apparent contradiction of the woman's orders. Giles had been rude with her, and yet the words the woman had chosen during the spanking suggested exactly the sort of contempt Céleste would have shown Sarah had the circumstances been real, and which Giles knew nothing about.

She even looked up those of the French ones she could remember, including *salope* (slut) and *cocotte* (trollop), neither of which were flattering, as they implied that Sarah's behaviour was equivalent to selling herself. *Putain de merde* was the same but stronger, with a disgusting literal translation of 'shitty little whore' or 'dirty little tart', but for sheer humiliation *turbulente* was worse still, which compared the fuss Sarah had been making as she was spanked with a temper tantrum from an unruly child which, given the circumstances, was so grossly unfair it left her open-mouthed with indignation.

It also confirmed her supposition that the entire thing had been set up. No woman, she was sure, could have behaved with such callous disregard for another's feelings, at least, not without being well paid and coached by somebody with a mind as perverse as it was scornful of modern values. Save for the occasional moment in the most fevered and private of her own sexual fantasies, the attitude was beyond anything she could imagine anyone taking, with one possible exception: Giles Compton-Bassett.

She finally managed to screw up her courage enough to confront him. When she rang he sounded genuinely pleased to hear from her, without either the suppressed snigger or guilty tone she had been expecting to pick up. Using the pretext of another story conference, she asked if he would meet her at the weekend in a city wine bar and he agreed.

Hot Gun came out the next day, and Sarah's copy arrived in the morning post. Despite what had happened, her fingers were trembling with anticipation as she opened the big brown envelope, and she immediately turned to the back where she knew their cartoon would be. Just one look at it put a smile on her face, and she stayed as she was, standing in the open doorway as she drank in every familiar detail. Whatever her qualms about the rude scenes she was

43

required to draw, she knew she would continue, the pride swelling within her as she admired the first published example of her own artwork acting like a euphoric drug.

She was still on a high two days later as she took the short tube ride into the city, which she knew was going to make dealing with Giles Compton-Bassett a great deal easier. He would have no choice but to listen as she explained clearly and calmly that she knew it was him, and that what he had done was totally unacceptable. She would then ask for an apology and, if it was forthcoming, promise to take no further action as long as nothing of the sort ever happened again. Once that was sorted out she would point out that their relationship was strictly professional, and that there was no place for childish pranks. Their afternoon of sex together didn't need to be mentioned at all, although it was probably a good idea to drop Rebecca's name into the conversation to show that she knew.

Her resolve lasted all the way to the Two Quart Jug, where they had agreed to meet. It was on the first floor, looking out over the street, and Giles had chosen a window seat, in which he was sprawled, as lazy and handsome and louche as ever. The idea of admitting to him that she had been given a bare-bottom spanking, even if he already knew, suddenly seemed no more feasible than giving him the details of her latest visit to her gynaecologist. He raised a hand in greeting and pushed the open bottle of red wine across the table towards a second glass.

Sarah sat down, completely lost for words as she poured herself some wine. Giles gave no more sign of what he surely knew than he had on the phone, his voice absolutely casual as he addressed her.

'How was Paris?'

'Great, thank you,' Sarah managed.

'Did you pick up any good material?'

'I've got lots of sketches, yes.'

'Great. So what do you reckon? I think we need to get the story going a bit, but we can't let them down, so maybe the first page is Céleste du Musigny giving the guy in the office a blow-job . . .'

'Monsieur d'Orsay.'

'The guy?' Giles answered without a flinch. 'That's a great name, but does he really need one? I only put him in as somebody she could get dirty with.'

'Whatever you think,' Sarah answered, 'but does she have to go that far with him? Couldn't she just show off a bit?'

'I can't see it,' Giles answered, 'not the way you've drawn him. He's a bastard, and he'd want his pound of flesh. I've already cleared it with Hugh, and while you can't show him erect, or her with him actually in her mouth, you can show him limp and make it very obvious she's down on him. Weird, I know, but we have to follow the guidelines.'

Sarah made to speak, thinking of the woman's threat, only to dismiss her worries as ridiculous. There was no Monsieur d'Orsay to have his cock sucked, just as there was no Céleste du Musigny to force her to suck it. Giles continued, apparently as oblivious to her feelings as ever.

'So that's plenty of good smut on page one. Have her kneeling, okay, with plenty of bum on show, and with women's bodies we can include every detail. Then on page two we need to move on. She's sucked the guy off and she's got the information she wanted. We know that, so we don't need to see her reading the files or anything. I don't think we need to know how she's picked up the threads of the case either, so let's go straight to the graveyard.'

'We should link the scenes,' Sarah said, forcing herself to think about the cartoon instead of being held down by the hair as she was forced to take the greasy Frenchman's erection in her mouth. 'Maybe with a frame cut diagonally, the top half showing her reading a paper with the dead man's name on it and the bottom half showing the gravestone.'

'You're right, that works,' Giles responded after just a moment's hesitation. 'So what does the reader know? That Céleste is prepared to suck some guy off to get the information . . .'

'Which means it's extremely valuable,' Sarah put in.

'I don't know if our readers will see it that way,' Giles answered her. 'Hugh says it's important to cater to our readers' fantasy lives, so girls ought to give out blow-jobs without making too big a deal over it.'

'Not Céleste,' Sarah pointed out, 'and certainly not with Monsieur d'Orsay. In fact I can't really see her doing it for anything.'

'Every woman has her price,' Giles answered.

'Who says?'

'Hugh Bowle. It's one of the maxims I have to work to when I'm writing.'

'That's outrageous!'

'It's not like that. We can't show sex without consent, so the girl either has to be horny or getting something out of it. If it's just a lot of people shagging we're not going to get much of a story, are we?'

'I suppose not,' Sarah admitted. 'Maybe I could have a couple of text boxes, to say how much is supposed to be in the coffin?'

'Okay,' Giles agreed. 'So we have Céleste looking at the grave, and then in the last frame you show that she's got a shovel in her hand. We don't have to have a sexual ending twice.'

46

'She wouldn't dig it up herself!' Sarah protested.

'No? Why not? She's supposed to be tough.'

'Yes, but grave robbery, on her own? She just wouldn't, and anyway, it would be really hard work. She'd hire people.'

Giles thought for a moment, then spoke again, more enthusiastically than ever.

'Yes. You've got it. She hires three guys, real scumbags, gets them to do the dirty work, then pins it on them while she walks off with the money. That's a great opening! She'll have to fuck the three scumbags, obviously –'

'Three men?' Sarah broke in, appalled. 'And why do they have to be so awful?'

'To keep the readers' sympathy with Céleste,' Giles explained. 'Anyway, guys love to see a posh girl getting it from some real dirtbag, and we've got to keep the sex up. It doesn't have to be completely gratuitous. Maybe that's the way she sets them up or something, but we don't need to worry about that yet. So what about that last frame? I know, we don't have to waste that d'Orsay guy. He might have grown suspicious, and followed her. We can show him with his face half lit and her in the background standing by the grave. How's that?'

Sarah managed a weak nod, horrified by what she was going to have to draw, and yet unable to deny that the readers would appreciate it. Giles had sat back, looking thoroughly pleased with himself. She still wanted to talk about Paris, but if he did know anything then he was an amazingly good actor, while if he didn't he was the last person in the world she wanted to discover what had happened.

'Have you ever been to Paris?' she tried.

'No,' he told her. 'Maybe I should sometime. So, what are you up to for the rest of the weekend?'

'This and that,' she said cautiously. 'I'll probably start doing some rough sketches. I suppose you'll be seeing Rebecca?'

She felt the question was well timed, seemingly casual yet dropped into the conversation just when he might have been bringing it around to them getting together again. This time there was no mistaking the surprise in Giles' answer, although there was none of the guilt Sarah would have expected.

'Rebecca?' he answered. 'I am, actually. She's coming up tomorrow and I promised to take her to the V&A. Would you like to come?'

Sarah didn't answer, very surprised indeed at his response. He was bold, but to want to introduce his girlfriend to another woman he'd slept with seemed extraordinary, unless he got some sort of strange kick out of it, which seemed all too likely. She wasn't going to put up with it.

'I'm not sure I should,' she finally answered him. 'It's not very fair on her, is it, after . . . it's not very fair on me either, after we . . . you know, after we slept together.'

'I don't understand,' he said. 'Why would that bother you, or Rebecca?'

'Oh come on! Even if you've got an open relationship or something she's not going to like you going with me behind her back, is she?'

'An open relationship?'

For a moment he looked seriously alarmed, then he laughed as he went on.

'She's my sister!'

'Rebecca is your sister?' Sarah managed as the blood rushed to her face. 'Oh, I thought – I mean, Hugh said –'

Giles laughed.

'What, so Hugh Bowle told you I was with Rebecca? That's hilarious! When they met he was all

48

over her, and I was still trying to land a contract, so we pretended we were together so he'd leave her alone but not take it out on me. So he told you?'

'Yes.'

'Did he ask you out?'

'No . . . yes, sort of, but I was going to be in Paris. You don't think he'd have tried anything, do you?'

Giles laughed again, louder than before.

'Boobman Bowle? With a chest like yours? Come on, Sarah, don't be naïve.'

'That doesn't mean he fancies me, just because I'm . . . busty.'

'Oh no? You could be a slimy green alien with a pair like that and he'd still be after you. You're twice the size of Rebecca, and he was drooling all over her.'

Sarah was blushing, and a primly dressed woman at the bar had turned them a disapproving look. She refilled her glass to cover her embarrassment, then his as she spoke.

'I'd love to come then. Shall I meet you there?'

'Why not come over to my flat now? The tube goes straight there.'

There was no mistaking the implication of his offer. Sarah hesitated, trying to sort out the tangle of her emotions. It had been good before, dirty, rather humiliating, but good. If Rebecca was only his sister, and if he hadn't been responsible for her spanking, then there was no reason not to. There was no denying the attraction he held either, both physically and for the way he was completely open about his desire for her. Yet there was still a nagging uncertainty. She struggled for a clever question, something that would make him give himself away.

'What does "turbulent" mean?' she asked, giving the crucial word a French intonation.

'Turbulent, do you mean?' he repeated, using the English form and sounding mildly surprised at her apparent ignorance. 'Rough, maybe, like a patch of rough water on a river.'

'No, I mean in French,' she told him.

'The same, I suppose,' he answered her, 'but if you're thinking of putting any French in the text, don't. The guidelines say we should assume our readers are monolingual.'

Sarah nodded, now almost convinced that Giles was not the guilty party, but if not him, then who?

'You didn't answer my question,' he said.

Sarah smiled.

'Let's go.'

'One day . . .' Giles said as his hands traced the shape of Sarah's hips.

'No,' Sarah answered, trying to sound firm while resisting the urge to purr, 'but you can lick.'

'I intend to,' Giles told her, and he took hold of the waistband of her jeans.

Sarah closed her eyes in pleasure. She lay face down on the bed of his South Kensington flat, which he rented for almost nothing from his wealthy parents. Her top was off, her naked breasts squashed out beneath her chest. Giles was straddling her legs, and had been massaging her neck and back, a little clumsily, but in a firm and methodical way that brought her arousal gradually higher. She could guess why he was being so patient, in the hope of bringing her to such a state that she'd allow him to sodomise her, but she was determined it wouldn't work. Her bottom hole was simply too tight, but that didn't mean she couldn't enjoy his attention.

'I think you'll have to undo them,' she said softly, lifting her bottom to let him get his fingers to the button of her jeans.

His arms came around her, clasping her bottom to himself, and Sarah sighed as he found the button. It felt good to be undressed by him, liberating yet pleasantly naughty too, for what he wanted to do. Her zip was pulled down, the front of her jeans tugged open. His fingers pushed in at the sides, catching hold of not only her jeans but the big white panties she had on beneath. She sighed again as he began to pull, enjoying the feel of having her bottom stripped, the full swell of her cheeks now a pleasure as they were exposed, to be massaged, stroked, fondled, licked, spanked . . .

Sarah caught herself just in time, before the awful words could spill from her lips. It was wrong, completely inappropriate for a woman to be treated in such a way, and far worse for her to actively want it. Yet there was no denying the desire in herself as he eased down her jeans and panties to bare her bottom, a desire to have the cheeky globe smacked, and smacked well, while he sat on her, telling her she was a naughty girl, punishing her, just as the woman calling herself Céleste had done.

'Relax,' Giles told her.

Her bottom had tensed automatically at the thought of what could be done to her, but she forced herself to do as he asked. His hands were already on her cheeks, massaging gently, and as she went limp he pulled them apart, stretching out her anus. Sarah felt a flush of shame for being exposed so rudely behind, but only for a moment, before his face pushed in and his tongue was burrowing up the tight little star between her cheeks. It was still shameful, or she was telling herself it was, but it felt too nice for her to want him to stop, far too nice.

She bit her lip, trying not to whimper for the pleasure of having her bottom licked, but quickly giving in. He had her stripped, everything that mattered showing, and his tongue was up her bottom, helping get her ready for his cock to be put inside her for their first fuck, even if not where he really wanted it. She was ready, completely, and she could hear him pulling at his cock as he licked.

'You can fuck me,' she sighed, worried that he might decide to come over her bottom and leave her disappointed.

'Yes, please,' Giles answered, pulling his face from between her bottom cheeks.

Sarah made to roll over, but he was still on her legs and had taken her by the hips, lifting. She let him, telling herself that it wasn't really undignified to allow him to have her in doggy position for their first time, although it would have been nice to kiss as she was entered. With her bottom up he wasted no further time, pushing himself to her so that his cock was briefly wedged between her cheeks before taking it in hand and pushing it down.

For one awful moment Sarah thought he was going to force her anus whether she liked it or not, and then the rounded bulb of his helmet was pressing to her sex, opening her, pushing in, sliding deep, a sensation so good she cried out in ecstasy. As he began to fuck her she was wondering how she'd managed to go without it so long. She began to push back, rocking her body on his cock as her excitement rose. Her breasts began to swing to the rhythm, her nipples rubbing on the woollen bed cover. His hands closed on her hips, holding her firmly as he fucked her, to make her gasp and pant, already desperate to come.

She snatched for his pillows, pulling them under herself and reaching back for her sex almost in the same motion. Her hand found his cock, feeling the hard slippery shaft as it moved in and out of her body, with his heavy balls slapping on her knuckles. There was a man in her, fucking her, knowledge enough to send a shock of ecstasy through her, quite separate from the physical sensation of him moving inside her. Her fingers pushed in between her sex lips and she began to rub, her inhibitions completely gone as she masturbated herself with him in her.

'You bad girl!' Giles gasped as he realised what she was doing.

'Tell me,' Sarah gasped, 'tell me what a bad girl I am.'

Giles gave a low dirty chuckle and changed his grip, moving his body up a little so that he was pumping into her from above, with his lean hard belly smacking on the upturned meat of her bottom.

'You're very bad,' he puffed, 'really bad. How bad can you get, wanking while I fuck you? You dirty girl . . . you bad dirty girl . . . you dirty little tart . . . you fat-bottomed dirty little tart . . . you –'

He broke off, gasping. Sarah began to rub furiously hard, sure he would come at any moment, too far gone to care if he did it up her, but desperate to get there first. He'd called her a bad girl. He'd called her dirty, a dirty tart, a fat-bottomed dirty little tart. It was true. She wanted it to be true, and as she started to come his pace picked up inside her, his body smacking down on her bare bottom, just as if he was spanking her. Yes, it was perfect. That was what should happen to bad girls, bad girls like her. She should be spanked and fucked, put on her knees with her big bottom bare and spanked and fucked.

'Yes!' he grunted. 'That's you, Sarah, my dirty little tart . . . my filthy dirty fat little tart.'

She was in orgasm, his words burning in her head, her resistance gone, and she was babbling, the awful words breaking through a final pang of despair.

'Spank me, Giles . . . spank my bottom . . . fuck me, spank me, punish me . . . oh shit!'

Her orgasm exploded in her head, the awful admission only making it stronger, and she was still rubbing at herself and sobbing in ecstasy as he pulled his cock from her vagina and finished himself off all over her upturned bottom cheeks and in the crease between. As she sank slowly down onto the bed she could feel his spunk trickling down into the tight dimple of her bottom hole, for the second time. He spoke.

'You are such a trollop, Sarah. I think I'm falling in love with you.'

Four

The rest of the weekend passed in a rosy haze, spoilt only by the memory of what had happened in Paris and the obligation to admit, if only to herself, that it had not merely excited her physically, but that it represented the deepest craving of her sexuality. Giles seemed not to have noticed, and possibly he hadn't, as he'd been on the edge of orgasm himself when she spoke the fatal words.

Whether he'd heard or not, he had clearly decided that now they were officially together he could give free rein to his obsession with her bottom, taking every opportunity to squeeze her, stroke her, pinch her, fondle her, pull down her panties, lick her, and beg to be allowed to teach her to accept his cock in her anus. Embarrassed but also flattered, Sarah accepted everything except the final surrender, and had soon begun to wonder if asking him to put her across his knee and apply a few firm swats to her bare cheeks would be so bad after all.

She couldn't bring herself to do it, the act of asking simply too undignified for her to accept, yet she found herself hoping he would do it anyway, taking the decision out of her hands. He didn't, but his constant attention to her cheeks made it harder and harder to resist, building an awareness of her bottom as the focus of her sexuality and making her feel appreciated as she never had before. There was no lack of attention to her breasts either, and by the evening she was wandering around the flat stark naked, not merely unconcerned, but actively enjoying being in the nude.

The following morning they were still in bed, with Sarah giving Giles' cock a leisurely suck as he fondled her bottom cheeks, when the bell rang. Sarah was blushing pink as she ran for the bathroom, but Giles was as casual as ever, merely slipping on a dressing gown before going down to answer the door and let his sister in. Rebecca proved to be rather different to the picture Sarah had built up of her; she was red-haired rather than blonde, pretty, with a splash of freckles across her nose, nearly as tall as Giles and notably busty. She also shared something of her brother's character, friendly and open, yet self-confident to the edge of arrogance and apparently indifferent to the opinions of others.

Rebecca stayed for dinner, which Giles put together with a skill that surprised Sarah. Afterwards they walked her to the tube, Sarah kissing Rebecca goodbye in a way that felt entirely natural before she descended to the Piccadilly Line. Left alone with Giles once more, Sarah wondered if he would want her to spend another night, and if she should do so rather than getting back to her flat.

'Time for bed?' Giles asked as his hand moved down from her waist to the swell of her bottom.

'Why not?' Sarah answered, smiling as he began to steer her back towards the street.

She moved his hand from her bottom as he began to fondle, South Kensington tube station being a little too public for reality, however appealing it might be for a fantasy. He complied, but took her firmly by the hand instead, leading her back across the street and up to his flat without ever once letting go. The moment the door was closed behind them he was tugging her top out of her jeans and trying to kiss her, making her giggle and put a restraining hand on his.

'Not so fast!' she urged. 'There's no rush.'

'After eight hours?' he answered. 'There's plenty of rush.'

Sarah squeaked as her top was jerked high, and with the thrill of sudden exposure she gave in, holding it up for him as he began to work on her jeans. They were soon down, and he was turning her around and easing her forward across the telephone table.

'Couldn't we go to bed?' she asked, but gave no resistance as she was put in position.

'Sod the bed,' he answered. 'Right, bra up, knickers down.'

He suited action to words, grasping the wires of Sarah's bra and flipping it up to spill out her breasts. A brief squeeze and his hands went lower, to the waistband of her panties. He sank into a squat as he began to pull them down, his face just inches away from her bottom as she came bare. A sigh escaped Sarah's lips as she was unveiled, then a second, deeper one, as her cheeks were spread and his face pushed between. She stuck her bottom out, her eyes closed in bliss as he licked her anus.

She bent over fully, resting her arms on the telephone table as she gave in to the idea of being taken across it. He was clearly urgent, fumbling his cock out as he licked her, already erect, and quickly standing to press it between her cheeks. For once he didn't suggest buggering her, but simply spent a moment rubbing himself in the wet valley between her sex lips before pushing himself deep. She gasped as she was entered, and he immediately began to pump, the slapping of his belly on her bottom cheeks once more bringing thoughts of spanking into her head.

Determined not to give in to her need, she bit her lip, telling herself she'd think about it but not say anything. Maybe she could come while he fucked her, imagining him making her bend over the table to be punished, punished with a good firm spanking delivered to her bare bottom cheeks. It would be done the way he'd said, bra up and knickers down, to add to her exposure and shame while she was beaten. The thought sent a shiver the length of her spine, and she pushed her bottom out onto his thrusting cock as her hand began to sneak back between her legs.

'Too much,' he gasped suddenly and his cock was out, hot spunk spattering Sarah's bottom as he brought himself off over her. 'Sorry . . . sorry, Sarah but I just cannot resist that darling bum.'

'That's okay,' she answered, a little surprised.

'I'll make it up to you later,' he promised, still puffing a little from the sudden vigour of their fucking.

Sarah shook her head, reaching back to take hold of her bottom cheeks. They felt heavy, a little warm from the way he'd been pushing into her, and wet with his come.

'Watch me,' she said, and began to stroke herself, rubbing his come into the chubby globes of her bottom.

Just a moment of rubbing his come into her hot slippery skin and one hand was back between her legs. He made a little choking sound as she began to masturbate and she turned to see that he was watching, his eyes wide in delight, his cock still in his hand. Made bold and rude by his attention, she pushed her fingers down between her cheeks, deliberately spreading them to show off her anus.

Giles gave a low sigh and called her a tart as she shut her eyes, concentrating on her fantasy as she masturbated. The first part was real enough, having her top lifted and her jeans pushed down, then turned around and made to pose. The only difference was that she wanted it as a punishment, and for him to say those same rude words to shame her before she was spanked, bra up, knickers down, such a rude intrusive thing to say to a girl as she was stripped.

He'd done it too, lifted her bra and pulled down her panties, and fucked her. It was only a shame he hadn't spanked her first, and made her hold her bottom cheeks apart to have her anus inspected. Yes, that was it, the way she should be handled, in an exquisitely dirty sequence, her body put on show, front and back, her big cheeks spanked just as it'd been done in Paris, her anus inspected to really bring home her shame to her, then fucked and spunked over by the man who'd punished her.

She came, her teeth still set tight against her lower lip as wave after wave of ecstasy swept through her body, her bottom cheeks still held wide to show Giles the dirty little star between, holding a state of bliss until at last her legs began to give way and she was forced to stop, sinking to her knees on the floor.

'That was something to see,' Giles breathed from behind her, 'but if you tempt me like that, Sarah Shelley . . .'

He left the sentence unfinished, but she knew exactly what he meant.

Sarah felt her cheeks tighten in her panties as for maybe the thousandth time the thought of being either spanked again or sodomised entered her head. Yet for now it was irrelevant. She had to draw, and that was what mattered. Picking up her pencil, she focused on the blank sheet of A2 spread out in front of her. Her mobile was off, the landline was on answering machine and out of hearing. Everything she could possibly need was within hand's reach, including an open bottle of the same rich Australian Chardonnay that had helped her complete the first sheet. There was even a second one in the fridge just in case one was not enough, and she suspected she might need it. To draw Céleste stripping for a man was bad enough, but to draw her on her knees and sucking his penis was a vastly greater outrage.

Her attitude had changed over the few days since she had been with Giles, his lust, and maybe even love, increasing her confidence and making it easier for her to accept the very male-oriented sexual thrust of the story, while her own responses made her better able to appreciate the dirtier elements of the story, although they still shocked her. Only Céleste's character remained immune from Giles' influence, hence the wine.

She poured a glass and took a healthy swallow, then began to pencil in the frames, setting out both pages at once. As before, the work was fully formed in her mind, needing only to be transferred onto the page. This time, it was the right hand page that was easier emotionally, involving no sexual imagery at all, yet it was a challenge artistically. She needed to convey the darkness of the graveyard and the sinister aspect of Monsieur d'Orsay's face, yet leave detail visible and not show Céleste as too much of a ghoul.

Nearly two hours later she was satisfied with her efforts and could achieve nothing more without ink. The bottle of wine had barely been started, but she finished her glass and poured another before turning her attention to the other page. In the first episode Céleste had been left with her panties just beginning to come down, so the readers would be hoping for a bare bottom. At least that was Giles' reasoning, and Sarah could find no fault. A bare bottom it had to be.

The first frame would show Céleste posed as before, only with her panties pushed down and the full beauty of her perfect buttocks on show. Maybe she would even be bent a little to hint at the rear shape of her sex lips between her thighs? No, it was too much. Sarah took another swallow of wine. Yes, it was perfect, guaranteed to get the boys' blood pumping. Monsieur d'Orsay would be visible in the background too, the bulge in his crotch showing plainly beneath the desk.

As Sarah began to work, all the questions she would have to answer to complete the page were running through her mind. Would Céleste put up a fight, or would she consider it beneath her dignity to bargain? Exactly how much should she show? Perhaps smudged lipstick would add a dirty touch, or was that just a female thing? What would Monsieur d'Orsay's cock be like? The last question was the easiest to answer. He would be big, big and ugly, with lots of veins and a thick, wrinkly foreskin, and huge balls, which he would pull out of his trousers as well. The thought made her wince even as her pencil began to move over the paper.

The idea of taking him in her mouth was repulsive, and as his genitals took form on the page it grew more repulsive still. If there was a certain horrid fascination as well, then she knew that was only her dirty mind working. Maybe, just maybe, if she was provided with a really good excuse, she could have sucked him, and secretly enjoyed it. Sarah, yes, but Céleste could never have so debased herself. Yet that was exactly what Céleste had to do in the story, and kneeling with her bottom to the reader so that the rear view of her sex and her anal star showed, just as Giles had described.

Sarah paused, shocked by what she was about to do. She remembered what the woman in Paris had threatened, and had to tell herself not to be ridiculous. Yet it was true: for her to put Céleste's anus and vaginal pouch on display to one hundred thousand lecherous men deserved a spanking to end all spankings, to say nothing of the cock-sucking.

'I am a professional artist doing commissioned work,' she told herself, out loud. 'Céleste du Musigny does not exist and cannot take her revenge, no matter how much I deserve it.'

The last few words came out as a mumbled afterthought, but Sarah had begun to draw, holding her mind deliberately blank. Shapes quickly began to come to life on the page in front of her: Monsieur d'Orsay's face, the mouth slack with pleasure as he was sucked, a little drool visible at one corner; the look of disgust on Céleste's face as she bent to take the heavy dirty penis in her mouth; the shape of her bottom sticking out from beneath the desk with the slim cheeks slightly parted to hint at a tight, brownish anus and pouted sex lips, a sight at once ridiculous and thoroughly indecent.

It was also arousing, and Sarah found her hand going between her thighs, to press at the plump bulge of sex beneath her jeans as she admired her handiwork. Yes, she had it right, Céleste's anus would be dark, and very tight, undoubtedly virgin, just like Sarah's own, the only difference being that while the immaculate young Frenchwoman was clearly inviolable, the plump English slut had begun to feel that a good buggering might not be so very inappropriate for her after all.

Then again, why shouldn't Céleste be buggered? What was so precious about her? A lot of men would like to do it, that was for certain. Yes, if she was going to entertain three scumbags, men rough enough to accept money to rob a grave, one of them was sure to bugger her. After all, she had three convenient holes, just like any other woman, so why should she be exempt from taking a cock in the dirtiest of them?

Sarah knew that the wine was getting to her, but it was still a satisfying thought. Unfortunately the script didn't call for Céleste to be buggered by Monsieur d'Orsay, or the stuck-up French bitch would be over his desk with her cheeks bulging and her eyes popping in a truly comic expression designed to show that her rectum was being crammed with fat ugly cock, that part of the shaft still protruding from her anus wet with spit from her own mouth. Better still, she could show Céleste in breathless ecstasy, her precious dignity well and truly lost as she clutched at her breasts and sex while the foul greasy Monsieur d'Orsay buggered her.

There was no room, and the scene probably exceeded the guidelines anyway; but there was something Sarah could do, a minute touch designed to show that, deep down, precious perfect Céleste du Musigny was a slut, a *salope*, *une cocotte*. With her face set in a wicked smile, Sarah carefully began to pencil in the tips of Céleste's fingers, shown pressed to her sex as she sucked on Monsieur d'Orsay's cock under the table. Céleste was now masturbating as she gave fellatio.

Sarah was laughing as she sat back in her chair. She wasn't going to need her second bottle. One was plenty. In fact, just a half, which was all she had drunk. Now grinning, she went back to work, accentuating the full pear of Céleste's out-thrust bottom; adding beads of sweat to Monsieur d'Orsay's corpulent face; and last, on the second page, where Céleste stood reading the document she had sacrificed so much to obtain, smudged lipstick and a trace of spunk in her raven-black hair.

'You know something, Sarah doll,' Hugh Bowle said, 'and I don't want you to take this the wrong way, but when I hired you I thought maybe, just maybe, there was a risk you'd turn out to be a bit prudish for this kind of thing. I take it back. You're the best.'

Sarah found herself blushing and smiling as he threw the copy down on the desk. She had come in on the promise of another long afternoon lunch, but made sure that Giles was invited as well, ostensibly as he was part of the team, but in practice because she didn't want the embarrassment of having to turn Hugh Bowle down if he propositioned her. Now, as he sat behind his great polished desk with his hands folded over his paunch and his eyes moving alternately between her chest and the copy, she was sure she'd made the right decision.

She had also decided that as Giles had obviously had nothing to do with events in Paris, Bowle had to. However unlikely it seemed, however inscrutable his motive, there was no other choice. Evidently his friendly manner hid more than a shifty desire to exploit her for her breasts, knowledge that created odd and highly disturbing feelings as he continued to talk.

'There's good news too. You are going to be syndicated.'

'Excellent!' Giles responded immediately. Sarah threw him a puzzled look.

'You'll be in more than one magazine,' Bowle explained. 'Our sister publication in the US, some outfit in France, and another in Japan. That pushes your readership up to over half a million, so there'll be a nice fat increment in your next pay cheque and all.'

'Wonderful,' Sarah breathed, her delight tempered by shock. 'Half a million people are going see my work?'

'That's sales,' Bowle explained, 'so maybe a million readers, maybe more. You've been well on time too, and you haven't given me any bullshit, so I'm giving you a little treat, and the chance to soak up some atmosphere. Two tickets to Paris, Eurostar, plus accommodation in a five-star hotel, on the house.'

'Thank you,' Sarah managed, and meant it, despite the alarm bells already ringing in her head.

'Lunch then,' Bowle said, slapping his hands on his desk as he rose. 'Sid's coming along.'

'Sid?' Sarah queried.

'Bloke I told you about,' Bowle answered her. 'Photographer.'

'I don't remember, I'm afraid,' she said as she left the office.

'You know,' he explained. 'You said you might like to pose for *Boobie Babes*, and I said I'd introduce you.'

'I did?' Sarah responded, very sure that she hadn't.

She cast an imploring look at Giles as they entered the lift, but he merely shrugged.

'I – I'm not really sure I'd have the confidence for that sort of thing,' she said, not wanting a confrontation.

Bowle didn't answer immediately, but pressed the button to hold the door as a pair of young women made a dash for the open lift. Both were exactly the type who made Sarah feel most self-conscious: slim, smart, with tastefully applied make-up and dyed blonde hair, so alike they might have been sisters. They squeezed into the lift, thanking Bowle and giving Giles appraising looks that brought Sarah jealousy, but more pride, until Bowle began to speak again.

'You don't need confidence, darling, you need boobs, big boobs.'

He smacked his lips as he spoke, his eyes fixed on her chest. Sarah found herself going scarlet as one of the girls giggled, to which Bowle responded immediately.

'I don't know what you're laughing at, darling. I've seen bigger fried eggs than what you've got.'

'Cheek!' the girl answered, and smacked his arm.

Bowle laughed, and Sarah forced a smile, trying to be part of what was obviously no more than bawdy good humour. Giles put his arm around her shoulder, at which Bowle did a rapid double take, speaking again as they left the lift.

'What's all this then? You two an item?'

'Yes we are,' Sarah confirmed.

'Good for you,' he responded. 'You're a jammy bastard, Giles.'

He finished with a laugh and slapped Giles on the back as they left the building. Sarah wondered if he would say something about Rebecca, but a male voice called out from behind them and Bowle stopped. Sarah turned to find a man coming towards them, stocky and white-haired, with a mild disarming smile and kindly eyes – kindly eyes aimed directly at her chest, perhaps, but she would have been surprised if they hadn't been.

'Sid, there you are, you old bastard,' Bowle said, greeting the newcomer. 'You've met Giles double-barrel, and this is the girl I was talking to you about, Sarah, ace artist and A1 boobie babe. Sarah, this is Sid, who's been taking dirty pictures since before you were born, maybe since before your mum was born.'

'Pleased to meet you.' Sid extended a hand towards her.

Sarah took it, smiling, but wishing she could stop herself blushing, and wishing too that they wouldn't be so casual about her body. Determined to say something, she was still trying to find the right words when Sid spoke again.

'Hugh didn't do you justice, Sarah. You're perfect.'

'Thank you,' Sarah answered, 'but you know I'm not.'

Sid shook his head.

'Uh, uh. Here's the thing, see. Show a guy some girl who looks like she's been picked up down King's Cross with her tits out and unless he's got a freak for that sort of thing he's going to reckon: so what? She looks like she spends half her time with her tits out, so it's no big deal. Show the same guy a girl who looks like she works in an office, or she's his best mate's bird, and she's got her tits out, and he'll love it. Now you, you look right, you've got it all there, but you look far too brainy to be showing them off in a jazz mag, so it's a real treat. I'm going to need to do at least two sets here, a big one for *Boobie Babes* and another for *Hotties at Home*.'

'I haven't actually agreed to have any pictures taken,' Sarah pointed out.

'Come on, Sarah doll, don't make me look a prat,' Bowle put in as Sid gave her a puzzled look.

'Um . . .,' Sarah began. 'Giles, could you help me out, please?'

'If she doesn't want to do it, she doesn't want to do it,' Giles told Bowle, but then glanced at Sarah. 'I don't see why not, though. You love showing off.'

'Giles!' Sarah squeaked. 'That's private!'

'You don't have to worry about us,' Bowle said. 'We're trade. Sid and I must have seen enough boobage to sink the *Titanic*.'

Sarah didn't answer, rendered speechless by their casual discussion of her breasts, and the assumption that merely because the two men had seen a lot of other girls naked the exposure of her breasts was inconsequential. There was Giles' revelation of one of her most private fantasies too and, worst of all, the sudden fluttering in her stomach and tightening of her sex at the thought of showing herself bare in a men's magazine.

'Think about it over a couple of jars,' Bowle suggested, rubbing his hands together as he angled for the pub door.

There were only two outside tables free, and Sarah went to one, Giles joining her as the others went inside.

'What a pair of old perverts!' Sarah protested as she sat down.

'I thought you'd love it,' Giles answered her. 'You said you –'

'Not you too! That was private, and while we were making love. Anyway, don't you mind?'

'Not at all. I'm proud of you.'

'So you'd like several thousand men ogling me naked!?'

'Yes, why not?'

'Why not? My last boyfriend used to go nuts if another man even glanced at me.'

'Probably insecure.'

'That's true enough,' Sarah admitted.

'Why not go for it?' Giles urged. 'I'd love to see the results.'

'Pervert,' Sarah answered, her resolve weakening, only for another objection to occur to her. 'What if my Dad sees, or my brothers!'

'Do they read *Boobie Babes*? If they do, they'd be hypocrites to object to you being in it and, if they don't, then it doesn't matter.'

Sarah made a face.

'I'm not sure Dad would see it that way.'

Bowle emerged from the pub, clutching a bottle in one hand and four glasses in the other. Sid was behind him, with a second bottle in a bucket of ice, which he set down on the table as Hugh spoke.

'Champagne, to celebrate your syndication. You can do the honours, Giles.'

'You're just trying to get me drunk,' Sarah said, half joking.

'Usually helps,' Hugh admitted as Giles began to work on the bottle.

Sarah hid a sigh. All three of them wanted to get her breasts bare for the camera, even her own boyfriend, and as usual she found the pressure hard to resist. Rebecca would have laughed in their faces. Céleste would have slapped them. Sarah was going to end up doing it.

The cork popped under Giles' hand, emitting a froth of Champagne bubbles that made Sarah think of an ejaculating cock. The image made her sex tighten again as she thought of a young man masturbating over a picture of her naked, his cock in his hand, hard and virile as the spunk pumped from the tip and spattered his belly and the magazine, maybe all over her picture, unable to control himself for his excitement.

'Cheers, boy and girls,' Bowle announced, taking up the glass Giles had put down in front of Sarah.

She took the next and raised it in return, still thinking of spunk as she put the bubbling liquid to her lips, so much so that she was surprised to find it sharp and fresh instead of salty and hormonal and ended up choking on her mouthful. Giles patted her on the back, but only succeeded in making her cough up Champagne down her front. Hugh Bowle laughed.

'Well, you're going to have to take it off now, darling.'

'That's a thought,' Sid put in, 'we could start you off getting your top wet. You'd look great.'

'Will you all please shut up about my breasts!' Sarah snapped, finally losing her temper as she tried to mop up the spilt Champagne with a serviette.

'We're only kidding about, Sarah doll,' Bowle answered her.

There was a period of embarrassed silence, which quickly replaced Sarah's irritation with guilt. The men began to discuss sport, leaving Sarah to her thoughts for a while as she sipped Champagne and wished that she was better at imposing her personality on situations. Whoever she met, whatever the circumstances, she always seemed to end up allowing others to make her decisions for her, or basing her own decisions on what other people would think.

She drank her Champagne and a second glass. Giles opened the next bottle and half of that had gone too before Sarah reached a decision. She would do it, and enjoy it, not because they wanted her to, and certainly not for the money, but because she liked to be exposed. She would do it, but she would do it her way, following one of her favourite fantasies.

'Okay, I'll pose for you,' she said, speaking suddenly before common sense could get the better of her, 'but I decide how we do it.'

'Best leave that to the pros, love,' Sid suggested, and would have continued, but Sarah cut him off.

'Sorry, but we do it my way or not at all. I don't want to be deliberately exposing myself, I want it to be accidental.'

'What, like Peeping Tom stuff?' Bowle asked.

'No,' Sarah explained, 'more as if I've had an accident of some sort ... maybe torn my dress or something. The sort of thing that always used to happen to Carrie, or Annie Fanny . . .'

She was blushing as she said it, and trailed off, unable to continue. Sid was looking puzzled, but Hugh Bowle was grinning from ear to ear.

'I've got you,' he said. 'It's simple, Sid. She goes out. She loses all her clothes. She ends up all embarrassed.'

'That sounds fun,' Giles put in, and squeezed Sarah's thigh under the table.

'All we need is some sort of story,' Hugh said reflectively. 'I know, how about you're walking and you spill something down your top, just like you did then, only more so.'

'That works,' Sid put in, 'and we've got to get her in a wet T-shirt, can't miss that.'

'She could be near a stall selling cheap tops,' Giles suggested, 'so she decides to find somewhere private to change.'

'In a phone box,' Hugh added.

'Not very private, a phone box,' Sid pointed out.

'She's in a flap,' Hugh retorted. 'She would be, wouldn't she, with her tits on parade in the fucking street! Wouldn't you love? Tits out in a phone box is great, 'cause you can show 'em squashed up on the glass and that, and she knows that people might see, so she's in a real hurry.'

'Only her bra's all wet,' Sid put in.

'Yeah, so off that comes too,' Hugh went on with rising enthusiasm, 'only the new top's too small, so she's getting in a right flap, wriggling about and everything, so her titties are jiggling about like crazy.'

'Nice,' Sid agreed, 'but that would be better on film.'

'So let's do a DVD,' Hugh suggested, 'and stick it on the cover of *Boobie Babes* as a bonus, with Sarah

71

on the cover and all. If that doesn't give us an extra ten thou on the circulation, I'll buy the returns myself.'

Sarah sighed, openly this time. Her attempt to take things into her own hands had lasted rather less than a minute.

Five

With the trip to Paris booked for the Friday, Hugh
Bowle wasted no time in arranging for Sarah's film to
be made. Giles was full of enthusiasm, also Mak, and
with nobody to disapprove of what she was doing she
found herself swept along by events and very quickly
beyond the point at which she might have backed
out. Just two days after agreeing to play out what had
been one of her favourite fantasies for as long as she
could remember, she found herself standing in an
East End street, absolutely terrified.

It had seemed really quite easy the night before, as
she lay in Giles' arms. While they masturbated each
other she ran through the fantasy, telling him how
much more exciting it would be if she had to go fully
nude. He'd been in full agreement, and had come in
her hand as she described herself trying to pull up a
pair of impossibly small jeans over her bum, with
nothing on but a pair of minuscule panties already at
breaking point. Now it was real, real to an extent far
beyond what she'd expected.

From what Hugh Bowle and Sid had been saying,
she had expected everything to be done in a studio. It
wasn't, it was to be done in the street. They had
explained why: that the budget would be impossibly
large for a convincing studio set and all the minor

actors and extras they'd need. It was much cheaper, and easier, to simply play through the scenario for real, the only problem being to select a quiet street where there was an old-fashioned phone box in which she could do her strip. The rest was straightforward. As Hugh had pointed out, there was no law against a girl spilling beer down her chest, or filming it.

Giles was now talking to Hugh while Sid checked the light and adjusted his camera, but broke away and came over to Sarah, his face lit up by a happy wicked smile.

'We're ready if you are,' he said, 'only Sid's getting in a flap over how to get enough on your top to make a really good show. This is how we do it. Instead of you just spilling your drink, I'll be sitting with you at an outside table with a jug of Pimms. We argue, you throw your drink over me, and I throw the jug over you. Okay?'

Sarah managed a nod.

'It won't be real Pimms of course,' Giles continued blithely, 'just water with some fruit and stuff in it. We'll drink the real Pimms.'

They were already outside the pub they'd chosen, the Sparrow, an old-fashioned East End pub with benches out on the pavement, safely tucked away off the main thoroughfares and just beginning to cater for City tastes. Sarah went to sit down, trying to behave as if nothing unusual was going on as Giles and Hugh went in to get the jug of Pimms. Sid was already filming, and she realised it had begun.

'Here we are,' Giles said as he put the tray down and passed her a glass. 'Smile, chat, act natural. We haven't started arguing yet.'

'OK,' Sarah answered. 'What shall we talk about?'

'Sex?' he suggested. 'It might help if you were turned on.'

'That's true,' Sarah admitted and took a swallow of Pimms, draining nearly half her glass.

'Last night was good,' Giles said. 'I think I could watch you pulling your knickers up and down for ever.'

'No you couldn't,' she answered, 'you'd come. Anyway, it was really unfair of you to make me do that. I felt so embarrassed.'

'I know,' he told her, 'that's half the fun. It's going to turn me on when your knickers come down in the phone box too.'

'They're not,' she answered, wondering why he had raised his voice. 'We're only doing my top, aren't we?'

'No, every fucking stitch is coming off, you unfaithful bitch!'

He had screamed the last words, and as he did so he hurled the full contents of the jug into her face and across her chest. She gave a shriek of surprise as the chilly liquid hit it, her mouth going wide in an involuntary gasp, just in time for Giles to push in half a lemon that had been floating on the Pimms.

'So you can just fuck off!' he yelled and turned on his heel.

Sarah was left dripping, too surprised to react for a moment as Sid zoomed in on her, first her face, then her chest. She looked down in horror. Her top was soaked, her nipples poking up through the wet cotton and every detail of her rounded lacy bra visible as well. Her jeans were wet too, and she could feel the cold liquid soaking through onto the skin of her thighs and into her panty crotch.

'Great shot,' Sid said happily, taking the camera from his eye. 'Sorry about that, love, but it's hard to get a really good look of surprise on a girl's face if she knows what's coming. Now, slap your hands on your titties and run off. Action.'

She obeyed, too numb to resist, and again, and a third time as he made sure he had plenty of film of her wet breasts. People had stopped to look, while she was shaking badly and her nipples wouldn't go down, all helping to make her feelings ever stronger. By the time Sid was satisfied, she was on the edge of panic, and immensely grateful for Giles' fleece.

Five minutes later she was wishing she was still sitting outside the Sparrow with her top wet, or just about anywhere else. The stall they had chosen was the end one of a row in a side street, manned by a surly-looking woman who had grudgingly accepted twenty pounds not to argue with Sarah when she came to buy her clothes. Without the fleece, but with one arm clasped over her wet breasts, Sarah didn't need to act as Sid called out for her to start the scene.

'I – I'd like a top please,' she managed, 'and some jeans. Bra and panties if you've got them.'

'Looks like you need 'em,' the woman answered, 'but I ain't got a bra in your size. What are you?'

'Thirty-six F,' Sarah admitted. 'Please, can we be quick?'

'Can't do you a bra,' the woman insisted.

'That's okay,' Sarah answered, snatching a pair of frilly-edged white panties from the tray marked 10, sure to be too small, 'and these, and these.'

She'd picked the clothes they'd decided on in advance: black low-cut slim-fit jeans she had no chance of getting her bottom into, and a garish Union Jack top with a picture of a bulldog smoking a cigar on it, cut for a man and utterly inadequate to hold in her breasts.

'Thirty-one fifty,' the woman said, holding her hand out.

Sarah passed over the notes with trembling fingers. A lot of people were looking, and she was forced to take her arm away from her chest to pay over the money, leaving the full wet bulges of her breasts on show until she could snatch her purchases and run for cover. Sid followed her wobbling bottom with the camera, then made her do it again so that he could film from the front.

'In the can,' he said as she reached him. 'Nice one. Now for the big finale.'

'You were great,' Giles put in, handing her the fleece once more.

Sarah grimaced, wondering how she could ever have wanted to be exposed in public and yet unable to deny her rising feelings. Now came the phone box, public striptease, a thought that made her tremble so bad she could hardly stand up. Giles guided her, past the stalls and around one corner, then a second, to where an old-fashioned red phone box stood in a corner between two walls of dirty red-brown brick. A railway embankment rose behind the wall, and the street was empty, a tightly packed line of cars providing extra concealment from anybody who happened to look out from the houses opposite.

'Let's do it,' Hugh prompted.

Her nerve was about to fail her, and the moment Sid called for action she was hurrying into the phone box with no need for pretence. Stripping was harder, a bubble of panic growing in her throat as she jerked up her top, only to find the wet cotton stuck to her flesh, forcing her to jerk it high and wrestle it off her arms with her boobs squashed to the glass even before she was supposed to.

At last her top came away and she was in her bra in public. Still nobody was visible, and her hands went behind her back, her panic now so strong that she was stamping her feet in agitation as she struggled with the catch. It came loose, she felt the weight of her breasts loll forward and before she could stop herself she had flipped the cups up and she was topless.

A punch of shame and excitement hit her as her bare breasts came on show to the camera. She was doing it, bare in the street, or almost, and squashed to the glass as she went into the foolish sexy little routine she had agreed in advance, squashing herself to the glass so that Sid could film her flesh pressed flat through the panes. Her nipples were painfully stiff, aching as she pressed them to the warm hard glass.

Next came her jeans, and the moment she felt she'd given Sid enough of a show she was pulling the button open and wriggling them down, only to realise that she couldn't get them off without removing her shoes. That meant undoing the laces, and as she bent down her bottom was squashed to the glass, the tarty red panties they had insisted she wear already half-down over her ample cheeks, and Sid was still filming, from just inches away.

One shoe came, then the other. Sarah shoved her jeans to her ankles and wrenched one leg off, then the second, leaving her nude but for her wet panties, which had to come down too. The bubble of panic burst as she thrust them down and off. She was nude, stark naked but for her socks in a public phone box, her breasts on show to the world, her fat pink bottom wobbling bare behind, and as she bent to snatch up the bag with her new clothes in it she knew she was showing off even more, the plump rear purse of her sex – thrust out straight at Sid's lens.

A sob escaped her lips as she remembered how she'd been made to give the same rude display over the woman's lap in Paris. That had been worse, but at least she hadn't been filmed, and as she desperately tried to untangle her new panties she was promising herself that she'd get dressed just as fast as she possibly could.

Only as she jerked the panties up did she realise that she had one foot in a leg hole and one in the waist hole. Sobbing and muttering curses, she took them off again, once more with her nude bottom pressed to the window. At last she got them right, only to realise that the tag didn't say Size 10, but Age 10. It was too late, they were already halfway up her thighs, but that was as far as they would go.

Sarah swore, wrenching desperately at the tiny garment, but the panties wouldn't even come up to her bottom cheeks, let alone over them. She was in too much of a frenzy to admit defeat, bouncing up and down to make her bottom wobble and her boobs jiggle, until the cheap panties gave up the unequal battle and split, leaving her with a single pathetic scrap of cotton and elastic wrapped around one leg.

She kicked it off, willing herself to be calm as she pulled her new jeans out of her bag. Again she glanced out of the box, and to her horror saw that three young black men were walking towards her along the pavement, directly towards her. They hadn't seen her, merely joking among themselves, but they were going to at any moment. Sid either hadn't seen, or didn't care, but was still filming, while Giles seemed to have vanished completely.

Now demented with panic, she thrust one leg into the jeans, pushing her foot through and extending a hand to steady herself as she tried to find the second hole, only not on the wall, but on the door, which swung open. Sarah gave a single long shriek as she tumbled backwards out of the phone box and a yelp of pain as she landed on her back on the pavement, to lie kicking like an upturned beetle, her breasts wobbling in every direction, her naked sex and rolled-up bottom on full show to the camera, anus and all.

More by luck than judgement her foot had gone into the right hole, and she forced it through and dragged the jeans up, squeezing her bottom in. The button wouldn't do up by a long way, but her cheeks were covered, and that was far, far more important. That only left her breasts, but the door had already closed, leaving her topless in the street, with the three young men staring at her open-mouthed from a distance of a few feet and Giles nowhere to be seen.

'I'm sorry, I'm really sorry,' she babbled, slapping her hands onto her breasts. 'That's enough, Sid, I can't –'

'Just the top, love, just the top,' he urged.

'No I ...' Sarah stammered. 'Oh bloody Hell! Here, have a good stare, you bastards! Aren't I big and fat? Wouldn't you just love to stick your cocks between them and come all over my face, you dirty bastards! Come on, have a good grope, why don't you!?'

She was holding her breasts out to the three black youths, but they just stared. She wrenched the door of the phone box wide, snatched up the Union Jack top and tugged it on over her head. As planned, it wasn't easy to get on, and even when she'd finally managed to cover her breasts the cotton was stretched across them with her nipples showing as two straining bumps. Yet she was covered, and a moment later Giles was there, putting the big fleece around her shoulders.

'Good one,' Sid said, as Giles quickly gathered up Sarah's things. 'How about a last flash and a cheeky grin, just to show it was all in play?'

'Give her a chance,' Giles responded. 'Better put your shoes on, Sarah.'

He helped her, then began to steer her away. The two men didn't follow, Hugh Bowle holding Sid back, and Sarah let herself be led through the streets towards her own flat. She felt weak, and confused, not sure even what to think, let alone how to respond to the conflicting demands of her mind and body. Only when she was indoors did her tension at last begin to drain, and she let herself collapse onto the bed.

'Coffee? Something stronger?' Giles offered.

Sarah shook her head.

'No. Cuddle me, like you did last night.'

'Are you . . .'

'Do it, please.'

Giles complied, climbing onto the bed beside her. Sensing his uncertainty, Sarah pushed the over-tight jeans down, not off but to her ankles. Her hands went to her hips, her belly, her bottom cheeks, feeling the bare skin.

'No panties,' she sighed. 'I've got no panties on and they saw me like that, bare . . . Hold me, Giles, kiss me.'

Giles nodded and moved in closer, opening his mouth to hers. Their tongues met and Sarah closed her eyes, imagining herself back in the phone box, topless, then naked, stamping her feet in her growing panic, struggling to get the tiny panties up her legs, falling out to roll naked on the pavement, her breasts bare, her bottom bare, her sex bare.

She'd begun to masturbate, teasing her open pussy with her fingers to bring her pleasure slowly up as she tried to focus on the full power of what she'd done, on what she'd been made to do. Having her wet top plastered to her breasts in the street seemed mild now, even the hideously embarrassing experience of buying the clothes little stronger. Stripping was anything but mild, each moment of agonising embarrassment now providing her with a jolt of pleasure.

Giles' mouth pressed harder to her own and she responded, kissing urgently as her back arched in pleasure. She put a hand to her chest, stroking her breasts through the taut fabric. With no bra, they felt huge and soft, her straining nipples so sensitive she could hardly bear to touch them, even with her orgasm already approaching. She thought of how rude she'd have looked in the street, even in her top, but that was nothing to having been bare.

She crushed her mouth to Giles' as she started to come. One quick motion and she'd jerked her top up, spilling out her breasts, fat and soft and naked in her hands. Her fingers began to make the little clutching motions she preferred and her mind fixed on the most exquisite, most unbearable moment of the entire experience – when she'd tumbled out of the phone box to roll on the pavement, her breasts naked to the three astonished young men, her legs up, no panties, nothing to shield the fleshy folds of her sex and the rude pink star of her anus, not only on view to Sid and Hugh and Giles, but shortly to be exposed to thousands upon thousands of men.

Six

Peering carefully left and right, Sarah surveyed the platform of the Gare du Nord. It was clear, so far as she could see, with no sign of anyone resembling Céleste, but there were altogether too many people about for her liking. Exposure was one thing, but what she was worried might happen to her was another altogether, while recognising that it would ultimately excite her only made it worse. She'd felt thoroughly ashamed of herself for masturbating over the first time she'd gone nude for a men's magazine, but Giles hadn't understood, and for him to see her get a public spanking would be far worse.

'What are you waiting for?' Giles asked, nudging her bottom with the bags he was carrying.

'Nothing,' Sarah replied quickly, and jumped down onto the platform.

Giles followed, in no hurry at all, finding a trolley and piling the bags onto it before starting slowly down the platform, so that Sarah was obliged to follow at the same pace. Nobody was taking any real notice of them, and she tried to tell herself to relax. It wasn't easy, and if there was no sign of the Céleste woman on the concourse either, there were all too many places from which she could be ambushed, from the tall green pillars supporting the roof to a highly suspicious-looking set of tables outside a café, each with a red and white striped umbrella and chairs just right for a woman to sit on as she dealt with a naughty girl's bottom. Still nothing happened, and they reached the main exit without incident.

Thick pillars flanked the doorways, and Sarah froze as she saw the woman standing with her back to the nearest of them. She was tall, slim, naturally elegant, dressed in smart expensive clothes, all black, including a neat pork-pie hat exactly like the one Sarah had drawn Céleste in for her visit to Monsieur d'Orsay. Sarah could already feel her panties gliding down to expose her bottom as the woman turned, lazily, showing long, chiselled features completely unlike those of Céleste.

'Are you all right, darling?' Giles asked.

'Fine, really,' Sarah answered. 'I just need the loo.'

It was true, because when she'd seen the woman leaning against the pillar she'd very nearly wet herself and, if being spanked bare-bottom in public and in front of her boyfriend was a prospect of agonising humiliation, then having the same thing done wearing pissed-in panties defied description.

She ran back into the station and used the ladies', returning to Giles as quickly as she could. As they waited for a taxi she was telling herself that she was being silly, that nothing would happen or, if it did, Giles would put a stop to it. That didn't prevent her constantly scanning the faces of passers-by, and even in the taxi she found it impossible to relax completely.

If Hugh Bowle had set her up – and she couldn't see who else it could be – then he would know where they were going, having chosen the hotel personally. That made it all too likely that she was going to get it in the hotel and, if it seemed absurd to think of the staff permitting such a thing, then it was not much more absurd than the attitude of both staff and customers at the café on the Île St. Louis, and surely not all of them could have been paid off, because if so it must have been a very expensive joke.

A horrible thought occurred to her: that Hugh Bowle and possibly Sid too might have created the incident not as a joke at all, but to get some juicy footage for one of the magazines. No doubt there was a title devoted to spanked girls, as there seemed to be a title devoted to everything else, and yet there was the issue of model release forms, which they'd been very careful about for her phone-box strip.

As they drove she was constantly looking around her. Paris seemed different from her previous visit, although the day was much the same and nothing obvious had altered. Somehow it seemed more mundane, bland even, certainly less romantic, which was odd as she was visiting with her new boyfriend. The hotel was superb, immensely grand and impressively appointed, but with far less atmosphere than the poky family establishment in the Latin quarter.

Their room was excellent too, large, well furnished, but strangely sterile, despite what should have been a classic view across the Seine to the Eiffel Tower. She put it down to nerves and began to unpack, telling herself that she was at least safe, only to change her mind. What if Giles was in on it after all? If he was, they really had her where they wanted her. At any moment the Céleste woman might come in, perhaps even with a Monsieur d'Orsay look-alike. She'd be put over the knee and spanked bare. She'd be forced to suck d'Orsay's cock while she was punished, with no let-up until he'd come in her mouth. She'd be sat on and have her red bottom cheeks held wide so that Giles could bugger her while Céleste looked on, smoking a Gitane and giving a soft musical laugh every time Sarah pulled a particularly stupid face or squealed in the pain of her sodomy . . .

Giles was looking out of the window with a faintly critical expression on his patrician face, completely oblivious to her thoughts.

'I always think there's something inherently vulgar about French architecture,' he remarked. 'Shall we go down and have tea?'

Sarah agreed, telling herself not to be paranoid. Giles had some difficulty in making the hotel staff understand exactly what he wanted, to Sarah's intense embarrassment, but he finally managed it, and they sat for a while in comfort, allowing the stresses of the journey to dissipate. Slowly, Sarah began to relax. There was a very modern bustle about the hotel, while it was impossible to imagine the staff allowing a guest to be assaulted in the main lounge.

Having had tea, Giles was full of energy, and suggested walking along the Seine. Sarah readily agreed, pushing aside her worries in her determination to enjoy another of her long-held ambitions, to walk through the streets of Paris arm in arm with her lover. As they walked south and crossed the river on the Pont d'Iéna, something of the atmosphere she had noted earlier remained, and yet her determination to enjoy the experience began to win through.

Giles let her steer him, past the Eiffel Tower and along the bank, before striking in among smaller streets. Soon she was lost, navigating only by the occasional glimpse of the upper parts of the tower between buildings. She was no longer glancing fearfully at every woman who even slightly resembled Céleste du Musigny, although in her imagination it was just the sort of area in which she might have met her heroine, the Paris of locals rather than tourists.

They had been walking for over an hour when she turned back in roughly the direction of the hotel, intending to find the river and follow the bank. The buildings quickly became grander again, but in a different style, more municipal than commercial. Many of them were decorated with *tricolores*, but one in particular was so heavily hung with flags and bunting that there was more cloth showing than stone or glass. Sarah paused, read the inscription above the door announcing it as a war museum, and was going to walk on, but Giles held back.

'I wouldn't mind a look around, if you'd be interested?' he suggested.

'Not really,' Sarah told him, 'but you go in. I can amuse myself for a bit.'

'Are you sure?'

'Yes, I'll be fine. There's bound to be a stall selling paintings or something.'

Giles glanced up and down the street, made a doubtful face but moved towards the doorway of the museum.

'Thanks,' he said. 'I promise not to be more than half an hour.'

'Fine,' Sarah answered, slightly piqued but determined not to spoil their first day in Paris with a row or to give Giles any reason not to be content with her.

He answered with a slightly sheepish grin and went inside. Sarah paused, wondering what to do with herself as there were no stalls of any sort in sight, nor anything else of any real interest. She turned on her heel, wondering which way to go, only to realise that she had been wrong. There was a line of stalls, a little way down the street, partially obscured by trees. It was a scene that might very well have been painted by Pissarro, but for the traffic and other modern paraphernalia, of which there didn't actually seem to be a great deal.

She walked towards the stalls, hoping they'd be selling paintings and even wondering if with her now quite good income she might not treat herself. If there was something good enough it would be irresistible, a lifelong treasure to remember her visit with Giles, whatever came later. As she crossed the road she was picturing herself as a grandmother, explaining how she had come across some wonderful painting to a cluster of grandchildren lost in the romance of a Paris by then fifty years gone, just as when she was a child the Paris of the pre-war period had so inspired her.

Only as she approached the stall did she realise that she was passing a distinctly familiar building, tall, imposing, with fine *tricolores* crossed above the door, so similar to the one she'd drawn for the first episode of 'Graverobbers' that for a moment she felt uneasy. Then again, she had drawn it from her studies of Parisian architecture, and it was Parisian architecture, also no doubt a government building of some kind, so the similarity was hardly surprising.

On reaching the stalls her qualms were immediately forgotten. Not just one but all three sold paintings, and from many artists, with a broad range of styles unified only by an atmosphere that seemed to encapsulate her elaborately constructed image of romantic France. She was immediately entranced, both by the paintings and the other people around the stalls, every one of whom possessed something of the characteristics she so admired. Next to her was a girl in a blue cape and a smart hat, no more than thirteen or fourteen and clearly a pupil at some nearby *lycée*, yet discussing the influences behind the various paintings with a portly man of over sixty who wore a waxed moustache. Further along an elderly couple were in conversation with a young man who seemed to be one of the artists, while a small beetle-like man in a black coat listened with an expression of austere intelligence.

Sarah turned to the paintings, intent on choosing one, or possibly more than one, as the prices seemed surprisingly reasonable. Directly in front of her was a series using a particular blue to good effect, among which one instantly drew her attention. It was a view of the Seine, showing the upper works of Notre-Dame rising beyond the Île St. Louis, but made wonderful by the use of blue in the water and sky. Not only that, but the café outside which she had been spanked was plainly visible, with tiny figures at the table, including one, seated, elegant in black, who held another across her knee, anything but elegant with a plump pink bottom bare to the world and quite obviously being smacked. Her mouth came open in astonishment as a young man in a red and white striped top came towards her, evidently the artist, his expression aloof, as if insulted by her attention to his work.

'When did you paint this?' she asked.

'It is among my most recent works,' he answered her, his tone implying yet more strongly than his expression that she was incapable of fully appreciating it.

Sarah made to reply, but another voice broke in from directly behind her, a voice at once intensely feminine, haughty, confident, and instantly recognisable as that of Céleste du Musigny.

'You should purchase it, *cocotte*, and if you do not, I shall, on your behalf. *Réservez s'il vous plaît cette peinture dans mon nom, Armand.*'

'*C'est ça, Céleste,*' the artist replied.

Sarah had begun to stammer, immediately scared and confused, and as the woman took her by the ear she found herself unable to resist, despite the certainty that she was going over the knee and her panties would be coming down in front of Armand and the entire street. But it didn't happen. Céleste moved quickly away from the stalls, towing Sarah behind her, now squealing as the pain of her pinched ear broke through her initial shock.

'Where are you taking me?' she managed, catching the panic and self-pity in her own voice. 'Please, I –'

'Be quiet, you little whore,' Céleste snapped back. 'I warned you what would happen if you went on with your dirty scribblings, and now it will.'

'What?' Sarah asked. 'What ... Monsieur d'Orsay? No, not Monsieur d'Orsay, please ... you – you cannot do this to me!'

'No?' the woman queried, her voice cold with anger. 'You did it to me though, no? How do you think I felt, like that, like you showed me, on my knees to that ... that cretin!'

'I – no – look,' Sarah stammered, 'that wasn't you! That was just a cartoon! That – ow!'

Her cry of pain came as the woman wheeled on her to plant a stinging slap across one side of her face. Sarah was left gasping and clutching her hurt cheek, dizzy with shock as she was dragged stumbling towards the door of the building she had seen before, now held firmly by the wrist. She wanted to protest, but she knew it would make no difference and very likely earn her another slap in the face, while underneath her boiling feelings a strong sense of guilt was rising, guilt that made no sense, yet which she was unable to push down.

She was pulled up the steps and into the building. An elderly man in a blue uniform sat behind a great marble reception desk in the foyer, but he scarcely troubled to look up from the magazine he was reading as Sarah was dragged stumbling across the polished floor to a cage lift. The Céleste woman pressed a button, never releasing her grip on Sarah's wrist. The lift arrived, Sarah was pulled in and the door closed behind them. As the lift began to rise she finally found her voice.

'I – I don't understand, but if I've upset you in any way –'

'Be quiet!' the woman snapped. 'You were warned of the consequences if you continued your vile behaviour, and now you will accept those consequences.'

'Yes, but,' Sarah began, struggling with her own frustration at the woman's refusal to talk sense. 'I didn't do anything to you! I mean, if I had, then –'

'Nothing?' the woman responded, her eyes blazing. 'Nothing? You call being made to – to striptease for Monsieur d'Orsay nothing? You call being made to take the old toad's penis in my mouth as half a million people look on at my degradation nothing!? You . . . you are extraordinary . . . *incroyable!* We shall see, shall we, how you feel, and without even the audience. *Sacrebleu!'*

Sarah once more found herself speechless in the face of the woman's fury, and shied away for fear of another slap. The lift stopped and the door slid open onto a corridor. The woman gave Sarah a firm push, sending her stumbling out, and once more took a firm pinch of one ear. Squealing and babbling inanities, Sarah was frogmarched down the passage, past doors each marked with a name on a discrete brass plaque. They stopped outside one of the doors, no different from the rest save for the name – Monsieur d'Orsay.

'Please?' Sarah managed as the woman rapped on the door.

A voice answered, thick as oil, inviting them in. The Céleste woman pushed the door wide and Sarah was dragged in and sent forward with a shove, into the centre of a room furnished exactly as she had pictured it – even the pattern on the carpet was identical – and with the same design of desk. Beyond the desk was a man who looked as exactly like the Monsieur d'Orsay of her cartoon as the woman looked like Céleste du Musigny; greasy, florid, balding, complete with nasty little moustache and a sweating face which he dabbed with a monogrammed handkerchief as the door closed. He smiled, revealing a row of large yellowish teeth.

'Ah ha,' he said, 'so this is our little *artiste*, eh? Quite the little butterball, is she not?'

'Look, I don't know who you are . . .' Sarah began, only to stop as he laughed.

'Oh, but you do!' he said, seeming vastly amused by the situation. 'Myself, I am Monsieur Vivien d'Orsay, and beside you, Mam'selle Céleste du Musigny.'

He was grinning as he finished, and Sarah was gaping. She had decided that d'Orsay's Christian name would be Vivien, but only on the train. Giles knew, but they had been together every moment since. More confused than ever, she found herself completely lost for words as the man continued, now addressing the woman.

'Well, Céleste, my dear, let us proceed, eh! I trust you are going to spank her first? There is nothing these English girls like more, you know, than a well warmed bottom before sex. It is, I imagine, a device to defray their guilt, for which they may feel they have been punished in advance.'

He finished with a dirty chuckle and folded his hands across his paunch. The woman had pulled out a chair and placed it purposefully in the exact centre of the space in front of the desk, sideways on to Monsieur d'Orsay. Sarah could do nothing, her body limp as the woman reached out to take her wrist once more. A great bubble of shame and consternation was forming as she was placed gently but firmly across the knee, her bottom to Monsieur d'Orsay. Yet she was too shocked to fight, while two voices seemed to be whispering directly into her brain, one cold and full of disgust, telling her she deserved what she was about to get and more, the other warm and seductive, telling her what a lucky girl she was to be spanked in such exquisitely humiliating circumstances.

'You say she fought before?' Monsieur d'Orsay remarked from behind her as the woman took hold of the hem of Sarah's dress. 'Perhaps she has begun to learn her place after all?'

'We shall see,' the woman responded, and the pretty summer dress Sarah had put on in the hotel was lifted onto her back.

With the exposure of her panties Sarah was finally shocked out of inaction. She tried to get up, but the woman immediately caught her wrist and twisted it hard up into the small of her back, as before. A squeal of pain and misery broke from her mouth, followed by babbled protests against the monstrous liberty about to be taken with her. Monsieur d'Orsay merely laughed, then spoke again.

'Oh ho, she still has some fight in her, I see? Excellent! Take her knickers down slowly, Céleste, make her feel it as she is unveiled.'

'That is my intention,' the woman stated. 'Be calm, Sarah, you will only make it worse, while if you have a gram of decency in you then you must realise that you fully deserve this.'

'No I don't!' Sarah squealed, still kicking and wriggling despite the woman's words, already near to panic as a thumb was hooked into the waistband of her panties. 'No! Please, not my panties! Not in front of him! No!'

'*Hoopla!*' d'Orsay declared. 'How she kicks! Slowly, Céleste, very slowly, to see a girl's bottom exposed is a moment to be savoured, like a fine wine.'

'You are a filthy old *roué*, Monsieur,' the woman responded, but it didn't stop her beginning to take Sarah's panties down, and just as slowly as he had requested.

He merely chuckled, and Sarah's babbled entreaties broke to a long moan of despair as the top of her bottom crease came on show. She could feel the tension in her panty elastic as they were eased low, and the exposure of every inch of smooth pink bottom skin, the swell of her cheeks and the plump crests, the meaty tuck and between, where she knew full well her sex lips would be peeping out backwards between her thighs.

'*Magnifique!*' d'Orsay sighed as Sarah's full rear view came on show. 'She is fine, yes. I do like them big, womanly. What is the word the English use? That is it, porky, to compare her with a pig, which is appropriate, *n'est-ce pas?*'

'Fuck off!' Sarah sobbed, surprised to hear the words in her own mouth.

'Yes,' d'Orsay continued, ignoring her completely, 'she is certainly porky, ideal for spanking, not that I in any way wish to denigrate your own derrière, Céleste. No, where she is porky, you are pert, and –'

'Kindly keep your observations on my anatomy to yourself, Monsieur,' Céleste said coldly. 'That was our agreement, was it not? Now, if you have looked your fill?'

'Oh ho, not quite,' he replied. 'Have you forgotten how she made you expose your breasts? She needs the same treatment, no?'

'That is true enough,' the woman admitted, and immediately began to tug Sarah's dress higher.

'No, not my breasts!' Sarah squealed. 'You don't need my breasts bare to spank me, Céleste, you don't! You just don't!'

She'd snatched back, trying to keep her dress from being pulled up, but Céleste immediately let go, and before Sarah realised what was happening the zip at the back had been tugged down. Immediately she made a grab for her front, only for her dress to be turned up further still. Again she snatched back, and immediately the woman's hand was under her chest. Sarah went wild, full of panic and frustration as she fought to protect herself, with d'Orsay laughing and slapping one fat thigh in merriment behind her. It did no good, Céleste was too clever and too quick, so that before long Sarah's dress was up around her neck, her bra catch was opened and finally the cups were pulled up, to flop out the full fat meat of her breasts. They jiggled and bounced beneath her chest as she continued to fight, now with both arms twisted up into the small of her back so that she was unable to cover her shame at all.

'Superb!' d'Orsay chuckled, breathless with laughter for the display Sarah knew must have been as ludicrous as it was erotic. '*Vraiment superbe!* Ah, but she is a fighter, no? Yet it was worth your trouble I think, Céleste. What a pair she has, true *bloblos*, such as you seldom see on a French girl.'

He had got up, and walked around his desk to get a better view of Sarah's dangling breasts. Céleste – and Sarah now found herself thinking of the woman as her heroine – made a small adjustment in her position, bringing Sarah's bottom up a little and leaving her breasts swinging free.

'*Bloblos*, my fat little English tart,' she explained, 'are heavy pendulous breasts, such as, perhaps, you might think to find on an overweight peasant girl who has just given birth.'

As she spoke the spanking began, Céleste's hand smacking down on Sarah's bare wriggling bottom. Overwhelmed by her emotions, she gave in to it, merely kicking a little in her pain and sobbing for all the bitterness and self-pity in her head. Monsieur d'Orsay stayed on his feet, giving the occasional cluck of satisfaction as he walked around the spanking scene. Sometimes he would pause, to admire Sarah from behind with her bottom bouncing to the slaps and her sex and even her anus on show, or to duck low to take a look at the faces she was pulling as she was punished.

Céleste paid little attention to him, spanking to a firm methodical rhythm that never allowed Sarah so much as an instant to compose herself before the next smack fell. If anything it hurt more than before, and her bottom began to warm more rapidly, until before long the same awful helpless feelings of strong sexual arousal had begun to steal over her. She tried to fight it, but she knew her own body was betraying her; her nipples were hard, her sex moist and swollen.

D'Orsay was still making a close inspection of her spanking, and she knew that not only could he see, but he would be fully aware of what the changes in her body implied. Sure enough, when he finally went back to his desk he gave a lewd knowing chuckle as he sat down, then spoke.

'You were right, Céleste, she is a whore at heart. Enough, I think. She is rosy and obviously warm, while I think I would burst at a touch.'

Céleste didn't answer, but the spanking stopped and Sarah's arm was released. Panting, she slid to the floor in a kneeling position, massaging her wrist briefly before putting her hands back to her hot bottom. Her skin was aglow, thick and hot and rough, her sex puffy and urgent between her thighs, so that she was shaking her head in furious and futile denial of her own feelings as d'Orsay continued.

'Just as she made you, Céleste. *Ça c'est juste, non?*'

'Do it,' Céleste ordered, looking down at Sarah, her voice full of cold satisfaction. 'Do it as you made me do it. Crawl to him on your knees with your pants down behind and your breasts showing bare. Get under the desk with your bottom stuck out behind and take him in your mouth, as I had to. Suck him, suck his horrible penis and make him come in your mouth and in your face, as you had him to me. Go on, do it, you little bitch, you dirty slut, you –'

She broke off suddenly to stand back, angry and yet still fully in command as she looked down. Frightened, her emotions a mess, Sarah could only obey, crawling on her knees to d'Orsay's desk and beneath it, all the time acutely aware of how she would look from behind with her panties down over her smacked bottom and her wet sex showing between her thighs. Once she was under the desk it was worse, her legs bent and cocked wide, her bottom splayed open to show her anus, the exact same rude pose Céleste had been in, and with Monsieur d'Orsay's taut lumpy crotch right in front of her face.

'Take my penis out,' he ordered.

'Do it!' Céleste snapped, and bent to plant a stinging slap on Sarah's outthrust bottom.

'Ow!' Sarah complained, her voice breaking close to tears as she went on, all sense of reality now abandoned. 'I didn't do that to you!'

'No,' Céleste answered her. 'You did not. You had me masturbate, you filthy *salope*, and you are going to do the same as you suck him. Now take him out, and I want to see those fat fingers on your cunt.'

Sarah bit her lip hard as Monsieur d'Orsay spread his legs and came a little forward in the chair to make

97

it easier for her to take his cock out. A long thick bulge showed under his trousers, which he squeezed and adjusted into a more central position before folding his hands over his paunch. He was looking down as Sarah put trembling fingers to his fly, his face redder and sweatier than ever, his eyes bulging with delight, just as she had drawn him as Céleste prepared to undertake the same degrading task.

'Come on!' Céleste urged, and planted another hard smack on Sarah's bottom.

With her face set in a scowl of consternation, Sarah began to undo Monsieur d'Orsay's fly, first peeling the zip down, then opening the buttons higher up. As she worked, her fingers would occasionally brush the turgid lump of his penis, making her flinch and bringing a sickly feeling to her stomach at the thought of taking it in her mouth. She hesitated as his fly fell wide, but again Céleste smacked her, and with a wince of distaste she tugged down the front of his underpants.

His cock sprang free, fat and fleshy and dirty, an obscene thing, exactly as she had drawn him. Remembering the picture, she let a hand burrow into his underpants and pulled out his balls, the heavy scrotum every bit as fat and wrinkled as in her imagination. Now in a trance, she rocked forward, taking his cock in her hand, and with a final mental effort, feeding it into her own mouth. A strong taste filled her senses, both masculine and sour, making her gag. She sucked and swallowed, knowing she'd be sick on his cock if she didn't, and he spoke.

'Oh ho, she is truly eager! Not like you, Céleste.'

Sarah pulled back, wanting to deny his words but forced to draw in air before she could speak.

'No, I –'

Céleste immediately leant forward across the desk and twisted her hand cruelly into Sarah's hair. Forced to take the big cock back in her mouth, Sarah's words broke off in an odd gulping noise. Monsieur d'Orsay gave a pleased cluck and Sarah began to have her face fucked, Céleste pulling her up and down by the hair and talking as she did it.

'Not eager enough,' she said. 'You suck, you little *cocotte*, like you made me. Take it deep, Sarah, as deep as I did, go on!'

With the last order Sarah's head was pushed down harder still, forcing the thick bulbous head of d'Orsay's cock down her throat. She was gagging immediately, with her cheeks bulging and her eyes popping as her head was held down and her hands flapping ineffectually at the Frenchman's legs. Only when her face had begun to go red did Céleste relent, pulling Sarah's head up, and off, to leave her gasping for breath once more before she could find words.

'Don't, Céleste, please! I didn't do that to you, did I? I'll do it, but let me do it my own way.'

Céleste gave a contemptuous grunt and kept her hand twisted in Sarah's hair, but gave up her control. Sarah took hold of the thick cock, full of self-disgust and shame as she began to tug on it, and telling herself she was only doing it to stop Céleste hurting her, to get her ordeal over quickly, because she had no choice – anything but that she wanted to do it and have him come down her throat and in her face the way she had drawn Céleste getting it.

'That's better,' Céleste admitted grudgingly. 'Yes, Monsieur d'Orsay, she is eager. She is a slut. Now, Sarah, why are you not masturbating? You must want to, or why make me do it? Go on, rub your cunt, you little tart. We don't mind.'

Her voice was rich with mockery as she spoke, and Sarah found herself reaching back immediately, to touch her puffy sopping vulva. Her clitoris ached for her fingers, and after one half-reluctant motion she gave in, masturbating freely as she tugged on d'Orsay's now rock-solid penis. He gave a grunt of pleasure at her added attention, Céleste a snort of contempt, and Sarah a last bitter sob of shame as she let her feelings go.

It was right, what they'd done to her, spanked her bare bottom and made her suck cock on her knees. She deserved it. She loved it. She wanted it done again, only for the spanking to be longer and harder and more humiliating, done in public, for her to be made to suck any man who wanted attention to his penis, to have her hair twisted and her face fucked the way Céleste had just done.

As if in response to her wish, Céleste once more tightened her grip in Sarah's hair, painfully hard. Her head was jammed down, the fat cock forced into her gullet, and again, deeper, making her gag, and yet she was still rubbing at her sex, still wanking on what little cock stuck out between her lips. She started to come, thinking of what was being done to her no longer with self-pity and misery and resentment, but in ecstasy as her sex went tight. Again her head was forced down onto the swollen cock, harder still, and Sarah was coming even as a great gush of spunk erupted into her throat.

D'Orsay grunted loudly as Sarah tried desperately to swallow, failed, and coughed up the full mass of what had just been done down her throat. It went all over his trousers as he tossed himself into her face, spattering her cheeks and hair, smearing it direct from his jerking cock tip onto her nose, filling the pits of both eyes until she was completely unable to see.

She didn't care, revelling in it as she snatched at her sex, with the same words running over and over in her head, stripped and spanked and made to suck, stripped and spanked and made to suck, stripped and spanked and made to suck, until at last she screamed out in her ecstasy, completely out of control as her face was forced down on Monsieur d'Orsay's genitals by Céleste.

'That is the way,' Céleste crowed as she smeared Sarah's face into the rubbery spunk-soiled flesh, 'all over you, you little trollop, as you come, you filthy *salope, putain!'*

Céleste's voice was no longer calm but full of glee, and she kept Sarah's head firmly in place even when the spasms of orgasm has subsided. Sarah's nose was clogged with spunk and mucus, forcing her to open her mouth over d'Orsay's slippery balls in order to breathe, but as she tried to pull back Céleste's grip tightened once more, keeping her firmly in place.

'Stay as you are,' Céleste ordered, 'and listen. You liked that because you are a wanton, a natural whore, but when you come down you will not be quite so proud of yourself, no?'

Sarah shook her head, her lewd feelings already fading with her ecstasy and desperate to be allowed to take her face out of Monsieur d'Orsay's crotch.

'So I thought,' Céleste confirmed. 'Understand this then. You will never make me do anything of this sort again, never! You will treat me as I deserve, as a lady, and show due respect for my status and my modesty. You will not depict me naked, nor in any situation of disadvantage, with Monsieur d'Orsay or anybody else, do you understand?'

Sarah nodded frantically, her face now too comprehensively coated in slime for it to make any difference.

'*Bon*,' Céleste responded. 'If you do, I suspect you can imagine what will happen to you, yes?'

Again Sarah nodded.

'*Bon*,' Céleste repeated. 'Let us get your painting, then, and perhaps we shall see if young Armand has the skill to depict the same scene in rather more detail, and perhaps with rather more of the realist perspective.'

She laughed at her own suggestion as Sarah's head was finally released. Monsieur d'Orsay gave a pleased chuckle and put his cock and balls away after making a few perfunctory dabs with his handkerchief. Sarah was allowed to use her compact and some tissues from her bag to wipe the mess from her face, then she was escorted downstairs.

The stalls and street were as before, Armand now seated on a high stool, smoking a reflective cigarette. He and Céleste conducted a brief negotiation in rapid French, with the occasional gesture towards Sarah, who stood sulkily to one side. Presently the painting was wrapped up and changed hands. Sarah took it, feeling oddly numb and quite unable to disobey, recognising also that what had been done to her was entirely reasonable, however horrid. After all, she had done the same to Céleste, and while it made no more sense than before, she could no longer deny the woman's identity, nor that of Monsieur d'Orsay.

Seven

Just a month before, if asked how she would feel about being dragged into a building, spanked, and made to suck a man's penis, she would have been horrified by the very thought, and if she had provided an answer at all would have said she'd be traumatised. As it was, she found it impossible to accept what had happened as real, despite the warmth of her bottom and the lingering taste of man in her mouth. She had the painting too, and yet from the moment she had seen Giles standing outside the museum her memories had been closer to those of a dream or a fantasy than reality.

His reaction removed any last doubts that he might have been in any way involved. As they walked back towards the river and then the hotel, his conversation focused entirely on the museum, the painting and whether they should eat in the hotel restaurant or visit somewhere from the Michelin guide he had brought. Sarah said very little, somewhat bemused and wishing the warmth of her smacked cheeks hadn't once more begun to send urgent signals to her sex.

Back in their room Giles grew amorous, to Sarah's alarm as she knew full well that her skin would still be red and that given his obsession with her bottom he could hardly fail to want to turn her over, and notice. She was not ready to admit what had happened, let alone that it had been done by two fictitious characters of her own creation, and ended up pretending that she was not in the mood.

After dinner and a brief inspection to ensure that her bottom had returned to a normal healthy pale flesh pink instead of spanked rose, she made up for her earlier refusal, first allowing him to have her on her knees and then tossing him over her own bottom. Delighted by her lewd behaviour, he took her back down to the bar and ordered Champagne, leading to more sex later that night.

The next few days followed a similar pattern, sight-seeing and shopping and sex. Sarah was nervous at first, constantly on the lookout for both Céleste and Monsieur d'Orsay, but neither appeared and, to her intense chagrin, her worry began to give way to longing. Céleste had been wrong, at least in part. The punishment had scared Sarah and made her contrite, also filled her with self-disgust for enjoying it so much at the end, but it had also left her with an empty sensation that no amount of sex with Giles could fill, however good.

She needed something more, and that something was to be spanked. It had to be done properly too, taken across his knee and held firmly in place as her outer clothes were disarranged and her panties pulled down, then her cheeks smacked without thought for her protests until she achieved that glorious glowing feeling that came no other way. Unfortunately it didn't seem to be something he was interested in. Plainly she was going to have to ask and, if that rather spoiled the fantasy, then at least she would be getting what she now needed more than any other part of sexual pleasure save orgasm itself.

A week had passed before she decided she could wait no longer and would have to overcome her embarrassment. They were due back the next day, and she had decided that it was important to take her first spanking in Paris or, at least, her first spanking from somebody other than Céleste du Musigny. Giles was keen on a grand meal for their final evening, and while Sarah wasn't sure if that was a good idea if she was to be put across his knee afterwards she immediately accepted, telling herself she would eat very little and drink plenty.

They chose the Café d'Arles in Montmartre, once the haunt of artists, now refurbished to one of the finest and most expensive restaurants in the city. Giles ordered the *menu gastronomique* and Sarah quickly became lost in the succession of delicacies brought to them, and thoroughly drunk due to Giles' insistence that each and every one should be accompanied by a different wine. By the end she was having difficulty standing and badly in need of the loo.

Leaving Giles to a final glass of Cognac, she made her way as best she could to a ladies' toilet exactly as fresh and fragrant as she would have expected, only to freeze with the door held half open. Céleste du Musigny stood at a sink, washing her hands in a fastidious manner. Sarah's head filled with awful visions, of being bent across the sink to have her big bottom smacked as a procession of elegant French ladies came and went, or dragged out into the restaurant for a public spanking, or taken into the kitchens and made to suck off the entire male staff . . .

She was unable to run, unable to resist, and Céleste had seen her, the mirror behind the sinks reflecting both their images which contrasted so glaringly that Sarah suddenly felt how impudent of her it was to even come to such a place. Céleste might dine at the

Café d'Arles with impunity, but for Sarah it was like using bone china at a chimpanzee's tea party. She waited to be addressed, and at last Céleste turned around.

'Aping your betters, Sarah?' she remarked.

'I – I'm sorry,' Sarah said, the words slipping out despite herself. 'Are – are you going to spank me?'

'Spank you?' Céleste replied, her voice tinged with amusement. 'No. If the patron has the poor taste to admit you, then it is no affair of mine, while so far as your behaviour to me is concerned, I trust you have already learned your lesson?'

'Yes,' Sarah lied, then continued. 'Céleste . . . may I ask you a question?'

'No,' Céleste answered simply as she finished drying her hands.

'But –' Sarah began and stopped.

Céleste had left, without so much as a backward glance. Sarah stood still for a moment, staring at the door through which her heroine had disappeared, before the urgency in her bladder brought her back to her senses. There was considerable relief as she sat down, not merely for easing the strain, but because she had escaped a spanking, yet the feeling that it would have been fully deserved would not go away.

As her pee gushed into the bowl she closed her eyes, imagining how it might have been. Being put over the sinks would have been deeply embarrassing, and she could picture herself so easily, held down with one arm in the small of her back, her dress trapped beneath her badly twisted wrist, her panties down to her thighs as Céleste applied a firm spanking. Other women who came in would see, but would barely notice, any more than the customers at the café on the Île St. Louis. After all, Sarah was only some fat-bottomed English slut being spanked for impudence, it was hardly important.

She shook herself, fighting the urge to slip a hand between her thighs and bring herself to a badly needed orgasm. Only the bloated feeling in her stomach prevented her, but she allowed her fingers to stray there and to the heavy mounds of her breasts as she considered how much lewder it would have been to be taken out and spanked in the restaurant. That way the other diners could have seen the consequences of her appallingly gauche act in daring to show herself at the Café d'Arles, a bare bottom-spanking in public. Yes, that was what she deserved, to get it in front of all the elegant beautiful people in the restaurant, with her dress pulled up and her bottom bare, the biggest roundest bottom in the restaurant by far, a fat wobbling English bottom, so utterly different to the perfectly pert posteriors of the French ladies. Afterwards, when she was rosy and snivelling, she would be taken out to the back, stripped nude, put on her knees among the refuse bins and made to suck off every single male member of staff, until her entire body was plastered in spunk as she masturbated.

Again she shook herself. Her nipples were hard, poking up through her dress, and the urgency between her thighs was hard to deny. She had at least finished peeing, and quickly dabbed herself with a piece of toilet tissue, promising not to go further but to wait for Giles. Drunk, aroused and desperately in need of attention to her bottom, she knew that she could ask, that she would ask, because if he refused he wasn't worth being with.

Out in the restaurant she glanced around, looking for Céleste, but there was no sign of her heroine, while the customers were not the wealthy French exquisites she had been imagining at all, but mainly tourists. Nor would hers have been the biggest

107

bottom in the restaurant, an honour that went to a middle-aged woman, obviously American, who not only had a backside of truly stupendous proportions but was wearing pink lycra trousers. Several others also exceeded or equalled her own dimensions, leaving her in perhaps seventh or eighth place.

Giles had finished his Cognac and dealt with the bill, offering his arm as she reached the table. She took it, allowing herself to be escorted out and to a waiting taxi. The journey seemed to pass in an instant, and at the hotel she declined his offer of a last drink in the bar, suggesting they have a bottle sent up instead. Giles readily agreed, and she was soon propped on the bed, sipping cold Champagne with one hand resting lightly on her bulging tummy. Her bottom needed attention as badly as ever, and the sight of Giles in black tie was making her need more urgent still, but she knew she would have to wait at least a little. He seemed to have other ideas.

'Wouldn't you feel better doing that nude?' he asked, settling himself into a chair.

Sarah simply smiled and put her glass down, enjoying being told what to do and more than happy to be naked for him. Knowing how he liked her, she knelt up on the bed and turned her back, her eyes on his as she eased her dress up to show off her bottom. His response was a pleased nod and she pulled the dress right up, and off, telling herself that he had said nude, so she would go nude, without a stitch, although it was a shame not to have her panties peeled down the way Céleste did it.

Her shoes were already off, and her bra came next, unclipped at the back before she half turned to show Giles as she let the cups free, spilling out both big breasts into her hands. Throwing the bra aside, she spent a moment teasing her nipples to full erection,

108

then reached back to push her thumbs into the waistband of her panties. He was watching, comfortably seated with his glass in one hand and the other gently massaging his cock, which he'd pulled out as she took off her dress.

She closed her eyes, thinking how nice it was to be told to strip, and how much nicer it would be to be told to strip for a punishment spanking, preferably across his knee with several other people watching. As she began to ease her knickers down she was thinking of how it had felt to be bared in front of Monsieur d'Orsay, and wishing he was there too, to enjoy her shame, perhaps even for Giles to order her to suck the filthy old lecher off and take his spunk in her face.

A strong shiver ran through her as her panties came down over the tuck of her cheeks. Leaving them around her thighs, she went down on all fours, to show off her bottom with her back pulled in to make her cheeks spread and expose the rear views of both her sex and her anus. Her belly felt heavy, her breasts heavier still and, after a moment she rolled onto her back, giggling for her own naughty behaviour as she reached for her glass.

Giles was erect, nursing the long pale penis sprouting from his fly, with his balls out too, which Sarah found a delightfully rude contrast to his immaculate dinner jacket and perfect bow tie. That was how it should be, she thought, he fully dressed, decent save for his cock and balls, her stark naked, nothing hidden and ready to pleasure him in any way he pleased, only preferably after having her bottom smacked up to a glowing ball. Now was the time to ask, surely?

She rolled over, propping herself on the long bolster at the top of the bed as she looked back, knowing that the view would appeal to him and sure he could be tempted. He immediately began to tug harder on his cock.

'Do you like my bottom?' she asked.

'Do I like your bottom?' he echoed. 'Sarah, I adore your bottom, you know that. I could spend hours with my face between your cheeks, just licking you. I worship your bottom, I only wish you'd let me teach you how to take my cock up your hole.'

'I know,' she told him, 'and I would let you, but I could never take it. Now . . .'

'You could,' he interrupted, 'it just takes a little practice. I could train you.'

The idea of being trained to accept a cock up her bottom made Sarah shiver, and before she could pluck up the courage to bring the conversation around to spanking he spoke again.

'Try a finger, go on. Suck it first.'

Sarah pursed her mouth, but the thought of teasing herself between her cheeks as he watched was too much. Lifting her body, she rolled the bolster down the bed and laid herself over it, now with her hips raised to lift her bottom into full prominence, her cheeks a little parted, an excellent position to show off her anus to him, also an excellent position to be spanked in. It also left her bloated tummy clear of the bed, a sensation that brought some of the humiliations inflicted on her by Céleste to mind, especially how she'd been made to feel about having such a full bottom and big breasts.

'Why don't you come and do it?' she suggested.

'I want to watch you,' he said. 'I want to see the expression on your face as your finger goes in up that dirty little hole.'

Sarah swallowed and nodded, his rude words too compelling to resist. Deliberately turning her head so that he could see, she stuck a finger in her mouth, sucking it as the thought of how indecent she was about to be raged in her head. No decent girl would touch her own bottom hole save to wipe herself or in the bath, and certainly not in front of a boyfriend, only she wasn't a decent girl. She was a slut, just as Céleste had said, only too willing to show off her bottom and tickle the tight little hole between her cheeks, even put a finger inside.

She reached back to stroke her cheeks and between, feeling her open crease and shivering at the thought of what Giles could see. Her bottom hole was on plain show, and he wanted her to touch, to put a finger in. A moment to overcome a last barrier of decency and she'd done it, tickling the puckered bumpy flesh of her anus, a sensation at once so rude and so good that she was quickly sighing in pleasure.

It was almost too much, to have a man behind her as she teased her anus, even her boyfriend, so utterly indecent, but far too good to stop. He was erect, thinking how his cock would feel in that same tiny hole. She felt a touch of fear at the prospect. Her hole was so tight, her anal ring a puckered knot of muscle, completely closed, even with her spit-wet finger caressing and pushing at the central pit.

'Relax,' Giles advised, 'let yourself open, as if you were on the loo.'

'I can't!' Sarah sobbed. 'I'll poo myself!'

Giles chuckled and stood up. Sarah twisted around, wondering if he was simply going to climb up on the bed and have her anyway, his patience lost as he forced her anal ring, buggering her on the bed whether she liked it or not. He didn't, but went into the bathroom, emerging a moment later with a tube of toothpaste.

'This will help,' he told her. 'Hold your cheeks apart.'

Sarah obeyed, her feelings of exposure and shame growing stronger still as she reached back to haul her meaty cheeks wide, stretching out her anus. There was a maniacal quality to his grin as he climbed on top of her, straddling her legs to pin her down as he poised the tube over her open bottom. He squeezed, extruding a fat green worm of toothpaste from the tube, which broke and fell, landing right on her anus with the faintest of squashy sounds.

'Rub it in,' he instructed. 'I'll hold you wide.'

His hands found her bottom cheeks, spreading them wider still. She shut her eyes again, shivering with shame-filled pleasure as her finger went to her anus, squashing the little coil of toothpaste onto her ring. A little went in up her hole, more squashing out around her finger. She made a face, the slimy feeling at once disgusting and intensely pleasurable as she begun to rub it in, only for the cool moist sensation to start to grow warm, then hot.

'Ow!' Sarah protested. 'That burns!'

'I know,' Giles said happily, 'but it's made you nice and loose, hasn't it?'

Sarah's answer was a gasp, aghast at the trick he'd played on her, and yet there was no denying it was true, the toothpaste had not merely begun to lubricate her anus, but the now ferocious burning sensation was making her sphincter go loose, and she knew it would no longer be hard to get her finger in.

'You bastard, Giles,' she sighed, and she'd done it, slipping one finger in up the well-lubricated ring, and deeper.

Her mouth had come wide as she began to finger her bottom, the burning sensation, the feeling of being penetrated and the impossibly improper knowledge that here she was touching her own bumhole all coming together in a rush of wanton ecstasy that broke what little resistance she still had. Not that it made much difference, with Giles pinning her to the bed, his rock-hard erection towering over her naked vulnerable bottom and sure to be plunged deep up her now-open hole as soon as she vacated it.

Another touch of fear hit her at the realisation that she was now going to be buggered, and with a cock thicker by far than the finger now working urgently in her burning anus.

'Wait,' she managed, breathless, and gasped as she eased in a second finger alongside the first, then a third.

She was whimpering as she felt her anal ring stretch wider still, with reaction and for the thought of how she must look, bottom up over a bolster in a French hotel room, her bottom cheeks held wide and three fingers inserted up the slippery gaping hole between. Giles' cock touched, prodding the softness of her thighs, and higher, into the groove between leg and buttock.

'Okay,' Sarah gasped as she pulled her fingers free. 'Do it, Giles . . . gently, but do it . . . right up my bum . . .'

Her voice broke to a moan, of despair for her dirty feelings and of pleasure as she felt the rounded rubbery bulb of his cock tip press between her thighs but not to her sex, to her anus. She buried her face in the bed, clutching the sheets in an agony of emotion as she felt her virgin bottom ring start to spread, slimy and hot around his invading penis, taut, so taut she was sure she would split, only for her muscle to suddenly give and a good half the length of Giles' cock to jam suddenly up her bottom.

'I'm in you,' he gasped. 'I'm up your bum, Sarah . . . God you're so lovely, so tight, so hot, so meaty, so fat . . .'

Sarah felt a touch of chagrin for his words, even as he wedged another inch or so of penis into her rectum. His balls touched between her thighs, the hair tickling her, and where his pubes were between her bum cheeks, but one more good shove and he was right in. Sarah was unable to resist a moan of pleasure as she felt the mass of his ball sack press to her sex. He was in her, up her bottom, his stiff cock moving in the cavity of her rectum, something so unspeakably rude she was shaking her head as much in reaction to her emotions as to the sensation of her buggering.

Still she was wishing she'd been spanked, but first, after a little ritual of punishment, put across the knee, her panties taken down, her bottom spanked, made to open her own anus with a finger as he watched, and finally buggered. She was saying the word over and over again as he picked up his pace in her rectum, his hard belly now slapping her bottom and his balls beating a rhythm on her empty cunt. Already she knew she was going to want it again, and not merely as a surrender to his lust, but for her own sake, or best of all, as a punishment.

As the thought hit her she was fighting to get her hand to her sex, desperate to rub off while she was given her first ever buggering. She couldn't do it, the bolster was in the way, but with Giles now grunting and panting on top of her, thrusting so hard that her anal ring was pulling in and out on his cock, every slap of his balls on her sex made her more urgent still. She sobbed in frustration, only for her mind to find a way out, telling her that it was for the best, that if a man buggered her as a punishment she shouldn't be allowed to come. Yes, that was perfect. When she did something wrong in future she would be spanked and then buggered by the man who'd spanked her, the ideal way to handle a naughty girl.

114

'So good,' Giles moaned, suddenly slowing his pace, 'so, so good ... God I love you, Sarah, you gorgeous fat-bottomed little trollop, and now I'm going to spunk up your bum.'

'Yes,' Sarah gasped as he once more started to thrust, 'do it up me, Giles, and tell me what a bad girl I am. Tell me how you like my bottom ... my fat bottom. Tell me how you're going to ... to punish me, Giles, to spank my fat cheeks and stick your cock up my bottom hole ... punish me, Giles, spank me and bugger me and spunk in my bottom!'

She was screaming the words out as she finished, and he'd done it, finishing off up her bum with a crescendo of furious shoves then going suddenly still, his cock held as deep as it would go. Her body was being crushed down into the bed, but the instant he had finished and began to relax her hand was burrowing back and her knees coming up, lifting herself into a kneeling position as she began to babble.

'No, no, keep it in, Giles ... keep your lovely cock in, deep up, and smack me ... smack me ... spank my naughty bottom while I come, Giles, go on, you bastard, do it!'

Her hand was on her sex, clutching at her swollen lips, and higher, thrusting two fingers into her vacant cunt with a third raised to touched the junction of his cock and her anus. A jolt of pleasure not far from orgasm hit her at the feel of her taut ring, stretched out around the intruding penis, and she began to masturbate with the palm of her hand as her fingers groped at his balls, her empty cunt and best of all, her straining buggered anus.

'You are such a little slut, Sarah,' Giles laughed, and brought one hand down on her bottom. 'Imagine wanting your bottom spanked!'

At his words her muscles tightened, the first contraction of orgasm, brought on by the exquisite shame of being spanked and laughed at while she was spanked. He began to beat out a rhythm on her bottom cheeks, chuckling as he did it, and she was there, the contractions now violent as she pictured how she would look, on her knees, stark naked, her fat pink bottom stuck in the air, his cock deep in her bumhole as her big wobbling cheeks were spanked.

Eight

After the ecstasies and unrealities of Paris, London felt mundane to Sarah, even in the company of Giles. The events of the previous week already seemed remote, her virgin buggering little less so than the encounter with Céleste du Musigny and Monsieur d'Orsay. She knew at a rational level that the latter was impossible, but she found herself unable to acknowledge that as important. She had been smacked across Céleste's knee as surely as she had been buggered, both events sharp in her memory, while she had the painting to prove it.

One of the first things she had done on getting home was to hang it, in her own room where she would be able to admire it for the sake of inspiration and to remind herself of what had happened. The only drawback was that it also reminded her of why she had been punished, and Céleste's threats of further punishment, but even there her reaction was ambiguous. The spanking had hurt, sucking Monsieur d'Orsay off had been utterly disgusting, both experiences had been deeply humiliating, yet she found herself craving more of the same, in turn guilty for being unfaithful to Giles, and in turn again craving punishment from him in the form of spanking and sodomy.

That at least she got, in bed together on their first night back, with him slipped in from behind her, first in her vagina and, when a little juice had run down to lubricate her anus, up her bottom. She was still bruised and sore, so it hurt more than the first time, but she felt she deserved it and made no complaint, especially when he pushed back the covers and began to smack her exposed cheek.

In the morning she was waddling somewhat, and had to make him promise to leave her bottom alone for a while, although it seemed a shame to abandon what had already become a craving. She had agreed to go down to Berkshire with him at the weekend and meet his parents, a prospect she found both flattering and alarming, but both turned out to be very different from her expectations, while she also found herself enjoying Rebecca's company.

On the following Monday they met with Hugh Bowle, who told them he had secured yet another syndication, this time in Korea. Giles stayed that night but left in the morning as Sarah needed to work, and once more she found herself seated in front of her drawing board with a pure white sheet of A2 in front of her and her pencil in her mouth as she considered the third episode of 'Graverobbers'. They had been through it, and in theory it was simple, and extremely rude. The first frame was to show Céleste meeting with the three roughs in a Parisian back alley, the last to show her standing in the half light of the graveyard while the men began their gruesome task. All the other frames were supposed to show her having sex with the three men and, while she was only supposed to hint at what was really happening, both Giles and Hugh wanted her to imply that Céleste not only took one of the men up her bottom, but that she actively enjoyed her buggering.

After a few minutes of tapping her teeth with the pencil and making a few tentative lines, Sarah gave in to the inevitable and went to fetch a bottle of wine. For all her change in attitude over the last few weeks, she simply could not bring herself to draw Céleste being not only so lewd, but with such men and in such an environment. It was utterly sordid, the exact opposite of Céleste's character, while it was all too easy to imagine what Sarah's own fate might be.

The least she could expect was to be dragged into an alley and put through her paces by three men in her mouth, sex and anus, and while Céleste watched. Just thinking about it made both holes tighten in her panties, and telling herself not to be ridiculous made no difference at all. It had happened before, and so it could happen again, while she couldn't even be sure if not going to Paris would be a defence.

It was hardly being faithful to Giles either, but after two glasses of the strong Chilean red he'd brought over a few days before, she was telling herself that he'd written the story, so he could hardly complain if the consequences were that his girlfriend got gang-banged in a Parisian back alley. If it didn't happen then there wasn't a problem, but if it did, then it was plainly his fault.

She tried to start drawing, but found herself unable to put the pencil to the page. It was just too strong, to think of how she'd find herself unable to disobey Céleste's orders, probably taking down her own panties and pulling up her top to show her breasts, unless of course Céleste chose to spank her first, or simply threw her to the men. They'd soon have her clothes off, probably torn off, or left hanging in rags around her body as they used her, one big cock forced down her throat, another pushed to the hilt in her pussy, a third jammed deep up her straining anus.

It was outrageous, unthinkable, but then so was being spanked in public and holding her bottom open for her boyfriend to bugger her, and she had done both. There was also the prospect of revenge, because as the wine began its work she was feeling rather less passive about what had been done to her. After all, she hadn't shown Céleste being spanked, just doing what any girl might do, although admittedly with a fairly gross man. Yes, the punishments had been completely out of proportion. Perhaps if Sarah had been made to take down her panties and hold her top up for Monsieur d'Orsay the first time, and to suck him the second, then that would have been fair, but to spank her, and in public! Céleste had it coming, and the fact that Sarah had come to crave punishment made it worse. After all, what a terrible thing to do to somebody, to make them yearn for their own degradation.

Slowly, carefully, she began to draw a rat. He was a nasty rat, a big rat, fat and sleek, with great chipped incisors and an evil gleam in his eye. Another, smaller rat lay nearby, dead, the victim of a disputed fish head which the first was now eating. Beyond the rats were a pair of dustbins, overflowing with refuse, and beyond that four dark figures, three male, the fourth female, Céleste, with her face lit by a single dim lamp at the end of the alley. Money was changing hands.

Already she had done enough to give the prissy little bitch a fit of the vapours, and Sarah was grinning as she continued, knowing she had already gone too far, much too far. She began to pencil in more detail, now working fast, first the leering expectant face of the leader of the three roughs as he suggested sex. Under no circumstances was it possibly to show Céleste simply accepting, so Sarah drew the second rough leaning in to make her an offer she had little choice but to accept. There was no room for anything more subtle or more elaborate, that was that, Céleste was going to have to satisfy all three, right there in the alley.

They were a fine trio, real pigs, a father and two sons, right out of the gutter. Raoul was the father, middle-aged, hard-faced, with an ugly scar running down his forehead and one glass eye. He was dressed in coarse workman's clothes, his cock a monstrous thing, huge and wrinkled, lying on a bulging scrotum as he presented himself to Céleste and demanded she suck him.

Marcel was the eldest son, a lean vicious creature whose features Sarah modelled on the king rat she had drawn in the top frame, taller than his father and with genitals to match, his cock unnaturally thin and long and bent. He could appear in the background of the third frame, easily visible as Céleste sank to her knees to take Raoul in her mouth, waiting his turn with his erect penis in his hand.

The younger son would be Lamond, as tall as his brother but bigger by far, obscenely fat with a stupid drooling face and a great stubby cock, short in proportion with an outside helmet already taut and shiny with blood as he watched his father's penis grow in Céleste's beautifully painted mouth.

With all three roughs pencilled in, Sarah swallowed what remained in her glass. The scene was coming on nicely, but it remained to show Céleste first trying to get it over and done with, then losing control and making an utter slut of herself, just as Sarah had done with Monsieur d'Orsay. First a few clothes would have to come off, which meant a series of small frames, with Raoul's dirty fingers digging into Céleste's immaculate blouse, pulling, tearing it wide and turning up her expensive designer bra to expose her breasts, the nipples already erect.

That left room for one more good-sized frame, showing the expression on Céleste's face. It was one of utter revulsion as she sucked on the now rock-hard penis in her mouth, with Raoul pawing one pert breast to leave dirty finger marks on the smooth white skin. Marcel was watching with a cruel grin. Lamond was giggling inanely as he pointed out Céleste's erect nipples as evidence of her excitement.

Sarah swallowed, imagining herself in the same position, breasts out and sucking cock, about to utterly disgrace herself as she gave in to her needs. Until that point she'd need to be made to do it, but afterwards ... afterwards she'd be playing with her breasts and rubbing her pussy under her skirt, she'd be pulling aside her own panties to offer her sex, she'd be sucking on Raoul's balls with a finger up her bum to get herself ready for one of his sons to bugger her.

Céleste was going to do all of those things, and more. Again Sarah began to draw, this time with one hand between her thighs, gently massaging the plump puffy mound of her sex. That made it easier, growing bolder as she masturbated. Four frames took care of Céleste's rising excitement, just as Sarah had imagined it, with the last showing Céleste's bottom with her black lace panties pulled aside, her sex wet with juice and a finger tip just about to be inserted into the tight brown anus.

A few quick lines took care of the final frame, leaving a big irregular white space. Now kneading her pussy with mounting urgency, Sarah began to fill in with two drawings, one showing Céleste from the front, now mounted on Raoul as she sucked on Marcel's cock, with the grotesque Lamond about to insert his stumpy penis between her open buttocks, open because she herself was holding them wide in expectation of a good hard buggering.

The second showed Céleste's final disgrace, Raoul pumping into her from beneath, Marcel with his hideous cock jammed deep down her throat, Lamond with his face set in idiot glee, her anus a taut glistening ring on his cock shaft, her fingers clearly busy with her sex as the men used her. It was good, and Sarah knew that her hand was going down her panties the instant she was finished, but it could still be better. She needed three close-ups as the men came, small frames positioned around the main drawing.

First was Raoul's, his cock deep in Céleste's gaping hole, the spunk exploding out around his shaft, her anus a gaping black hole as Lamond prepared to enter her again, her fingers plainly visible among the slippery folds of her sex. Next was Marcel's, his long cock in his hand, tossing great gouts of thick white spunk into Céleste's face, her mouth held wide to catch it, her expression one of dopey ecstasy as she revelled in being soiled. Last was Lamond's, cock in hand, pumping spunk into Céleste's open anal passage, from which it had begun to dribble down into her now vacant cunt as she brought herself to orgasm.

Sarah wasn't even going to have to put a hand down her knickers. The pencil lead broke as she sketched in the final lines and she had given in to her excitement, massaging her pussy through her jeans as hard as she could. It was enough, grinding the panty material to her clitoris, and she was coming, crying out again and again as the waves of ecstasy swept over her.

The moment it was over she knew she was going to have to get drunk again in order to pluck up the courage to ink it in, but that wasn't really a problem. For the moment she felt distinctly sticky and wanted a leisurely bath, which she ran while she undressed, finally climbing into it with the last of the bottle for company.

As she lay soaking it dawned on her that she was in fact going to have to tone her artwork down, not because of what she'd shown being done to Céleste, but because it was way beyond the limits acceptable in the guidelines. The thought put a wry smile on her face and she had closed her eyes, relaxing in the hot water, drunk and happy. After a while she heard the door bang as Mak returned, but she paid no attention save to call out a greeting, perfectly happy for him to come in and talk to her if he wanted to. It was ridiculous to be shy in front of a man for whom her body held no interest whatsoever.

Having him see a drawing she had done of a woman getting gang-banged by roughs was another matter, especially the final frames, but it was already too late. She heard him call out in admiration, and a moment later he had come in, looking down on her with his hands on his hips and an expression of mock severity on his face.

'You are one bad girl!' he told her. 'And one good artist. If only that was a guy you'd shown getting it three ways!'

He finished with a long whistle and Sarah found herself smiling and blushing for the compliment and what he'd seen, not, she told herself, because despite being low in the water her breasts still rose out of the bubbles like two enormous pink jellies.

'How could a man take it three ways anyway?' she asked after a moment.

'One in the mouth, two up his arse,' he replied casually. 'But I thought you said it couldn't get that strong anyway?'

'I have to tone it down,' she admitted. 'I got a bit carried away.'

'You bet you did!' he answered her. 'But you can't lose that, it's too good.'

'Maybe I'll ink it in anyway,' she said, 'just for myself.'

'You do that.'

She did, using her back light to create a less pornographic version of her artwork and inking in both over a period of several days and several bottles of wine. In the second version the men's erections were hidden in shade or visible only as bulges in their clothing, while she removed all the frames that showed close-ups of cocks and Céleste's body. The result was still good, but less so than the original, and for the first time she found herself wishing she could go beyond the guidelines rather than worrying about her work being strong enough for male tastes.

Hugh Bowle was delighted with the official version, but she kept the other to herself and Giles, who was so taken with it that they ended up having sex on the floor. It was hurried and passionate, but when she came with his cock in her mouth and her sex and bottom spread to his face, she was imagining how it would feel to be made to satisfy both him and the three roughs together.

The rest of the day was spent with him in her flat, watching two of Mak's old films and snacking, and for the first time Sarah began to feel that there was more to their relationship than a string of exciting sexual encounters. Giles ate at the flat too, and Sarah finally introduced him to Mak, who was better behaved than she had expected, neither trying to flirt with him nor making remarks about the sexual preferences of public school boys.

By the time she fell asleep after a long and intimate sex session that for once didn't involve her being rolled bottom-up for his orgasm, she had decided that she would be faithful to him, in practice, and in so far as it was possible in her fantasy life. Céleste, who she was coming to think of as real Céleste rather than cartoon Céleste, might have other ideas, but there was a way around it.

Céleste was a creature of Paris, cosmopolitan and quintessentially French. If the real Céleste was true to the cartoon Céleste, then she would avoid London and certainly never come to grimy grotty Stepney. Otherwise . . . but otherwise was too much to think about. The solution was simple. Sarah would avoid Paris.

They slept late, and Sarah was still drinking her morning coffee when she heard the letterbox go. Knowing that the house would be deserted save for the two of them, she ran downstairs in her bathrobe to check the post. Two letters were for her, a cheque from Ehrmann and Black that put a smile the full width of her face, and a thick brown envelope. She guessed what it was immediately and took it upstairs unopened and with her sense of embarrassment already rising.

Giles was slumped on the sofa, dressed in his shirt and a pair of boxer shorts, a cup of coffee in one hand. Sarah flashed the cheque in front of his face and sat down next to him.

'Pay,' she said, 'and this . . .'

She trailed off as she dug her thumb into the envelope flap, tearing it across to reveal the top of not one magazine, but two, with the titles visible as she tore the paper. One was *Boobie Babes*, the other *Hotties at Home*.

'I'm not sure I can look!' she said, the blood already rising to her face as she saw the top of her own head on the cover of the first magazine.

'I can,' Giles said eagerly as he snatched the magazines from the envelope. 'Oh my, look at her will you? I bet you don't get many of those to the pound! Oh, it's you, sorry.'

126

There was laughter in his voice and Sarah slapped his leg, blushing darker still as she saw the picture. Sid had managed to catch her with a still as she took her bra off in the phone box, so that her breasts showed through the main panel of the door. They looked simply enormous, lolling forward from her chest like a pair of great pink water balloons, and while her nipples were still concealed by the trim of her wet bra, it was obvious that they were erect. To make matters worse her face showed too, clearly recognisable in a frame of hair, her chagrined expression making it look as if she'd been caught out being naughty rather than posing on purpose.

'That's my Sarah!' Giles said happily. 'I'm going to frame this and keep it on my wall.'

'Don't you dare!' she exclaimed. 'What about your parents, and Rebecca!'

'They won't mind,' he assured her.

'It's the cover of a pornographic magazine, Giles, and a pretty smutty one at that!'

'All the better,' he answered, and began to flick through the pages.

Sarah snuggled close, embarrassed and worried for the possible consequences, but unable to look away. The DVD attached to the cover of *Boobie Babes* showed the same picture of her, but there were more inside, captures of her shoot including her with her top wet, changing in the phone box and, worst of all, when she'd fallen out onto the pavement, rolling on her back with every single private detail of her body on show, including her anal star and her puffy and all too obviously excited sex. Giles gave a pleased sigh and squeezed the bulge in his boxer shorts, which was notably larger than before.

'God you're a turn-on!' he said, dropping *Boobie Babes* and picking up *Hotties at Home* instead.

There was only a single picture, to Sarah's relief, the same one as on the cover of *Boobie Babes* and a great deal smaller, but as Giles began to read out the text beneath her feelings changed.

'What's this then? "Meet Sarah from *Boobie Babes*, the bustiest bounciest bubble-butt babe out and a flasher too. Her 36F chest is all natural and she loves to get them out for the boys. She'll be in next month's issue, bare about the house and in kinky corner too, so don't miss it!"'

'They might at least have changed my name,' Sarah sighed. 'Not that it makes much difference, but what's this about me being in the next issue? They don't expect me to pose again, do they?'

'It looks like it,' Giles admitted.

'Cheek! They haven't even asked.'

'No? Did you read the stuff Hugh gave you to sign?'

'No. He said it was a model release.'

'Yes, but maybe for more than one shoot. Check your pay slip too.'

Sarah quickly burrowed her hand into the smaller of the envelopes and drew out the payslip from Ehrmann and Black. Sure enough, at the bottom of the detailed list of what she had been paid for was two hundred and fifty pounds credited from *Hotties at Home*.

'Shit!' she swore. 'The sneaky bastards!'

'That's Hugh all over,' Giles agreed, rather more casually than she would have liked. 'Let's see what the kinky corner is.'

He'd been flicking through the pages as he spoke, and stopped, opening the magazine out to show a double-page spread of photos, all showing the same girl as she went about what would have been ordinary household chores had she not been gradually undressing, from the first shot which showed her panties beneath a short skirt as she did the hoovering, to the last, in which she was scrubbing the bathroom floor, on her knees, stark naked and photographed from an angle that left nothing whatsoever to the imagination. Giles turned back a page to show another picture of the same girl, fully dressed with the title 'Bare about the House' at the top.

'So I have to do that?' Sarah said, knowing full well that she did, and would.

'It looks like it,' Giles agreed, flicking forward to another full-page picture, the same girl again, but bent into the bath with her bottom lifted and both pussy and anus on blatant display. 'She's cute, isn't she? Nice bumhole.'

Sarah slapped his leg for a second time, harder than before.

'Not as cute as you,' Giles said quickly. 'You'd look great like that!'

'Thanks a lot!'

'You would,' he insisted. 'Your boobs are twice the size of hers for one thing, and you've got a much bigger bum.'

'You really know how to flatter a girl, Giles Compton-Bassett,' Sarah answered him.

'Any time,' he told her. 'Shall we watch the DVD?'

'I suppose we'd better.'

Sarah was trying not to sulk as Giles set up the DVD. It looked as if she was going to have to let her panties down again, if not actually in public then for a large magazine audience. Effectively she had been tricked into it, although she could already hear the mock hurt in Hugh Bowle's voice if she dared to complain, explaining how she should have read the papers she'd signed. She knew she wouldn't dare anyway.

Giles sat back down, putting his arm around her as the DVD began to play. Sarah watched with rising chagrin as she appeared, seated at the pub table,

129

having Pimms thrown all over her, and with her breasts looking huge beneath her wet top. Giles had been massaging his cock as he watched, and now pulled it out. It stuck up half-erect from the opening of his boxer shorts.

'Wank me off, darling,' he said, a casual instruction rather than a request.

Sarah hesitated only a moment before reaching out to take his cock in hand. It felt bizarre, masturbating her boyfriend over her own public exposure and humiliation, but there was no denying it was getting to her, just as it was getting to him. To watch herself strip in the phone box was hideously embarrassing, especially as she pushed her bottom and boobs to the glass. It made her look clumsy and foolish, and gave the impression that she was little more than a pair of outsize tits and a big round bottom.

Seeing her attempt to struggle into the impossibly small panties was worse still, but nothing to the moment when she fell out of the phone box, rolling up on the pavement with her bottom spread and the three black youths plainly visible in the background. She thought of all the men watching, some laughing at her, some with their cocks in their hands, some actually coming over the sight of her wobbling boobs and wet ready sex, or, like Giles, the rude pink star of her anus. And suddenly he had come, the thick white spunk running down over her fingers as his cock erupted in her hand.

She gave in to the unequal struggle between her arousal and her feelings of embarrassment and shame, sticking her fingers in her mouth to suck up Giles' come even as she was tugging her clothes open. Her hand was still dirty, and she smeared the mess onto her breasts, enjoying the sensation of soiling herself and wishing she was doing it in public or in front of a camera as her sticky nipples poked up between fingers and thumbs.

The DVD had finished, and she shut her eyes, imagining herself back in the phone box, nude and squirming with embarrassment and panic, her body seemingly all bottom and boobs. Giles was right, it was good. It was good to have great big heavy breasts and a round cheeky bottom. It made her sexy, it made her a woman, it made her the object of men's desire, not aesthetically perhaps, but at a deep primitive level. She wanted them to enjoy her too, to see her nude in some smutty magazine.

Her body tightened with her approaching orgasm, one hand clutching at her breasts, the other busy with her sex. She felt Giles' touch, his hand sliding under one thigh, to tickle the plump swell of her bottom where her cheeks stuck out over the edge of the sofa, and push between. Her thighs came wide, inviting him to touch her anus, which he did, starting to tease, one finger circling the tiny hole as her ring began to contract in sympathy with her sex and bottom cheeks.

She was coming, on a wave of ecstasy as she imagined hundreds and thousands of men all masturbating over her naked body, every single one erect for her, coming for her, making her suck them, fucking her, buggering her. As she cried out, Giles penetrated her anus, slipping his finger deep up with her own juice to lubricate her passage. Again she screamed out, thinking of taking three cocks at once with a great queue of men also waiting to enjoy her. Her orgasm rose once more, then it began to fade, leaving her with the thought that what she'd just come over couldn't exactly be described as faithful, then that Giles seemed to love showing her off to other men anyway, if not necessarily having her taken three at a time.

Nine

Hugh Bowle rang the next day, his voice bland and professional as he asked Sarah if the weekend would be convenient to photograph her for 'Bare about the House' and the 'Kinky Corner'. Having already surrendered to what she felt was inevitable, she agreed, telling herself that having been in *Boobie Babes* already there was no point in fighting to preserve whatever modesty had not already been stripped away.

She consoled herself with the thought that she would at least be on her own, not sucking cock or penetrated like the girls in the harder magazines. It was also helpful to have a boyfriend who encouraged her and supported her instead of becoming possessive or prudish about her body.

'Bare about the House' followed the same routine in every issue, with a girl stripping as she did her housework, from fully clothed in the opening shot to stark naked in the final one. It was rude, sexist and humiliating, an utterly inappropriate way to treat a woman and, for Sarah, intensely arousing. 'Kinky Corner' was simpler, a single full-page shot of a girl in a mildly unusual sexual situation. In the case of the issue Sarah had seen it was a buxom girl with her blouse pulled down around her waist as baked beans were poured into her cleavage from above. Just to look at it made Sarah think she could feel the mixture of beans and sauce slithering down over her breasts and pooling around her tummy as they got under her blouse, but she knew her own fate would be different.

Saturday arrived and she found herself no less nervous than the time before, blushing every time she thought of what was ahead, her nipples inclined to go stiff at a touch and her belly and sex tight with anticipation. Giles was coming over, and Mak knew what was going on and had promised to be there for her, but the prospect of having them watch only added to her embarrassment, for all that one was her boyfriend and the other was gay. When the doorbell went she was further horrified to discover not only Hugh Bowle and Sid, but lighting and sound technicians as well.

The men promptly took over the flat, Mak and Giles helping them with Sarah left to sit on the sofa and contemplate her coming strip. She knew it had to be all the way, and that the last couple of shots would show everything, and not as if it was accidental either, but on blatant display. Somehow that made it worse, with no excuse save her own lewd nature, and she was biting her lip as Hugh came in to the living room, rubbing his hands in satisfaction as he spoke.

'Okay, Sarah doll, we're ready for you. Now remember, think sexy, and eyes to the camera. You need to make every guy who reads the mag think you'd like to be his girlfriend. Look available. Got it?'

Sarah nodded and stood up as the others came into the room. Six men were stood around her and her clothes were coming off, slowly, top and jeans and bra and panties, until she was nude, and not one of them would have so much as undone a button.

'Dusting first,' Hugh said. 'Reach up nice and high, Sarah, make those gorgeous tits lift.'

He'd passed her a pink nylon duster on a bamboo pole as he spoke. She went to where the lights were pointing, reaching up to wipe dust from the picture rail, already acutely conscious of the way the pose made her breasts lift and loll forward in her bra. Sid began to take pictures and she did her best to follow Hugh's instructions, although it made her feel as if she were little more than some kind of sex doll, to be smiling and showing off as she worked around the house, presumably in the hope that some kind man would take pity on her and break the monotony by giving her a good stiff fucking.

'Nice,' Hugh confirmed when Sid finally stepped away. 'Nice bum in the jeans too. Knicks and top next, that always looks good, and we've got to leave the best to last.'

'What do you want me to do?' Sarah asked, her fingers going reluctantly to the button of her jeans.

Hugh thought for a moment, with his tongue prodded into one cheek, then spoke.

'You got a dustpan and brush?'

'Yes, of course.'

'And maybe an old mug or something you don't use?'

'I think so ... yes.'

'Make us a coffee then, doll.'

He laughed as he said it, and winked at Sid. Sarah felt a fresh touch of chagrin at being used as coffee girl, which seemed to confirm her status as skivvy, but as she made for the kitchen Hugh spoke again.

'Jeans off first, darling. This is part of the shoot, yeah?'

'Oh,' Sarah responded, blushing as all six men laughed, even Mak.

She pushed her jeans down and off, taking her shoes and socks with them. Her bottom felt huge in

134

the tight pink panties Giles had chosen for her, and seemed to wobble to every tiny movement as she waited for the lights to be moved. In the kitchen she went through the familiar routine of making coffee, something she had done for real in top and panties many a time, but which now felt sexual and somehow smutty in a way that would never even have occurred to her before.

'That's good. You're a natural,' Sid said as he finally stood up.

'I haven't really done anything,' Sarah pointed out.

'Exactly, love,' he answered her. 'We want you natural, not posing around like some tart. That's what the boys who read *Hotties at Home* like, see.'

'You're sure this is an old mug?' Hugh asked, picking up the freshly made coffee.

'Yes, it came with an Easter egg I think,' Sarah said. 'Hey!'

Hugh had dropped the mug, which exploded on the floor tiles, splashing Sarah's bare feet with hot coffee and scattering shards of pottery across the floor.

'Bra off, doll,' Hugh instructed, 'and clean it up like that.'

Sarah had opened her mouth to speak, but thought better of it, instead undoing her bra and pulling it off down her arms as the men watched with interest. They moved back to give her extra space as she began to clean up, first fetching the dustpan and brush and some kitchen roll. Her breasts were lolling heavy and bare beneath her top as she bent, so that Sid could see them from between her legs. They were both bending down and on all fours, and she was made to hold her poses repeatedly before he was satisfied.

Again what would have been perfectly ordinary positions felt intensely sexual, making her wonder if that was how men saw her all the time. The shoot had also begun to turn her on, leaving her nipples poking up through her top, which encouraged Sid to demand a few more pictures, first of her putting the dustpan and brush away, then peeling her top off and putting it in the wash basket. In nothing but tight pink panties she felt vulnerable and yet more excited, leaving her trembling slightly as the lights were moved once more, into the bathroom. Next, she was to scrub the bath in just her panties, then nude, and it would be done.

'I can't get the angle, Sid,' the lighting technician was complaining. 'The room's too narrow.'

'Outside the door?' Hugh suggested.

'It won't work. There'll be a bloody great shadow right across her bum.'

Sarah felt relief as she realised she was not going to have to crawl around on the bathroom floor in the nude, but this was closely followed by disappointment. Then again, her panties were coming off regardless.

'Maybe I could do some washing up?' she suggested. 'I don't mind doing that nude, and –'

'No,' Hugh interrupted, 'we've used the kitchen. I know, put the light at the end of the bath and she can do the loo.'

'The loo?' Sarah echoed.

'Sure,' he responded, evidently oblivious to just how humiliating it would be for her to be photographed cleaning the lavatory in just her panties, never mind naked. 'Bung some bleach in first, bent over, and you can start to show off a bit now, 'cause the readers'll be getting horny for you. Back in, bum out, yeah?'

Sarah nodded, hiding a sigh as she went to fetch the bleach. Sid took several shots with her bent over the lavatory bowl, both from behind and from the side to make the most of both her breasts and her bottom, which felt bigger than ever with only her panties for protection. They were coming down too, at any moment.

'Now give the bowl a good scrub,' Hugh ordered when Sid had finished. 'On your knees, a few shots, then knickers off, your nudies, and we're done.'

His tone was commanding, expecting an immediate response and no fuss, setting Sarah's whole body trembling as she obeyed. She shot a glance to Giles, telling herself it was only such a turn-on because he was there, but she knew it was a lie. It felt good to have men ordering her to pose in her panties, to scrub the toilet bowl, to go naked for her nudies, such a rude term . . .

'Perfect.' Sid's voice broke into her thoughts. 'Knees apart, bum up . . . yeah, that's good. Wet panty crotch, great! Like I said, Hugh, she's a natural.'

Sarah swallowed a sob at his words and began to scrub the toilet as she held her rude pose. It was no longer something she might have done anyway, certainly not with her bum stuck in the air and her knees apart as if just waiting for some man to come up behind her, whip her panties down and fuck her over the toilet, maybe even with her head held down the bowl . . .

She winced at the disgusting thought, which had entered her head from nowhere, just as Sid spoke.

'That's great. Now for your knicks. Roll 'em down a bit first, like you haven't bothered to pull them up properly.'

He didn't wait for Sarah to adjust herself, but reached out to tug her panties down a little, showing the first couple of inches of her bottom crease. Sarah held the pose, shivering with humiliation and arousal as he took more pictures, with the thought of all the men looking at her in her rude position now swirling in her head.

'Very nice, Sid,' Hugh remarked from somewhere above and behind her, 'the boys love a bit of slit, but don't miss out on those titties.'

'Too right,' Sid agreed. 'Kneel up, love, keep scrubbing the bowl, and make 'em swing a bit, yeah?'

Sarah obeyed, kneeling up and quickly finding the right motion to make her breasts swing in time to the motions of her brush in the toilet bowl. Sid was snapping away furiously, then stopped to make an adjustment to the camera. As she began again Sarah realised he was filming her.

'One for the website,' he explained when he had finished. 'Make a nice MPEG, that will. Off with your knicks then, and we're done.'

He had scrambled round behind her as he spoke, an oddly ape-like motion, and once more focused the camera on Sarah's bottom. She waited until he was ready before pushing her thumbs into the waistband of her panties and started to take them down.

'That's it,' he said, 'nice and slow, now come on, love, back in, bum up, I want to be seeing the old chocolate starfish as you pull 'em down.'

A jolt of shame and pleasure hit Sarah at his words and she obeyed, not only deliberately flaunting her bottom to make her anus show as her panties came down, but looking back over her shoulder as if to invite any man watching to take her, even up her bum. All six men were staring, only Mak even remotely calm, making her wonder if she would be expected to satisfy them once the shoot was over. Giles might stop it, but she knew she wouldn't.

'Ace shot,' Sid drawled. 'Now all the way, then down on all fours again.'

Sarah already had her panties around her thighs, and quickly pushed them right off, adopting the rude crawling position she had been told to, with her back still pulled in to make her cheeks spread as she went back to scrubbing the lavatory bowl. It was a ridiculous position, impractical for cleaning the lavatory, or anything else save to show off for men who liked to imagine girls doing their housework in the nude. That didn't stop it feeling good: her reservations were now lost beneath her excitement and, when Sid moved back after taking a last close-up of her now sopping pussy, her main emotion was regret.

'Is that it?' she asked.

'All done,' Sid confirmed. 'Nice shoot, love. Great tits. Great arse. Good and natural.'

'How about the one for Kinky Corner then?' Hugh asked. 'What do you reckon, Sid?'

'How about a bit of bondage?' Sid replied. 'Been a while since we've had a bit of bondage.'

'Could be,' Hugh agreed. 'You got a pair of handcuffs, Sarah doll?'

'No,' Sarah answered him, slightly aggrieved that his tone suggested it was more or less a foregone conclusion.

'We really ought to make the best of those tits, whatever we do,' Sid pointed out.

'Too right,' Hugh agreed, 'only we had Lindie with the beans all over hers last time, and we've got Yvonne with her nips clamped this month.'

'She likes to be spanked,' Giles put in, quite casually.

Sarah felt her face flare red and her sex tighten hard, but Hugh was shaking his head.

'No good. No boyfriends, that's the rule, not in *Hotties at Home*. It has to look like the girls are available.'

'I – I could spank myself,' Sarah suggested, hardly able to believe she was saying the words.

'Nice one!' Sid responded. 'Let's go for it.'

'With this brush, that's good,' Hugh added, picking up Sarah's big wooden bath brush, 'and bent over so we can get those titties hanging down and all.'

'Over the loo, not the bath,' Sid pointed out, 'or I can't get the light right.'

'Sounds good,' Hugh answered him, and passed Sarah the bath brush.

She was shaking so hard she nearly dropped it, and she felt weak as she got into position, bending down to rest one hand on the edge of the loo, the other back to lift the brush over her bottom, her naked bottom, with her equally naked breasts hanging fat and pendulous under her chest. She looked back, right into the camera as Sid started to take pictures, thinking again of how rude she would look, a naked girl spanking her own bottom over the loo, a girl so dirty she'd punish herself if there was nobody else to do it for her.

'Perfect,' Sid announced after what seemed to Sarah an eternity of holding her rude position.

Sarah stood up, reluctantly, wondering if she was about to be made to take all five straight men in her mouth, and in front of Mak. It seemed to make sense, now that they'd got her horny and seen every private crease and crevice and curve of her body. Surely they'd want their cocks attended to? Maybe not, as they were professionals, and her boyfriend was there, but it was tempting to imagine different circumstances, perhaps with her trio of seedy Parisians, taking rude photos of her for some cheap smutty magazine, then demanding she suck their cocks.

They'd begun to pack up, and Giles joined her as she made for the bedroom, his arm around her waist.

She was still nude, because she wanted to be nude and knew that as soon as she put her clothes back on the experience would be over, which she didn't want, not until she'd come. The moment they were in her room she put her arms around Giles, nuzzling his neck and wriggling her breasts and hips against him. He responded immediately, his hands moving down to cup her bottom, kneading her cheeks and pulling them wide, immediately making Sarah think of how she'd been made to show her anus for the camera.

'Make me suck you, Giles,' she whispered. 'I really want to.'

'Now?' he queried, even as she began to go down to her knees.

Sarah nodded urgently and gave him a push to make him sit down on the bed.

'What about Hugh and . . .' he began, but broke off as she began to nuzzle his crotch with her face.

'I don't mind,' she told him, 'even if they know. I just want you in my mouth. It feels so good, Giles, to be naked at your feet with my bum stuck out, and when they've all seen me, seen me nude . . .'

She broke off, filling her mouth with cock as she pulled him free of his trousers. He gave a sigh of pleasure and leant back on the bed, ruffling her hair as she began to suck, eager and dirty, one hand already back between her thighs. Soon Giles was hard in her mouth, and the temptation to bring herself to climax was close to overwhelming, yet she held back, hoping that the door would be pushed open and she'd get caught giving her boyfriend a blow-job, or better still, made to give blow-jobs all round. At the least she wanted the fantasy. She pulled off, taking Giles' cock in hand to masturbate him as she spoke.

'Hugh and Sid, do you think they normally make girls . . . you know, help them, afterwards?'

'I bet they'd like to,' Giles sighed, and paused. 'No? You wouldn't? You would wouldn't you, you little slut.'

Sarah nodded, blushing even as her fingers began to work harder on her sex.

'Do you want me to tell you about it, slut?' Giles asked, his voice full of cruel amusement.

Again Sarah nodded, more urgently, then took his cock back in, as deep as it would go, delighted to have her mouth well filled with erection as she masturbated.

'Maybe I'll let them,' Giles began. 'Maybe when I've finished with you I make you stay in here and tell them you're available. How would that be? They'd make you suck them off, Sarah, one by one, all four of them Sarah, in your pretty mouth, one after another, suck, suck, suck . . . oh you dirty little slut, I can't hold . . .'

He finished with a grunt and he'd come, deep in Sarah's throat. She swallowed as best she could and whipped his cock out, tugging furiously on the shaft with her mouth wide to make him spunk in her mouth so that she could see, and in her face too. He came forward, suddenly, to grab his cock from her and pull her back by the hair, finishing off over her breasts and rubbing his slimy helmet on her erect nipples as he began to speak again, hoarse and breathless.

'That's my Sarah, nude on your knees with my spunk all over you. I'd make you do it, I would. I'd make you suck them and let them fuck you between your tits, and between those fat bottom cheeks, maybe even up your bum . . .'

He broke off again as he hit a second peak, a last eruption of come splashing between Sarah's breasts as she too reached orgasm. She'd begun to smear his

142

mess over her breasts and face as she came, still holding his slippery erection in her cleavage as she imagined herself put on her knees in her own bedroom and made to satisfy the men who'd been taking dirty photographs of her. It was wonderfully, glorious unfair, that she should be made to do a thoroughly degrading sexist striptease, ending up stark naked as she scrubbed a lavatory bowl, then be expected to suck five men to orgasm because they'd got excited over what they'd done to her.

She cried out as she came, unable to stop herself, although she knew full well that they would hear and know what was going on, a thought that gave a final peak to her orgasm before she was done. Exhausted, she sank slowly down, one thigh still shaking hard from the power of her climax. Hugh's laughter sounded from outside the door, then his voice.

'You finished in there, you two?'

'Yes, thank you,' Giles replied casually.

Sarah's cheeks flared red once more and she was frantically shaking her head, sure that Giles was going to invite Hugh Bowle in to have his cock sucked. Giles merely laughed and ruffled her hair again, then spoke, now in a whisper.

'Don't worry, I wouldn't do that to you, unless . . .'

He trailed off, one eyebrow raised in query.

'No,' Sarah said quickly. 'It's just nice to think about, that's all.'

'Would you?' he asked quietly. 'Tell the truth.'

Sarah hesitated, not sure what the answer actually was. What he was suggesting sounded at once compelling and utterly disgusting.

'Would – would you mind?' she finally managed. 'I mean, I wouldn't want to do anything that you'd feel bad about.'

'You want to do it though, don't you?' he demanded.

'I – I –,' Sarah blustered, 'I'm sorry, Giles, I know I'm a slut, but I'd never ... I'd ... oh okay, yes, I would, if you told me to, but it would be for you.'

'Slut,' he answered, now laughing. 'I love you, and I wouldn't have you any other way.'

Sarah found herself smiling and simpering, absurdly grateful, and reaching out for a cuddle, only for Giles to pull away.

'Watch what you're doing, Sarah,' he protested. 'You're covered in spunk!'

'Your spunk, you bastard!' she laughed, and slapped his leg.

She cleaned up and dressed, still red in the face with embarrassment as she joined the others in the living room, both for what she'd done and the way she'd behaved afterwards. None of them seemed to mind, treating her as an absolute equal despite having just had her grovelling nude on the floor, Hugh even showing a new respect as he spoke.

'That was a great shoot, Sarah, especially when you're new. You're a natural, you really are, and I just know you're going to be popular. So how about a tie-in, to get readers buying new titles? This is how it works. We advertise you as a super-sexy new artist in the text for your shoot in *Hotties at Home*, which is great too, 'cause it shows you're not a professional model and that's important. Then in *Hot Gun* we say the artist for "Graverobbers" is appearing nude in *Hotties at Home*. How's that?'

'It seems to make sense,' Sarah admitted.

'Great,' Hugh went on. 'And then to bring the two together we'll do a big shoot for *Hot Gun*, just tasteful nudie stuff, nothing heavy but mostly outdoors, in Paris.'

Ten

With the next issue of *Hot Gun* in the shops and on the newsstands, Sarah found herself constantly looking over her shoulder and starting nervously at every sound. She knew perfectly well that she had only drawn a few pictures, and that even then she had shown Céleste as willing, if perhaps rather resentful, yet she felt as if she had committed some terrible crime for which justice was inevitable.

Despite not being in Paris, she expected at any moment to be set upon by three men identical to the horrid characters she had created, dragged into a suitably sordid alley and put to their cocks. Céleste, after all, didn't have to come herself, and would know that Sarah would feel too guilty to put up a fight. Telling herself that she was being silly made no difference whatsoever. To make matters worse, she was going to Paris at the weekend, and when one day and a second passed without incident she was soon telling herself that Céleste was merely waiting until Sarah came to her.

She hadn't told anybody, knowing it would only make her look foolish, especially if she tried to use Céleste as an excuse not to go to Paris. Giles and Mak, who shared a rational view of life, would think she was mad, while the more cynical Hugh would immediately assume she had got cold feet and was trying to back out of the contract she had signed. Her only hope seemed to lie in numbers, as it was hardly going to happen in front of five men.

As the weekend drew closer she found herself growing ever more nervous, and her resistance weakening. Part of her had always wanted it to happen, even as she drew the pictures, and she was repeatedly telling herself that if it was going to happen anyway, then she might as well give in. That in turn made her feel bad about Giles, because however liberal he might be about what she did, he was hardly going to be happy about her being taken into an alley and bonked senseless by three rough Frenchmen.

Her nervousness showed, but he put it down to apprehension at her coming photoshoot and having to strip off in public, which turned him on. Sarah didn't trouble to contradict him, but as she knelt with his erection deep in her sex from behind, while he told her how good he would feel watching her walk naked down a Parisian street, she was wondering if he'd be quite so happy watching her suck cock in a Parisian alley.

She was also delaying the next episode, sure it would only get her into further trouble, but once they were on the train there was no escaping it; with the full journey ahead of them, and Hugh and the others further down the carriage, there was nothing to do but talk to Giles.

'Where have we got to?' Giles asked as they began to gather speed through south-west London, speaking more to himself than to Sarah. 'We know Céleste has hired the thugs, and that d'Orsay knows what she's up to. Next comes the actual grave robbing.'

'I ought to make that a full-page scene,' Sarah responded, hoping to keep the sexual content to a minimum. 'After all, it is the scene we've taken the title from.'

'Yes,' Giles said thoughtfully, 'but if we do we'll have to have plenty of sex on the second page.'

'Couldn't Céleste entertain the men afterwards?' Sarah suggested, already picturing the scene in her mind, and the likely consequences, yet knowing she had it coming anyway.

'It would be too similar to the previous episode,' Giles objected. 'We need something different, something hard ... hmm, perhaps it was a mistake to let them get so heavy with her in the last episode.'

'That's true,' Sarah agreed ruefully.

'At least we should have spared her bottom.'

'Very true.'

'Never mind, it was a great scene. So what can we do? Come on, it has to be dirty and it has to fit the story.'

He was still addressing himself as much as her, and turned to stare out of the window as he finished. They were somewhere out in the suburbs, with long rows of brick houses at the bottom of the embankment and beyond, with the occasional clump of taller, concrete blocks of flats standing among them. Sarah tried to think, hoping to come up with something that she could at least cope with before Giles' devious perverted mind came up with something she couldn't.

'Maybe the roughs tie her up?' she suggested on sudden inspiration. 'That way we could make her more sympathetic to the readers because when she pins the crime on them she's just getting her own back. Obviously if they tie her up against her will they can't have sex with her, but her clothes could be a bit disarranged, maybe?'

'It takes the sting out of it,' Giles objected. 'I think we need to make her a real bitch, and that's definitely

147

how the readers will want to see her, only not as bad as the other characters. I like the idea of her tied up though, hmm . . .'

He went silent, then continued with sudden enthusiasm.

'I've got it, that's how she pins the blame on the roughs. Once she's hidden the money she says she'll go with them to celebrate. They already know she likes it rough, so they won't be suspicious when she asks to be had in bondage. That way they can tie her up and really use her without us getting into any problems with consent, then in the last frame the police burst in and in the next episode the roughs have been arrested, but because Céleste's been found tied up and well used the police are sure to believe her story. What do you think?'

'Good,' Sarah admitted weakly, 'great.'

'It is, isn't it?' Giles responded, immodest as ever. 'We don't really need a full-page graverobbing scene after all, but that's your area so I'll leave it to you, just as long as it's plain that Céleste has taken them back to wherever they live for sex, then you can get into the bondage. Perhaps finish with her tied up and sucking one man's cock while another cuts her clothes off, so the readers know it's going to get really hard next month.'

'What about the money?' Sarah asked, desperate to at least postpone her fate. 'Céleste would need to hide it somewhere they didn't know about, wouldn't she?'

'I suppose so,' Giles admitted. 'No, because once they'd been arrested she could come back and get it. After all, they're not going to tell the police where it is, not immediately, and they needn't even know she's set them up.'

'Surely –'

'No, because they'd just think she was trying to get herself off the hook by saying she was their victim.

But . . . but meanwhile, d'Orsay knows what's really happened. Maybe he's even got photographs, so he can blackmail Céleste into being his sex slave. Oh yes, wonderful! We can have her made to suck his balls, lick his arsehole, suck his cock after it's been up her bum . . .'

'I don't think Hugh would let us get away with that, would he?' Sarah queried, now completely horrified.

'No,' Giles admitted. 'Damn.'

He turned to stare out of the window again, now frowning. Sarah sat back, picturing a future of rough dirty sex and wondering just what she'd let herself in for by choosing Giles as her boyfriend. That morning she'd been buggered before breakfast, Giles applying some of the lubricant he now kept by the bed to his morning erection and prodding it up between her cheeks while she was still half asleep. Her bottom hole still didn't feel quite right, but she tried to tell herself that if the Frenchmen caught her at least Raoul or Marcel or Lamond would be able to penetrate her anally without it hurting too much.

She shook her head. There were no men, except in the cartoon, so they couldn't catch her and bugger her, or anything else. Yet there was no Céleste either, nor a Monsieur d'Orsay, and she'd been spanked by one and sucked cock for the other. It had happened, and therefore there had to be a rational explanation, simple logic as Giles would have said. On the other hand, if she threw logic out of the window, it raised some interesting possibilities.

Sarah frowned as she looked down the Rue Claude Magnien. It was simply not as it should have been, not as she saw it in her imagination, and therefore not the place she wanted to go nude outdoors in Paris.

She had accepted that she was going to do it, and that it could be done safely enough at dawn on a summer's day and on a quiet street, which left only the actual choice of location.

Most of the morning had been spent posing in the hotel room, from fully dressed to nude, with the windows open so that the Eiffel Tower was visible in the background just to make absolutely certain the readers knew she was in Paris. She had felt the same mixture of excitement and embarrassment as before, especially when they had made her go out on the balcony, which had left her not merely willing, but eager. She was also determined to get it right.

In her mind the scene was clear. It would be a narrow street somewhere in the Latin Quarter, with high buildings in the classic Parisian style and no hint of modernity. There would be a double line of trees and boxes of geraniums on the window sills, swept paving stones, a perfectly blue sky. There would be posters advertising ballet and theatre, perhaps clubs if sufficiently stylish. There would be a stall selling pictures, another selling flowers, tables outside cafés with chequered cloths. There would be no cars, but perhaps an old-fashioned delivery van.

She knew what she was going to do as well. The morning sun would be striking down the length of the street, illuminating her perfectly as she stepped forward, wearing nothing but a fake-fur coat and smart shoes. First she would shrug the coat from her shoulders, showing her cleavage and her legs as she walked, then let it drop, to walk naked and proud down the centre of the street as Sid photographed her, front, side and back.

They had agreed to everything she wanted as long as she could provide the location, which she had promised to do. Unfortunately it didn't seem to be as easy as she had expected, despite the fact that on her first visit she had seen half a dozen perfect streets just in the vicinity of her hotel. Now she couldn't even find the hotel, and the men were beginning to get impatient, Hugh Bowle in particular.

'What's wrong this time?' he demanded, seeing her expression. 'It looks all right to me, very froggy in fact. Look, there's even a big picture of a snail outside that restaurant.'

'The light will be perfect, first thing,' Sid added.

'It . . . it's just not right,' Sarah insisted. 'There are too many cars, and too much neon. I wanted more colour.'

'The neon's pretty colourful,' Hugh pointed out. 'Look, doll, all this arty stuff's all very well, but this looks like Paris to me, and what the readers really want to see is you getting your tits out.'

'I know,' Sarah admitted. 'I just want somewhere . . . somewhere special.'

Hugh glanced at his watch.

'All right, seeing as we're not doing it now anyway you can look around until it's time for tea, but if you don't find anything better we're going for it here, got it? And remember what Sid said about the light. Me, I'm going for a beer.'

He started towards the nearest bar, the sign for which was in pink neon, and to Sarah's taste completely unacceptable. She glanced up and down once more, but altogether too many details jarred with the image in her mind. Hugh and Sid disappeared into the café, Giles hesitating.

'Are you coming?' she asked.

'Actually I could rather do with a beer,' he admitted.

Sarah pursed her mouth, thinking of Céleste, who seemed to have a knack of turning up the moment

Sarah was alone. Then again, they had been zigzagging back and forth for ever since lunch and, had it not been for Hugh's detailed street map, would have been comprehensively lost. Besides, in the two days since their arrival there had been no sign of Céleste, nor Monsieur d'Orsay, nor any men closely resembling Raoul, Marcel and Lamond, despite the occasional shock.

'Wait here for me then,' she said.

Giles moved gratefully towards the bar and Sarah set off down the street. The far end looked promising, with a small fountain visible and at least one window box. On reaching the fountain she found that it was at a little crossroads, and that the street it crossed was perfect, almost exactly as she would have drawn it herself. So, in fact, was the continuation of the Rue Claude Magnien, better even, because it was closed to cars.

Yes, it was easy to imagine herself dropping her coat from naked shoulders and stepping free and nude into the morning sunlight, even the afternoon sunlight, because there were very few people about, and those that were didn't look as if they'd mind – just the opposite. Now feeling deliciously daring, she began to walk down the centre of the street, telling herself she'd do it both ways, so that Sid could get the best light for her rear view as well as from the front. After all, Giles insisted her bottom was her best feature and it would be a shame to disappoint him.

At the end of the street she turned sharply around on her heel, meaning to walk back exactly as she would need to in the morning, only to almost bump into somebody coming the other way. She had already begun to apologise when she realised it was Céleste and her words froze on her lips.

Céleste's expression was icy, save for a hint of a cruel smile as she looked down on Sarah. Already close to panic, Sarah glanced around, her fear rising as she saw Raoul, standing outside a café, Marcel, pretending to admire the paintings at a stall, and Lamond, idly picking his nose, each unmistakable. There was no direction in which she could run. As Sarah's helplessness sank in, Céleste gave a light chuckle and raised one aristocratic eyebrow.

'Why the trepidation, *cocotte*?' Céleste asked. 'This is only justice, no?'

'You're – you're not going to do this to me,' Sarah answered, forcing the words out despite the urge to sink to her knees and beg forgiveness.

'No?' Céleste queried as the men began to close in. 'You think, perhaps, that it is not just?'

'If you do . . .' Sarah began, and stopped.

Céleste had placed a single finger beneath Sarah's chin. As her face was tilted up to leave her looking directly into Céleste's eyes, Sarah found herself unable to speak.

'Do not threaten me, my little whore,' Céleste said quietly. 'What you had me do, I intend to have done to you. Is that not justice?'

All the things she'd planned to say were running through Sarah's head, but she found herself nodding meekly.

'Good,' Céleste went on. 'I am glad you understand, and perhaps this time you will learn your lesson, yes?'

Again Sarah nodded, unable to do otherwise. Céleste continued.

'I wonder. You enjoyed that foul old *roué* d'Orsay, didn't you? Perhaps you will enjoy these three dirty pigs as well, no?'

'No,' Sarah managed, struggling to tell herself it was true.

'And yet you made me?' Céleste answered, a touch of anger now showing in her voice. 'You made me do

'. . . do unspeakable things, and when I had expressly forbidden it.'

'I . . . can't help it,' Sarah responded, starting to babble, 'I really can't . . . Giles makes me do it . . . my writer . . . I just draw the pictures.'

'Yes,' Céleste grated, tilting Sarah's head yet further back, 'you draw the pictures, of me being despoiled in every way, for money, you filthy little whore!'

Céleste's voice had been rising, and as she finished with an angry click of her tongue she grabbed Sarah's wrist, twisting her around. Sarah squealed in dismay as her body was forced down over a large open litter bin, and in an instant her dress had been turned up and her panties whipped down, baring her bottom to the public gaze one more time. As she was exposed she began to struggle, but Céleste merely tightened her grip, forcing Sarah's face in among the litter, squashing a half-eaten custard tart over her nose and one eye.

'Hold her down,' Céleste snapped, and immediately strong male hands took grips on Sarah's body, her hair and her arms, pinning her down in the rubbish.

She was still struggling, in blind panic, with her thighs kicking in her lowered panties and her bottom cheeks wobbling frantically. The piece of custard tart was now smeared over half her face and her breasts were in among the rubbish too, with something cold and wet soaking into her top over one fat globe. A smack landed on her bottom and she gave a despairing shriek as the spanking began, only to stop almost immediately. She caught Céleste's voice.

'*Merci, Monsieur, ça c'est gentil.*'

'*C'est rien,*' a man's voice answered as a stinging pain lanced through Sarah's bottom.

All three of the men holding her in the litter bin laughed, and others joined in, bringing Sarah a harsh stab of shame as she realised her spanking was being watched by what seemed like quite a crowd. That didn't stop her squealing, kicking and generally making an exhibition of herself. Whatever she was being beaten with hurt too much, each stroke seeming to sting more than the last until she was writhing and thrashing in the litter, in which she was now so deeply immersed that her bottom was the highest part of her body.

Céleste continued to apply the strokes, with Sarah bleating pathetically into her faceful of soggy custard and pastry. Not one person moved to help her, or even spoke up for her; instead they were laughing at her and doubtless making crude remarks about how big her bottom was, how comic she looked, and soon how wet her sex was getting. At that her struggles renewed, the thought that they knew she was getting excited over her punishment too much to bear, while she knew it would be all to easy for Raoul or one of his sons to push a stiff cock up her once the beating was over.

It stopped. Again Céleste spoke, although Sarah's head was now too deep in the rubbish to hear clearly. The men's grip tightened. Sarah gave a wail of despair as her hot bottom cheeks were hauled wide. Something cold and slippery touched her anus, a bit of the tart, and she began to fight in earnest as she realised she was being lubricated for a public buggering. They merely laughed at her, holding her still as something touched her tightly clenched bottom hole, and her anus had been forced.

She cried out in despair as she was penetrated, only to realise that whatever had been stuck up her bum was far too thin for a man's cock, while there was nobody mounted on her either. Whatever it was, the crowd found it immensely funny, laughing at her and passing humorous remarks. Again Céleste spoke and the men let go of Sarah's wrists, only to catch her by the thighs and upend her into the litter bin.

Her legs were waving wildly in the air for a moment before she could recover herself, flopping out over one side of the bin to stand dizzy and dishevelled on the pavement as she struggled to pull herself together. Her face was plastered with custard and bits of pastry, her chest was smeared with some sticky yellow substance that had soaked right through to her breasts, and a long thick paint brush had been inserted in her anus, the sort used to put a wash on a large canvas, and obviously what she'd been beaten with. She pulled the brush out and glanced around her. Céleste had disappeared, along with the three men, there was no sign of the crowd who'd been laughing at her just moments before, but Giles, Hugh and Sid were staring at her from just a few feet away.

'What happened to you?' Hugh demanded as Sarah hastily pulled her panties up.

Sarah didn't answer immediately, wondering how much they'd seen, as Giles came forward to put an arm around her. Finally she managed to speak.

'Some bastard . . . some bastard tipped me into the litter bin!'

'And pulled your knickers down?' Sid asked in astonishment.

'Yes,' Sarah answered him. 'Could we . . . could we go back to the hotel now?'

'Don't you want to call the police or something?' Hugh asked.

'No,' Sarah said, 'don't, please. I just want to leave it.'

'You can't just leave shit like this,' Hugh insisted. 'There must be witnesses. Excuse me, do you speak English? Did you see what happened?'

The man he had addressed merely shook his head and walked on.

'Sarah's right,' Giles said. 'The police would only make it worse for her.'

Hugh hesitated and looked around. Only a few people were visible, and none of them were paying any attention.

'Don't, please,' Sarah said.

'Your call, doll,' Hugh replied doubtfully.

Giles hugged Sarah to him as they began to walk her away from the bin. Her mind was in a whirl, and for more than what Céleste had done to her. Not only had the crowd melted away with extraordinary speed, but in the brief period she'd been head-down in the litter bin the artist selling paintings had packed up his stall, at least two café owners had removed the chequered cloths from their outside tables and more than a dozen separate householders had taken their geraniums in from their windowsills.

Sarah sat in her bed in the hotel, sipping coffee and nibbling at a piece of toast liberally spread with apricot preserve. As before, what Céleste had done to her hadn't affected her nearly as badly as she would have expected, nor in the way that Giles and Sid evidently expected, to judge by their hushed serious tones as they talked together in the other room. Hugh was rather less sympathetic.

'I've heard of this sort of shit, in Japan,' Sid was saying. 'It's a bit like happy slapping, only instead of hitting somebody they creep up behind a girl, whip her skirt up and pull her knickers down, so the guy with the mobile gets a shot of her bare bum. Sharking, it's called.'

'I think that's just one video,' Giles put in, 'and even that's supposed to be a fake. I tell you, I'd kill the bastard if I'd seen him.'

157

'Ah, come on, it's no big deal,' Hugh urged. 'We used to do that, back in the 'sixties, just for a laugh. You go up on either side of a girl, right, at a party or at the bus stop maybe. Skirt up, knickers down, and her bum's bare before she knows it. You'd get a slap now and then, but most of the time they loved it.'

'Maybe as a joke, with a girl you know,' Giles pointed out, 'but this was a complete stranger!'

'You know he gave her a few across the arse and all?' Sid put in.

'I saw,' Giles confirmed.

'With that paintbrush she was holding, I think,' Hugh added, trying but not really succeeding in hiding his amusement. 'They must have scarpered pretty sharpish, you know. I didn't see anyone.'

'Pity,' Giles said. 'And what about the way people just pretended they hadn't seen anything!'

'Bloody Frogs,' Hugh agreed. 'But don't worry about it. She's a tough girl, your Sarah. She'll be all right.'

Sarah took another bite of toast. Hugh was right, it seemed. She felt perfectly OK, as if her experience had been no more than a dream, a dream somewhere halfway between a nightmare and the sort that left her panties sticky in the morning. There was even a vague sense of having been cheated out of something because she didn't feel worse, yet considerable satisfaction for the very same thing.

'So what about the shoot?' Hugh said quietly.

'We can't ask her to do it now!' Sid responded, Giles agreeing immediately.

'I suppose not,' Hugh admitted. 'Shit! Still, we've got the indoor shots. Those are good.'

'That's true,' Sid agreed, 'and we can get something else, maybe, while we're here. Hire some local models perhaps?'

Pushing her covers back, Sarah swung her legs off the bed. For days she had been preparing herself to walk nude down a Parisian street, until it had become one of the things she was determined to do. To let Céleste spoil that was a defeat, and very different to the defeat of receiving spankings, which she found impossible to deny. She pulled her robe on and stepped out into the main room, smiling at the three men.

'I'm ready, let's go.'

'That's all right, love,' Sid said. 'Don't push yourself.'

'I'm fine. I want to do it,' Sarah insisted. 'Just let me have a shower and I'm with you.'

They had begun to talk among themselves as she walked across to the bathroom, Giles and Sid arguing against Hugh, who alone wanted to take Sarah up on her offer. She paid no attention, showering and drying herself before coming back to find them much as before, still sitting down and still talking.

'Are you coming or not?' she asked. 'Because I'm going to do it anyway.'

'It's the middle of the morning, love,' Sid pointed out.

Sarah merely shrugged, knowing that if she began to discuss it she would quickly give in. As she went back into the bedroom she deliberately left the door open as she dropped her robe, walking nude to the cupboard where they'd put the coat and boots she was supposed to wear. She pulled both on, her heart already hammering in her chest but determined not to back out.

Back in the other room the men were on their feet, Sid with his camera, Giles looking doubtful, Hugh already by the door. Sarah beckoned to them and left, the men following behind. It took all her courage to keep walking, down the stairs and out of the hotel, across the road and in among the streets opposite. The Rue Claude Magnien was no great distance, but time seemed to have slowed to a crawl, every glance from passers-by seeming to penetrate her coat and see that she was naked beneath, every step amplifying her tension and arousal.

By the time she reached the end of the street she was barely aware of Sid's presence as he began to take photographs of her. She walked briskly to the fountain where the short stretch from which cars were banned began. It was less perfect than the day before, but she didn't hesitate as she walked to the end, now slowly. As she turned she found Sid down on one knee, the camera pointed directly at her, with Hugh and Giles standing to either side, the first looking pleased with himself, the latter with an expression close to awe. Sarah gave him a smile and began to walk forward, her chin held high and her hands on the edges of her fur coat.

The blood was singing in her veins as she shrugged the coat from her shoulders, the power of her emotions overwhelming as the moment came to go bare. She felt the coat slip down, and open, exposing her breasts, her belly, her sex and legs and, as it fell discarded to the ground behind, her bottom. Stark naked but for her boots, she stepped forward, her head swirling with embarrassment and pride, apprehension and delight, shame for her behaviour and a wicked joy for exactly the same reason.

People were looking, with astonishment, with enjoyment, with disapproval, very different emotions to the nonchalant amusement with which not dissimilar audiences had greeted her two public spankings. She ignored them, walking on down the exact centre of the street, step by step as Sid's motordrive clicked and whirred, until she reached the bin in which she'd been upended the day before.

She turned, presenting her bottom to Sid as she started back, now putting a sway into her walk. Her coat was just yards ahead, representing safety she had no wish for, then abruptly every wish for as a policeman stepped out from the nearest café. Sarah froze, and so did he, his face registering first astonishment and then outrage. He got over his shock first, starting forward as he began to sputter in French, not a single word of which Sarah managed to pick up. It didn't matter. His reaction to her going naked was all too obvious, and it contained not a hint of amusement, nor of tolerance.

He reached her, still speaking too fast for her to understand, and as she began to babble apologies he had caught her by one wrist, clipping a handcuff to it, pulling her arm behind her back and fixing it to the other. Helpless, feeling completely vulnerable and full of self-pity, Sarah could only stand still as he reached for his radio, then stopped, clicking his heels together and giving a smart salute as a silky smooth and all too familiar voice spoke from behind Sarah.

'*Bonjour, Monsieur l'Agent. Il y a un problème?*'

'*Mademoiselle du Musigny,*' the policeman replied. '*Rien du tout, ce n'était qu'un petit tapage.*'

'*Cette femme,*' Céleste continued with an airy gesture of her fingers towards Sarah. '*Je la connais, et on peut éviter les écritures par se charger du problème ici, sans de la formalité.*'

'*Quelle excellente idée, Mademoiselle,*' the policeman responded immediately, all his puff and outrage gone, to be replaced by a lewd good humour Sarah liked even less.

'Dealt with informally?' Sarah queried. 'I think I'd rather be arrested, please. May I have my coat too?'

The policeman merely gave her a puzzled look, and she was still trying to work out how to ask to be arrested in French when Céleste spoke again.

'*Une fessée sur les genoux, je pense.* Which for your benefit, Sarah, means an over the knee spanking.'

'You can't do that!' Sarah exclaimed.

'Whyever not?' Céleste responded, her voice full of amusement as she stepped back.

'You just can't!' Sarah wailed. 'Hey, no ... not again! Help!'

She looked frantically around, but there was no sign of Sid, nor Hugh, nor even Giles. They'd fled, leaving her to her fate and adding considerably to her consternation as for the third time she was taken over the knee for punishment in a Parisian street. Nobody else came to her aid, or even paid much attention, one elderly gentleman nearby not even bothering to look up from his copy of *Le Figaro*, but merely moving up a little on his bench to make room for Sarah's head as the policeman sat down.

Céleste had come to watch, looking down on Sarah as she wriggled in the policeman's grip, her face set in mingled amusement and contempt. The policeman was now hugely enjoying himself, all trace of his previous venom gone, as if he was a different person. He lifted a knee to hump Sarah's bottom up into a better spanking position, took a moment to adjust her breasts so that they hung down against his leg instead of being squashed on it, chuckled as he pinched one already hard nipple between forefinger and thumb, and laid a hand on Sarah's bottom, only not to spank, but to grope.

'Hey, come on!' Sarah protested as his thick, somewhat clammy fingers squeezed her cheek. 'Get off me, you dirty old bastard! Céleste, stop him, he's touching me up!'

He was, both hands now on her bottom and her body trapped beneath his elbow to prevent her escape. Céleste merely laughed at Sarah's plea, and again as the policeman's hands dug deeper. Sarah squealed as her cheeks were hauled wide, stretching her anus open to the warm air and the lewd gaze of the policeman, Céleste and a couple who had stopped to watch the spanking.

'Stop him, please?' Sarah begged, her face turned up to Céleste. 'This just isn't fair, not to touch me up, not . . . oh!'

Her squeak came as a blunt finger pressed to her bottom hole, tickling the little pit at the centre before moving lower. Sarah gasped again he began to investigate her sex, holding her lips open and probing her hole, until she'd begun to kick her feet and squirm in raw consternation.

'Stop!' she howled. 'Please, not up my fanny! Oh you – you pig, you dirty old –'

Again she broke off, this time with a gasp. He had inserted a second finger into her hole, then a third, and had now begun to masturbate her with obviously practised efficiency. Still Céleste did nothing, nor anyone else, merely watching as she was brought on heat, the policeman's fingers working her hole open and his thumb diddling her clitoris, until at last she could hold back no longer and had begun to gasp and wriggle herself on his intruding hand.

He stopped immediately, gave a knowing chuckle, and began to spank, applying his hand firmly to the cheekiest part of her bottom, but nothing like as firmly as he might have done. Sarah was already warm from being masturbated, and found herself enjoying it immediately despite her raging consternation. Only when Céleste made some remark in French, about the intention being to punish Sarah, did the spanking grow harder.

Now with the full force of the policeman's brawny arm being used on her helpless jiggling bottom, Sarah went wild, kicking and screaming in her pain, scissoring her legs to show off her cunt and bucking furiously so that her breasts slapped on his leg and the hard wood of the bench. The old man reading *Le Figaro* gave her a single dirty look and went back to his paper, but nobody intervened, with a few more people now watching, including, to Sarah's horror, Raoul, Marcel and Lamond.

Her despairing wail cut the air and she was immediately babbling pleas for protection from the policeman in between her squeals and yips as he continued to spank her. He took no notice, now peppering her bottom with single well-placed smacks, as if determined to give her an even glow all over. One last extra hard one right under her tuck and it was done, but she no longer felt relief, only trepidation.

'Please, Céleste, haven't I had enough?' she begged as the policeman helped her up. 'Please?'

Even as she spoke she was rubbing her hot bottom as best she could with her cuffed wrists. Céleste's mouth was curved up into a cruel smile as she met Sarah's gaze, then she nodded.

'Yes, my little *cocotte*, you have had enough, for now at any rate. Enough spanking, that is. *Allez, mes enfants, à l'allée.* To the alley, Sarah, where a little justice will be served up.'

'No,' Sarah responded as strong hands took her by the shoulders. 'Céleste, please, not that. I – I promise I won't do it again . . .'

'It is simple justice,' Céleste responded as the policeman and Raoul began to move her towards the black mouth of an alleyway very much like the one she had drawn. 'What you make me do, I shall make you do.'

'I haven't had you spanked!' Sarah squealed. 'Come on, Céleste, please!'

'Regard the spanking as a little extra, well deserved,' Céleste responded. 'Now come on, be a brave girl. Perhaps you can enjoy it as much as you made me, who knows?'

Céleste had stopped, standing with her arms folded and an expression of smug satisfaction on her face as Sarah was dragged into the alley. The bulk of Lamond blocked soon blocked Sarah's view of Céleste as she was pulled deeper in, where the air was cool dank and rich with the smell of decay. Marcel followed his brother, as did others, blocking the alley completely as Sarah was eased to her knees beside a pair of overflowing dustbins. It was not merely like the alley she had drawn, it was the very same alley, right down to the dustbins and the corpse of the rat, now somewhat decayed.

'Céleste!' she called out, now frantic. 'This isn't fair, it really isn't! I only made you do three! Céleste!'

There was no response, and her legs were pressed down to the cold slimy concrete of the alley floor, with both Raoul and the policeman looking down on her while the others stood beyond, their faces filled with lust, Lamond with his great stubby cock already out of his fly.

'At least undo my cuffs,' Sarah said miserably, looking back over her shoulder in an attempt to make her wishes clear.

The policeman looked at Raoul. Raoul looked at the policeman. Both shrugged. Both put their hands to their flies. Sarah drew a heavy sigh.

'Go on then, if you really have to,' she said, raising her voice as she continued. 'I'm going to do it, Céleste, but you wait, you just wait until the next issue, you – *glub*.'

She'd meant to call Céleste a bitch, but the policeman had put his cock in her mouth at that moment and the word had come out as a gulping noise. As she began to suck she was reflecting that it was probably just as well, and might even have saved her another spanking. The policeman was big, his cock a meaty brown rod with oddly slippery outer skin, so that as he began to come to erection it was like having an unusually large pork sausage in her mouth, raw.

He was growing quickly too, forcing Sarah to open her mouth ever wider as she struggled to come to terms with what was being done to her, the scene she had played over in her mind so many times since drawing Céleste put to cock in the same sordid alleyway, which she had masturbated over more than once. Now it was real, only with more men than she had ever imagined, each one determined to enjoy her, and with her hands cuffed behind her back to take away what little control she might have had.

The policeman said something to Raoul, a joke on Sarah's willingness. Raoul chuckled in response and he too took his cock out, which was every bit as huge and wrinkled and ugly as Sarah had drawn it. He laughed as he saw the shock in her eyes, and pushed close, offering himself to her mouth as he made a polite request to the policeman, who responded in kind, twisted a hand into Sarah's hair and pulled her off his own cock and onto Raoul's.

Sarah's eyes popped as the huge cock was fed into her mouth and down her throat. She was gagging immediately as the policeman began to move her back and forth by her hair, using her head as a fuck toy for Raoul's outsize cock. Marcel, watching, gave a cruel laugh at the sight, and as Sarah's head was finally pulled back a great gout of saliva exploded from her mouth, all down her breasts and belly.

Marcel immediately came round to the side, twisting Sarah's body so that he could get at her cleavage. The policeman's cock was back in her mouth as Marcel folded her breasts around his long bent erection and began to fuck them. Sarah felt an odd burst of pride, knowing that Céleste was physically incapable of what she was having done to her and she sucked harder, beginning to enjoy her ordeal.

The policeman promptly came in her mouth, unexpectedly and deep, so that she went into a violent coughing fit, a mixture of spunk and saliva and snot exploding from her nose, and more from her mouth as he withdrew to toss himself off in her face. As the mess slithered down into Sarah's cleavage, Marcel gave a pleased grunt and began to fuck in it. His father made a joke as he fed his cock back into Sarah's mouth and the two of them shared a grin as they began to use her together.

Lamond was pushing forward, cock in hand and eager for his go. The policeman stepped aside with a courteous gesture, Raoul withdrew, and Sarah found herself faced with the younger man's bulging hairy belly and short thick cock. She took it in, sucking quickly to get rid of a taste suspiciously like cheap paté and heavily mixed with unwashed man. He immediately took hold of her head, pulling her close to force his fat knob down her throat and making her gag again, now blowing spunk bubbles out of her nose as she struggled to breathe.

Raoul had got behind her, lifting her bottom in his hands as he slid his body in to make a seat for her, a seat with his cock sticking up out of the middle. She felt it press between her bum cheeks and her anus went tight by instinct, but he slid in up her pussy, allowing her to settle her bottom onto him. Abandoning one more level of dignity and self-respect, she began to bounce on his cock, the feel of his thick shaft inside her simply too good to resist.

Her new position made it hard for Marcel, who stood up, speaking rapidly to his father. Raoul grunted, settled himself to the ground and took a firm grip on Sarah's hips, holding her steady, his thumbs dug deep to spread her anus for buggering as Marcel straddled her. Sarah gave a muffled sob around her mouthful of penis as Marcel's bendy cock settled between her bum cheeks, briefly rutting in her crease before pushing lower. She felt his helmet press to her anus and forced herself to relax, knowing full well that it was going up her bum whether she liked it or not.

Marcel pushed as Sarah's anal ring spread on his cock, entering her with a sudden shove. She was already slippery, and loose from all the buggerings Giles had given her, and he went up easily, jamming the full length of his erection into her gut with a few firm shoves. All three were in her, rocking her on their cocks just the way she had shown Céleste getting it, save that the men were in different holes and with her hands securely cuffed behind her back she wasn't going to be able to masturbate.

She knew she'd have been doing it. Possibly she'd already have come, and as Raoul erupted inside her she knew that before they were done she'd be begging for it. Most of his come had squashed out around his cock, soiling her pussy and making her want to rub in it. Even her slimy breasts felt good, slapping together and bouncing wildly as with her cunt now vacant the thrusts of Marcel's cock in her rectum grew harder.

Raoul rolled out from underneath her and she was lifted, slipping off both cocks as the brothers bent her across one of the dustbins, her breasts and belly pressed to the filthy contents, her bottom and head sticking out to either side. Others had come close, creating a barrier of erect cocks between Sarah and the alley mouth, but it was the brothers who entered her again, bumhole and mouth as before, Sarah realising too late that they had swapped places.

Her eyes popped and her cheeks bulged as Marcel's cock went in, filling her mouth with the taste of her own bottom, and again as his brother's much thicker cock was jammed into her anus with a single hard shove. They began to rock her back and forth, Lamond fondling her rear cheeks as he buggered her and occasionally spreading them to admire the junction between cock and anus, Marcel with his hands pushed down into the rubbish to grope her breasts and plaster them with refuse.

Sarah was praying they'd come quickly, a wish she had granted as Lamond jammed himself deep to spunk in her rectum almost at the same instant Marcel whipped his cock out of her mouth and tossed off in her face, squeezing himself to control the jets of semen which he deliberately used to blind her, laughing as she was left with both eyes plastered with thick yellowish come and more running down her face.

Exhausted, dizzy and sore, Sarah could only lie helpless over the dustbin as more men moved in to take the brothers' places, a cock stuck in her mouth and another in her cunt almost before she could draw breath. She didn't know the men, she couldn't even see them, only suck as best she could and squirm her bottom on the belly of the man thrusting into her from behind. Others moved in too, one groping her breasts as he rubbed his cock on her now sweat-slick skin and tried to fuck her armpit, another masturbating over her bottom and slapping his erection on her still-hot cheeks.

Spunk erupted in her mouth and one cock was instantly replaced by another. One of them came all over her back and in her hair. The man inside her whipped himself free at the last instant to do it over her bottom, but instead of replacing him, the one who been wanking slipped a hand under her belly, rubbing her cunt as he positioned himself behind her.

Deep gratitude welled up in Sarah's head as she realised she was to be brought off, and she was immediately wriggling her bottom to encourage him. In answer, he poked the head of his cock up her bumhole and began to wank into her rectum even as he manipulated her cunt. It was too much for Sarah, who came instantly, a truly filthy climax to the way she'd been used, nude and in handcuffs, spanked in a public street, dragged into an alley and made to suck men off, fucked at their leisure, buggered and made to suck a cock just drawn from her rectum, and finally masturbated while a man she didn't even know tossed off up her bottom.

She was still coming as she was given a mouthful of spunk, which erupted all over the man who'd been in her mouth and she began to scream in ecstasy, her whole body jerking violently, her tits bouncing in the contents of the rubbish bin, her bumhole in spasm on the cock inside it as he too came, milking spunk into her full rectum.

Eleven

Sarah sat at her art desk, sucking meditatively on the end of her 4B pencil and staring at the sheet of paper before her, although her thoughts were not focused on the piece of artwork she was supposed to be doing but on Giles Compton-Bassett. He had let her down, so badly it had damaged her feelings for him beyond repair. Running off when the policeman appeared had been bad enough, but his pathetic excuses when she had finally returned to the hotel had been the last straw.

She had told him, and the others, that she'd managed to talk her way out of it, which they had readily accepted. Their excuse for deserting her was that she'd have been in bigger trouble if the police had realised she was being photographed, but it was quite evident to her that their main concern had been for themselves, the camera, and the pictures, in that order, with her welfare coming a long way behind. From Hugh and Sid that was bad enough, but from Giles it was intolerable.

Admitting to the truth had been out of the question, and not only because she preferred not to tell them that she'd been dragged into an alley and gang-banged. She knew that from their perspective it hadn't even happened, no more than the men who'd used her had helped her clean up in the nearest café and bought her a glass of absinthe to help her cope. The policeman had even shown her how to make it, pouring from a clearly labelled bottle and trickling ice-cold water into it over a sugar cube on a special spoon, an act illegal in France for nearly a hundred years, but not in the France of her imagination, which was where she had been.

How it worked she didn't know, and nor did it really matter. What did matter was that it worked, and of that there was no question. The alley had been the alley she'd drawn, right down to the dead rat, which could hardly be explained as a hidden memory from some earlier visit to Paris, leaving aside the fact that she was absolutely certain she had never visited the Rue Claude Magnien before. Also, the vivid and repulsive details of the Frenchmen's cocks existed only in her imagination and had never even been published. Every detail of the scene had been originally created in her own imagination, including, now she thought about it, what the men had done to her, but only in her darkest fantasies, which she'd never told even to Giles.

One in particular stuck out – having a cock withdrawn from her bottom hole and put straight in her mouth, something she'd never even considered until he'd mentioned it, and which had shocked her then. Yet while they'd been having sex that night, both of them thoroughly horny and drunk too, just before she came, with her mind less inhibited and more receptive to dirty thoughts than at any other time, she had thought of how it would be, only to dismiss it as too disgusting to bear thinking about. Yet Marcel had done it to her.

She winced at the memory, but at the same time she felt a sudden tightening of her sex. It was hard to understand how anything so dirty could turn her on, yet there was no denying that it did, and to accept that gave her power. Whatever Céleste did to her, she could cope – more than cope, in fact, because while knowing that whatever she drew would be done to her in revenge was frightening, it was also immensely arousing.

A touch of guilt lingered for what she was about to do to Céleste, but she knew the solution to that. On a small table by her desk stood a bottle of vivid green absinthe, a tall glass, and a bowl holding three sugar cubes and a spoon of the proper design, all purchased in Paris. If wine was enough to make her shed her inhibitions and push back her awe of Céleste, then surely *la fée verte* would be more effective still?

She began to set out the drawing, making light pencil lines to give herself a rough idea of where the frames would go. There was a lot to get in, from the first with Céleste and the three men robbing the grave to the last, in which the police burst into the room. As she drew she was thinking forward into the story and wondering how to bring Monsieur d'Orsay into it without breaking the guidelines. There was also the drug cartel, who hadn't even been mentioned.

Abruptly dissatisfied, Sarah sat back, her pencil in her mouth once more. It wasn't even going to be obvious why the money was in the coffin, and the sudden appearance of a South American drugs cartel was going to looked uncomfortably like a *deus ex machina*. Nor was it obvious how Céleste had found out about the plot in the first place. Giles hadn't done his job very well. Giles was useless.

The job still had to be done though, especially as Hugh knew what was going to happen in the episode. At least she could do that. Turning in her chair, she began to prepare a glass of absinthe, balancing a sugar cube carefully on the slotted spoon and pouring the green liquid over it, then water more slowly still, until her glass contained three fingers of cloudy pale-green liquid. She took a sip, letting the bitter-sweet, liquorice flavour fill her mouth as she considered how best to put Céleste in bondage.

It needed to look right to the police, something that left Céleste helpless for the men's use without giving the impression of deliberate erotic bondage. The men liked to use a girl every way, and preferably all together, a nasty habit Sarah had first created, then come to reap the consequences of, as doubtless she would again.

She paused, wondering if she really wanted to be tied into some awkward position and used by the three rough Frenchmen, maybe others too, and almost certainly after a spanking. As usual the prospect filled her with a mixture of longing and fear, arousal and self-disgust. Céleste would be furious.

Sarah took a swallow of absinthe, unable to start, yet knowing it was too late to back out. At the least she was going to have to wait a little, so she put the sheet of paper aside and took another. She began to doodle as she thought of how Giles should have behaved, coming to her rescue either by explaining the situation to the policeman or, better still, distracting him to let Sarah escape.

A real man, she decided, would have flashed the policeman, thus assuring full attention as he fled. Being tall and lean and young, Giles – or the imaginary Giles – would easily have outrun his pursuer, or escaped by some clever ruse. The others would then have helped Sarah to safety, both from the police and from Céleste, who never appeared unless Sarah was alone.

Better still, a real hero might not only have distracted the police, but looped around and saved Sarah from Céleste. Not Giles, obviously, but the man Giles should have been, just as Céleste's Paris was the Paris that should have been but was not. Yes, she could create her own *deus ex machina*, and there would be nobody to criticise, with the possible exception of Céleste.

Her imaginary hero would have come back, fought off the three Frenchmen and put Céleste across his knee for the spanking she so richly deserved. Sarah was smiling to herself as the absinthe began its work. Her thoughts started to take shape and her pencil to move on the paper, drawing rough forms, of the slender elegant Céleste across the knee of another figure, only to stop. Her expression changed to a sullen frown. It wouldn't work. Her hero would be captivated by Céleste. Men were always captivated by Céleste. Sarah would be the one who ended up getting spanked, in front of her new-found hero.

Another swallow of absinthe and the solution had come to her. No man would dare to spank Céleste, but a woman might, a British woman, tall and strong, with fiery red hair and a temper to match, a bit like Rebecca Compton-Bassett in fact. She began to draw again, filling in her geometric outline with female features instead of male; a glorious mane of hair, full breasts – although not so large as to be impractical – womanly hips and long well-formed legs.

Her new creation was not Rebecca, but a super Rebecca, Rebecca as a heroine, bigger in every way, but a little more down to earth, and called Becky, Becky Wellington. Becky Wellington was six foot tall, Sarah decided, and a champion equestrian of Olympic standard. She was exceptionally strong for a woman, absolutely certain of her place in the world, the daughter of an old and wealthy family, and, above all, British. She would deal with Céleste, more or less the way her namesake had dealt with Napoleon, bold, forthright, absolutely determined. Like Napoleon, Céleste would put up a fight and, like Napoleon, she would lose.

The voice of reason was no more than the faintest of whispers in Sarah's head as she began to draw in earnest. Only the occasional pause for a swallow of absinthe or to refill her glass was allowed to break her concentration as she sketched, and she quickly found that the legendary effect of absinthe was simple truth. She grew drunk, her inhibitions vanished, and yet her mind was still clear enough to think, and to allow her to ink in her sketches.

She completed the drawing of Céleste being spanked, then began another, adding yet more detail. Every humiliation inflicted on her had to be reproduced; the public setting, being held helpless as her bottom was laid bare, the deliberate exposure of both pussy and bumhole, every cruel subtlety of the spankings, including being masturbated and having her anus penetrated.

One by one, with drawing after drawing, Sarah filled in the details. There was Becky seated outside a café, the Café Anglais, having a cup of afternoon tea, with Céleste approaching in the background, as cool and haughty as ever. There was Becky giving Céleste a lecture on manners and telling her she was about to receive a dose of her own medicine for punishing Sarah. A close-up captured both faces, Becky's no-nonsense manner and Céleste's affronted dignity.

Then came the fight, with both women utterly convinced of their ability to win, and Céleste unwilling to concede defeat until she'd been forced face-down on the dirty ground. Becky was straddled across Céleste's back, her blouse ripped to show one heavy breast, her hair dishevelled, her face marked with scratches but set in triumph.

It took several pictures to convey Céleste's emotions as her bottom was unveiled: her face twisted into animal fury; disbelief at what was being done to her, and a consternation so vehement Sarah frightened herself with the result; and, last, screaming in rage as she came bare. Between each she put the reverse view: of Becky's fingers on the hem of Céleste's skirt; pulling it high to reveal the tops of seamed stockings; the skirt higher still, exposing the perfect apple-bottom clad in black silk panties with a border of finest lace. A whole series followed, showing the exposure of Céleste's rear cheeks, with the expensive black panties a further inch down in each frame.

Another full-size drawing showed Céleste with her panties properly down, bum bare to a sizeable crowd including not only Monsieur d'Orsay and a dozen fellow *roués*, but several fashionable young men and women, assorted Japanese and American tourists each of whom had at least two cameras, and a large group of English football fans complete with scarves, rattles and loo rolls, all watching with deep interest. Céleste's legs were scissored apart at a ridiculous angle, with her panties stretched taut between her knees. Her fists were beating on the cobbles in her fury, her newly-waxed cunt was on full show, and Becky was holding her trim bottom cheeks wide to display her tight brown anus.

With Céleste thoroughly humiliated, all that remained was to get her spanked. Now high, both on absinthe and her own arousal, Sarah drew with verve. A few of the footballs fans would help get Céleste over Becky's knee, and have a quick feel while they were at it. Céleste would then have her arm twisted firmly into the small of her back, just as she loved to do to Sarah, and her pert little bottom would be spanked, and spanked, and spanked.

Sarah drew picture after picture, showing Céleste from every angle as her bottom bounced and quivered to Becky's slaps. Some showed only Céleste's face, registering a dozen powerful emotions; more showed her bottom, in various ludicrous poses as she wriggled and squirmed, being smacked and about to be smacked, mostly with her cunt on show and as often as not her bumhole too, and growing gradually pinker as the spanking progressed.

Next came the rude part, with Sarah giggling drunkenly as she drew the now hot-bottomed Céleste being masturbated by Becky, not to turn her on, but to deliberately humiliate her by making her come with her bottom smacked to show that she was no better than Sarah. A detail showed Becky's hand between Céleste's legs, a thumb pushed in up her victim's vagina, fingers manipulating the moist fleshy folds below, with the clitoris sticking out between two.

Céleste tried to resist, her face showing first determination, then a consternation nearly as strong as when her panties had been about to come down, and finally a helpless ecstasy. In response Becky applied a few concluding smacks to Céleste's rosy bottom, and as a final indignity pulled the little cheeks wide once more and inserted the stem of a lily into the anus.

By the time Sarah was satisfied that she had exploited every possibility of Céleste's spanking she was too drunk and too horny to worry about anything but her own needs. Céleste, she decided, would give in once she had been brought off under Becky's fingers. She wouldn't even bother to take the lily out of her bumhole, let alone pull her panties up. Instead she would allow herself to be guided to her knees, now meek and apologetic as she was made to lick Becky's cunt, not for the sake of lesbian pleasure so much, but as a gesture of dominance.

That was the final drawing, of Céleste kneeling, knees wide, bare red bottom framed in dishevelled clothing, her cunt wet, the lily protruding obscenely from her tightly-puckered anus, kneeling in abject submission as she licked Becky, who had merely rucked up her skirt and pulled her panties aside to allow access to her sex without exposing herself unnecessarily.

At last Sarah sat back, feeling well pleased with herself and so aroused that her thighs and bottom cheeks were clenching of their own accord. She longed to bring herself to orgasm, but held back, promising herself she would finish the episode of 'Graverobbers' first. After showing Céleste spanked, the bondage was easy. The pictures flowed from her pencil, the discovery of the gold, the four of them drinking together, Céleste suggesting that she would enjoy being tied, and the bondage and sex itself.

Céleste was put on a chair, facing the wrong way, her thighs and ankles bound in place to keep her legs well spread and her bottom open, both cunt and anus available for fucking, her mouth too. Her arms were lashed tight behind her back, her torso fixed to the back of the chair so that her breasts stuck out over the top, leaving her body fully vulnerable.

Tied and helpless, Céleste was used in her mouth, in her cunt and up her bottom hole, in picture after detailed picture, the really filthy parts in insets so that Sarah could take them out for publication. She showed Raoul growing erect in Céleste's gaping mouth. She showed Marcel wedging his erect cock deep in to make Céleste choke. She showed Lamond with his hairy belly pressed to Céleste's face as he fucked her mouth. She showed Céleste fucked, each cock drawn in detail as it was pushed in up the increasingly wet hole. She showed the penetration of Céleste's anus, the tiny brown star forced wide until it made a straining ring of flesh around the first cock shaft. Last came the come shots – Lamond's thick cock withdrawn from Céleste's anus and stuck in her mouth for his orgasm, Marcel doing it in her face and smearing his mess in with his erection, Raoul coming deep in her throat at her own request, so that she choked and sicked up his come down her own breasts at the exact moment the police burst in.

It was perfect – unpublishable, but perfect. Sarah was in no mood to start toning it down. A last swallow of absinthe and she was grappling for the button of her jeans and pushing them down even as she flopped onto the sofa. She felt dirtier than at any time she could remember, wanting to do everything and have everything done to her all at once, but far too urgent to make herself take it slowly. Her jeans and panties came down, her top up and she was nude from her breasts to her ankles, her hands moving over her body to stroke her sensitive flesh as she let her mind run.

In the Paris of her imagination Céleste du Musigny would be kneeling in the street, her hot bare bottom on show with a lily stuck up it, her face pressed to Becky Wellington's sex. It was a glorious thought, and had Sarah wriggling with pleasure as she explored herself, repeatedly touching her breasts and sex, her belly and bottom, even between her bulging cheeks.

Touching her bumhole felt nice, also rude. Her finger went to her mouth and back between her cheeks without hesitation, her inhibitions completely gone. Her legs came up, rolled high as she fingered her anus, teasing the little hole until it began to come open, sucking her fingers once more, touching again, and this time pushing deep into the hot slimy cavity of her rectum.

She began to rub herself, jiggling her breasts at the same time and wishing there were a trio of men there to thoroughly abuse her as she brought herself off. They wouldn't do as they were told, but they would do as she really wanted, just like the men in Paris, using her and thus bringing her to an ecstasy she was quite incapable of achieving otherwise. She'd be made to suck their cocks until all three of them were hard. They'd fuck her and make her lick up her own juices from their straining shafts. They'd bugger her and make her suck their dirty cocks. They'd fuck her throat and make her choke, so that she threw up their mess all over her fat tits just like they'd made Céleste, only she, Sarah, would rub the spunk in as she brought herself to orgasm.

Her body was rolled right up, her finger as deep up her bottom as it would go, her other hand clutching at her cunt as she masturbated, wriggling in ecstasy for her dirty thoughts. As she started to come she pulled her finger from her bumhole and stuck it in her mouth, sucking up the taste of her bottom as her body jerked and trembled in an orgasm so powerful it left her slumped panting on the sofa long after she was finished, her mind fixed on one thing. Whatever else might happen, she was going back to Paris.

After a couple of days to get over her hangover, Sarah completed an official version of the bondage episode of 'Graverobbers' and took it in Hugh Bowle. He was more delighted than ever, and also keen to patch up the rift between Sarah and Giles. She declined, insisting that their relationship be purely professional in future, which left her feeling upset but also stronger and less emotionally vulnerable than before.

Back at the flat she sat down with a mug of coffee and began to wonder what, if anything, she could achieve. Was her imaginary Paris simply some elaborate trick, presumably played on her for the sake of profit as well as sadism? If not, how much could she change? Would she really be able to meet Becky at the Café Anglais? What if she were to draw a spire from Notre Dame falling on Céleste, or the Arc de Triomphe struck by a meteor, or Paris invaded by aliens for that matter?

The thought of killing Céleste caused a pang of anguish so sharp and so sudden that she immediately dismissed the idea, also telling herself that whatever she did it was not to be irresponsible. Not too irresponsible anyway, although now that she was sober, even the thought of Céleste getting her bottom warmed seemed an outrage. She bit her lip, thinking of the consequences, but experiencing an immediate flush of arousal. Sarah was the one who ought to be spanked, and regularly.

There was no escaping the truth. She wanted to be punished by Céleste. She craved it and she always had done. Céleste was not the woman she wanted to be, but the woman she wanted to serve, perhaps as a maid in her apartment; dressed in a skimpy uniform, spanked regularly, made to entertain male guests in her mouth, used as a sex toy at dinner parties . . .

A strong shiver passed through her at the thought. It would be perfect, the realisation of her true nature, and yet she hardly behaved as a good servant should, far from it. Instead she had put her exquisite Mistress through a series of humiliating sexual ordeals, so inappropriate for Céleste that no matter how often or how severely Sarah was punished, the balance could never be redressed. Céleste wouldn't want Sarah as her servant. She probably hated her.

The thought drew a tear from Sarah's eye and filled her with self-pity and remorse. She should never have accepted the commission to draw 'Graverobbers', while Céleste had been absolutely right to spank her for it, and everything else. In contrast, Sarah had been absolutely wrong to set Becky on Céleste, which had been the act of a pathetic vindictive little brat too self-centred and stupid to understand that she was in the wrong and that her punishment had been just.

Tears were trickling down Sarah's cheeks as she got up, not knowing what she was doing, but determined to make amends. She felt badly in need of a spanking, but knew it would never be enough. If she was spanked she would grow excited, and she wanted to be punished properly, because it was what she deserved, not to arouse her. Besides, there was nobody to do it and she would feel silly smacking her own bottom. She sat down again, pondering on what she could do, and how she could even begin to make up for what she'd done to Céleste.

Maybe she should put herself on the street? When angry, Céleste always called her a whore, so perhaps she would be satisfied if Sarah made herself one, out in the *banlieu*, offering to suck men's cocks for a couple of Euros a time? Then again, Céleste seemed to think Sarah was a whore anyway, not for prostituting herself, but for prostituting her art. No, Céleste probably assumed that Sarah would happily suck a man off for a couple of Euros already.

Maybe she should take a proper whipping, a couple of dozen strokes of the cane as she bent to touch her toes or, better still, a dose of the quirt, applied across her buttocks and back and legs as she hung helpless from her wrists. She was sure it would be more than she could take, but not sure whether or not it would turn her on anyway, while again, unless she went to Paris, there was the question of who would administer the punishment.

Maybe she should go to Paris, and beg Céleste to forgive her and punish her in whatever way seemed appropriate? She would surrender herself completely, allow anything to be done, no matter how painful, no matter how degrading. Céleste would know what to do, and when Sarah had fully redeemed herself she would be made Céleste's servant.

Another shiver of pleasure ran through Sarah's body, stronger than before. Evidently it was impossible for her to be punished by Céleste without becoming aroused, and she knew that would still be true right up to the point at which the punishment became dangerous, or beyond what was just. Whatever it was, it had to leave her whole and well.

Could Céleste be trusted? The answer had to be yes. Céleste was cruel, but only because Sarah needed her to be, and nothing had happened beyond what Sarah wanted. Yes, when she went to Paris she would give herself over to Céleste, completely, but she would punish herself first, in some way she genuinely disliked. She would even take photographs and show them to Céleste to prove that she was genuinely contrite.

Again she fell to musing, trying to ignore the fact that whatever she thought of, no matter how disgusting, sent a shiver of pleasure through her. Soon the need to masturbate was close to overwhelming, and yet she had still not found anything she could do safely that would not turn her on. The very act of punishment was exciting, regardless of the details, although some choices were less exciting than others, or so she thought until she remembered something Mak had seen in a gay club, which had struck her then as repulsive, and still did. A young man had been put on a lead, treated like a dog, and at the end of the night been made to eat a bowl of dog food.

The thought made Sarah's stomach turn, and yet she immediately knew it was what she should be made to do, what she was going to do. Everything else turned her on too much, or was actually dangerous, but the dog food wouldn't harm her at all. It was merely disgusting, and a highly appropriate and effective punishment for her. That was what she needed, a stomach full of dog food. She would eat it out of a bowl on the floor, in the nude except for a collar, and she would video herself to prove to Céleste that she had done it. Céleste would be disgusted, but also amused, and with luck would accept that Sarah's place was at her feet.

Sarah got up, determined to do it before common sense could get the better of her. Just to think about it made her feel sick, but she knew that was how it should be, and she didn't falter as she left the flat and walked around the corner to the local pet shop. Everything she needed was there, and she quickly chose a cheap red plastic bowl and a spiked collar. There were plenty of varieties of dog food, but she was determined not to cheat, and ignored the tiny sachets of luxury quality for the smallest breeds. Instead she chose the largest tin of economy dog food, the only appropriate choice for her.

As she walked back towards the flat she wasn't sure if she could go through with it. Her eyes already felt heavy with unshed tears for what she was about to do to herself, and a voice in the back of her head was screaming at her to have some self-respect. She ignored it, telling herself that it was selfish, the voice of a spoilt brat who could have another woman spanked and humiliated for money, that she deserved punishment and would go through with it no matter what.

Back in the flat she set up Mak's video camera on a tripod in the kitchen, with a field of view showing the entire kitchen floor and a new tape so that she could be sure of capturing her entire punishment. Now ready, she spent a moment rehearsing what she was going to do, and knowing that once the camera was rolling there would be no going back. She turned it on and came to kneel in front of the lens, her head bowed in contrition as she began to speak.

'Céleste,' she said, 'Mademoiselle du Musigny. I want to apologise to you, and apologise fully. My behaviour to you has been totally unacceptable, and I need to be punished. What you have done to me has been just, but you are right. I am a slut, and I can't help but enjoy it, especially when you spank me. So . . . so I'm going to do this, which I won't enjoy, as a gesture of apology to you and a punishment for myself. I beg you to accept, but I will understand if you don't.'

Sarah stopped, the tears now rolling down her face as she began to undress with trembling fingers. Her top came off and her bra. She already felt vulnerable with the exposure of her breasts, and more so as her shoes and socks and jeans followed. She left her panties until last, still kneeling with her head hung towards the camera as she pushed them down, then off. Nude, she lifted her chin and put on the dog collar, making sure it was clearly visible to the camera, held the big tin of dog food up for inspection, and peeled the lid off.

She winced as the cloying smell caught her nose and the glistening lumpy surface of the contents was exposed. Once more she wondered if she could really go through with it, but Céleste seemed to be watching, her beautiful face full of scorn and amusement, fully expecting Sarah to fail. Taking up the fork she had put out, Sarah began to scrape the contents of the can into her bowl, making sure what she was doing was clearly visible to the camera and that she got out every last bit of the disgusting brownish grey pulp.

With the tin empty, she showed it to the camera once more and put it down. She was forcing herself to go on as she got into a crawling position, the voice in her head now screaming at her to stop even as she adopted the dog-like pose, her face above the bowl, the smell thick in her nostrils, the tears pouring down her cheeks ... and then she'd done it. Her face sank into the dog food, her mouth opened around a big gelatinous lump, and closed.

Her stomach wrenched as the taste and feel of the dog food filled her mouth, but she'd done it and she was determined to go all the way. Turning her face to the camera, she forced herself to swallow and opened her mouth to make it quite clear she really had eaten the foul mess. Her face went back in the bowl, taking a bigger mouthful this time and she gagged again as she forced herself to swallow. A bit had stuck to her nose, more around her lips, but she ignored it, burying her face in the slippery smelly mess, sobbing and gasping between mouthfuls with the knowledge of what she was doing going round and round in her head, grovelling nude on all fours as she ate dog food.

It was right for her. It was what she should be made to do all the time, stripped and collared and fed cheap dog food out of a bowl, the cheapest dog food, suitable for a fat bitch like her. She didn't deserve to be Céleste's maid, she deserved to be Céleste's dog, kept in the nude and fed dog food and scraps, taken out for walks and made to pee and shit in gutters where everybody could see, made to sleep in a kennel, mounted in the street . . .

Sarah's face was pushed down hard in the plastic bowl, smeared with dog food as she eagerly lapped it up, swallowing one foul mouthful after another and licking up the pieces of jelly that had dropped on the floor. Her hand had gone back, to find her juicy ready cunt, and she clutched at herself in a frenzied masturbation as she brought herself off over what she had made herself do. As she started to come she was holding a full mouthful of dog food, some of it dribbling down over her lips. Her orgasm peaked and she swallowed it down, thinking of her full belly as wave after wave of ecstasy tore through her, calling herself a bitch and a slut in between screams and sobs as she let her emotions out, and knowing it was true, that there was no punishment too degraded for her to get off on.

Twelve

Two days later the remaining story for 'Graverobbers' arrived. The post was early for once, and Sarah was up late, still wandering around the flat in her robe with a cup of coffee. She was already in a crisis of conscience, torn between the conflicting demands of how she felt she should behave towards Céleste and her contractual obligations. The contents of the envelope made it worse.

First was a letter from Giles, apologising for his behaviour and asking for a second chance. Her initial reaction was outrage that he should dare to ask, only for her to pause. Just as he was asking for forgiveness from her, so she would be asking forgiveness from Céleste, for more, and for more again if she completed the cartoon.

There were three episodes, and to judge by their quality Giles was genuinely upset over their split. Gone was the ever-rising perversity and high sex content, to be replaced by a tepid tailing off of the story with quite a lot of violence and nothing exceptional in the way of rude behaviour. Céleste was to lose her clothes in a dramatic shoot-out with the drug cartel so improbable it reminded Sarah of the worst of Holywood action movies, while the difficulties with Monsieur d'Orsay were side-stepped by having him shot as he was trying to blackmail Céleste.

Sarah knew she could not do it. Maybe, after plenty of absinthe and with the rest of her life spent as Céleste's dog-slave, she could just about have continued to escalate the story, with increasingly dirty scenes and a perverted orgy as a climax, but she could under no circumstances draw Monsieur d'Orsay being killed, nor any other character. She was also sure that Hugh Bowle would be far from impressed, but that at least was a blessing. The story could be changed, and so long as Hugh liked her version, all would be well. Once it was done, she would go to Paris and offer herself to Céleste, who could do with her whatever was just.

Taking a pot of black coffee into her room, Sarah sat down to work. So far all the readers knew was that Céleste had somehow managed to find out that a large quantity of money was hidden in a coffin. She had bribed Monsieur d'Orsay to discover which coffin, and set up Raoul and his sons to do the dirty work and take the punishment, while she walked free. There didn't have to be a drug cartel, guns or killing.

The next episode would show the arrest of Raoul, Marcel and Lamond. They would then be safely out of the way, which was just as well, and for which Sarah felt no remorse whatsoever. She had enjoyed what they'd done to her, but she knew full well that they would have done it anyway and enjoyed her protests and tears too; after all, she had created them. That left Monsieur d'Orsay to be disposed off, and as Sarah began to sketch, an idea struck her.

Having successfully stolen the money and escaped prosecution, Céleste would want to celebrate. There would be a party, a glittering occasion with Champagne flowing freely, a string quartet and a dozen or so of Paris's most eligible bachelors all vying for Céleste's attention. One, Antoine Saint-Coeur, the most handsome, the richest, a man brilliant in every way, would win the privilege of a night with Céleste, a night of romantic tender lovemaking, just rude enough to keep the readers happy.

The entire episode was already complete in Sarah's mind, and taking shape on the page as fast as she could draw. Raoul, Marcel and Lamond were arrested and sentenced to long prison terms in double-quick time, their claims of Céleste's involvement met with derision. The party got under way, with Céleste the centre of attention for as many handsome young men as Sarah could fit on the page, each and every one of them pathetically grateful for the slightest glance or remark from her and hurrying eagerly to do her bidding. When it came to the bedroom scene, Céleste went on top, her back and buttocks and breasts and belly all shown half lit, and as pure elegance. Finally, in the last frame, Monsieur d'Orsay's face could be seen, also half lit beneath a street lamp as he looked up to Céleste's window in which her naked torso was visible in silhouette as she rode her beau.

Sarah's face was wreathed in smiles as she finished. It was good, and a fitting tribute to Céleste, although merely showing her naked would no doubt earn Sarah another well-deserved spanking, possibly in front of the handsome suitors. That was rather a nice thought, as was having to indulge all Céleste's rejects, taking them to orgasm in her mouth as they fantasised over the true object of their desire, with Sarah as no more than a convenient receptacle for their spunk.

She shook herself, promising not to get carried away until she had finished all three episodes. The next had to be Monsieur d'Orsay's blackmail attempt. He would accost her in the street, revealing what he knew as they leant on a railing overlooking the Seine, which gave Sarah a reason for a magnificent Parisian skyline drawn across the top of the page. Céleste, quite unruffled, would suggest that he might enjoy watching her have sex with another woman in return for a reduction in the amount she had to pay. Monsieur d'Orsay would accept with lewd enthusiasm, and Céleste would take him to a select brothel, which provided an excellent excuse for some gratuitous nudity. In the brothel they would select a girl, whom Céleste would spank and humiliate in various ways before making her suck Monsieur d'Orsay's cock as she used dildoes on herself in both vagina and anus. That girl would be Sarah.

As she pencilled in the last frame her excitement was close to unbearable, imagining herself as a girl in a Parisian brothel, sold for sex to all comers, and specifically Céleste and Monsieur d'Orsay, spanked, her anus opened, made to masturbate with dildoes in front of them, then to go down on his cock with her penetrated bottom and cunt stuck out behind. It was a fitting punishment for her, and would please Céleste, she was sure, especially if she masturbated over her own degradation, but that would have to wait.

She took a third sheet of A2, the climax to the story already clear in her mind. Having bought the girl, Céleste would take her back to d'Orsay's flat. There, she would bite down her disgust at him to perform with the girl as he watched, making her, Sarah, serve them naked, lick and kiss as ordered, sucking d'Orsay's cock and applying her tongue to Céleste's pussy.

The thought of being made to lick Céleste left Sarah feeling so weak and so aroused that she had to pause for a moment, her eyes shut tight as she struggled for control. She was telling herself she wasn't a lesbian, but she knew that for Céleste she would do anything, and that mere labels for sexuality had no meaning. Yes, she would lick, and gratefully, achieving an ecstasy as much submissive as sexual, and maybe, just maybe, Céleste would demand that Sarah's tongue be applied to her anus.

A violent spasm passed through Sarah, close to orgasm, and she was forced to take a swallow of coffee and count to a hundred before she could go on. The last episode could be almost pure sex, showing Céleste and d'Orsay putting her through her paces, including a good spanking, plenty of oral attention and, to make sure she was fully co-operative, the application of some unspecified drug. That would be done by Céleste, without Monsieur d'Orsay's knowledge, shown clearly in a small frame near the beginning, with an elegant gloved hand squeezing an ampoule into a glass with two bottles visible in the background, one of absinthe, one tiny and dark.

The drug explained her total willingness to perform, including the spanking and oral sex, licking Céleste's bottom, and being peed on. Another powerful shock of ecstasy passed through Sarah's body at the thought of kneeling naked on the bathroom floor as Céleste urinated on her, and her hand had gone to the V of her crotch as she continued to draw. Yes, she could be peed on, then made to mop it up, crawling nude on her hands and knees as Monsieur d'Orsay readied his cock for her body.

He'd lose control. He'd fuck her as she knelt in a puddle of Céleste's urine. He'd finger her bottom as his cock moved in her cunt, opening her anus. He'd bugger her and make her suck his dirty cock, only to stuff it back up her bottom and in her mouth a second time.

Sarah had lost control, wrenching her jeans open and stuffing her hand down her panties as she imagined the scene: her naked on all fours, wet with Céleste's piddle; d'Orsay scrambling ape-like back and forth as he alternately thrust his cock up her bottom hole and into her mouth, feeding her the juice from her own gaping anus; and at last his orgasm, which he'd do down her throat, forcing her to swallow his spunk.

She screamed out in ecstasy at the thought, coming under her fingers with the filthy image burning in her head. She subsided into her chair with her face set in a sleepy smile, but only for a moment. A few more pencil strokes were all that she needed to complete the cartoon, and she went back to work.

As Monsieur d'Orsay defiled her, Céleste would have slipped quietly away and, just as he came, the police would arrive to find him inflicting an act of unspeakable perversion on a girl he'd first purchased from a brothel as a sex slave, then drugged to make her compliant. The owner of the brothel, Madame Leboeuf, handsomely paid by Céleste, would support the story, while d'Orsay's accusations of complicity would fall on deaf ears. He would join Raoul and the others in prison, while Céleste walked free with the money and Sarah became her grateful obedient maid.

That was it, 'Graverobbers' complete, the final frame showing Céleste and Antoine Saint-Coeur standing on the balcony of the apartment, looking out over the moonlit Paris rooftops as they sipped Champagne. Sarah showed herself stood discreetly in the background, holding the tray with the ice bucket and bottle, the skirt of her maid's uniform so short that the tuck of her bottom showed, revealing a delicate tracery of lines from a recent whipping. That, she felt, was her destiny.

* * *

Not wishing to have to redo all three episodes, Sarah asked if she could take her pencil sketches in to show Hugh Bowle. He was as accommodating as ever, suggesting they meet at the Wharfingers rather than his office, to which Sarah agreed.

As she walked across the plaza beneath the Ehrmann and Black building two days later, her emotions were strong. It was only a matter of months since she had first been there, and yet it seemed as if an era was coming to an end. Her determination to go to Paris had grown with time, and with the story complete there would be nothing to hold her back. Only if everything she had experienced proved to be an elaborate hoax would she return, and she was convinced it was not.

Hugh was already in the pub, and evidently had been for some time, occupying the best of the alcove tables with a paper spread out in front of him and a pint of beer at his side. As Sarah entered he smiled and beckoned to her. Sarah returned a polite but slightly stiff nod, her feelings still somewhat bruised after the way he had deserted her in the Rue Claude Magnien. He seemed oblivious, insisting on kissing her the moment she had set her portfolio down on the table and planting a gentle pat on her bottom as she made for the bar.

Sarah ignored the unwanted intimacy, telling herself that once she was gone it wouldn't matter. At the bar she ordered a bottle of their best Chablis on Hugh's tab, sure it was the least she deserved. He appeared not to notice, watching her pour herself a glass before he spoke.

'So what's up, doll?'

'I wanted you to see my roughs,' Sarah explained. 'They don't follow the story Giles outlined, you see, and I want your approval before I start inking them in.'

'Fair enough,' he answered. 'So what, you still not made up with Giles?'

'No, I don't think so,' Sarah told him. 'He sent me a nice letter, but I really can't handle people who won't stick up for me when I need them.'

It was a pointed comment, aimed as much at Hugh as Giles, but as usual he failed to react.

'Pity,' he said. 'You made a great team.'

Sarah bit down her automatic disappointment at what sounded like the sack, telling herself that it no longer mattered. He had taken her portfolio, opening it to look at her pencil sketches, and she waited for his verdict, sipping Chablis and hoping he would be impressed.

'Looks good,' he said after a while. 'Looks great in fact. So what's with the tart looking like you?'

'I just thought . . .' Sarah responded, blushing.

'No, no,' he cut in. 'It's great. I mean, she's a looker, your Céleste, very catwalk, but our readers like a bit of T and A, and of course they've seen what you've got, so they'll recognise you. Nice. Oh yeah.'

He reached down to the bench at his side, to pass across the new issue of *Hot Gun*. Sarah quickly flicked it open, not to the cartoon, but to the pages before. Her cheeks were already hot, and grew hotter as she looked over the pictures of her posing nude in the hotel, with no detail of her body left private, and of her walking proud and naked down the Rue Claude Magnien.

Several passers-by were visible in the pictures, and in the last shot the policeman could just be seen as he emerged from the café, his face just beginning to register surprise. She already knew it was the last photo Sid had taken but there was no sign of Céleste, nor Raoul and his sons, nor even the old man who had been reading his paper on the bench while she was spanked. Without question the street had been different just a few minutes later.

'Thanks,' she said. 'May I keep this?'

'Sure,' he answered, 'but there's another one in the post. This is good stuff, as usual, but we're going to have to lose the pissing. Too kinky. Have her pour a jug of water over you instead if you want to be wet.'

'I'll just take it out,' Sarah promised. 'This is what Giles wanted. I hope you don't mind me making the changes?'

He took the storyline from Sarah, quickly read it through, then passed it back as he spoke.

'Not bad, and we did maybe need a bit of shoot-'em-up, but I prefer yours, more sex. You're not going to be a pain about the money, are you?'

'No, no,' Sarah assured him.

'Good girl,' he answered. 'You're a pleasure to work with, you know that, not to mention easy on the eye. So that's done with, what's next?'

'Do you still want me?' she asked, a little surprised.

'Sure,' he responded, 'course I do. Good artists are rare, and most of them are so fucking precious . . . pardon my French. Yeah, we want you, and if you don't want to work with Giles you can do the story yourself, full rate and all. How's that?'

'Very generous, thank you,' she replied, immediately feeling guilty for cutting Giles out, 'but I . . . I was actually thinking of going to live in Paris.'

He shrugged.

'No problem. We'll miss you around the place, but you can work from Timbuktu if you want, just so long as you get the copy in on time.'

'That shouldn't be a problem,' Sarah said cautiously, wondering what Céleste would say, 'but I may have to introduce a new character.'

'You do as you like, Sarah doll,' Hugh answered, 'only give this one a bit more up top, and a better arse. Slim, but with plenty of T and A, that's what the boys like. It's only poofs who're into the garden-rake look.'

'What about Giles?' Sarah asked.

'I think we'll put him on readers' letters,' Hugh said vaguely, 'not that it's my choice, but there's always room for a dirty bugger like him.'

'He won't lose out then?'

'Nah, not so's you'd notice, I wouldn't think.'

Sarah made a face, now feeling intensely guilty. At the very least Giles deserved an explanation and, as Hugh went on expounding the virtues of busty girls, she had already decided to pay a visit. Inevitably it would be awkward, and the wine was definitely going to help, so she swallowed her glass of Chablis and poured another.

Hugh had begun to talk about how popular she was following her appearances in *Boobie Babes* and *Hotties at Home*, how many letters she'd received from fans, most of who were apparently obsessed with her breasts, and how many hits they'd had on her page on the firm's adult website. She listened politely, feeling detached from it all, as if none of it really concerned her, and growing gradually drunk as the level in the bottle fell.

By the time the bottle was finished she felt ready to face Giles, or Céleste, or anybody else for that matter. She said her goodbyes to Hugh, promised to have a new story for him within a month or so, and went home to drop off her portfolio. Travelling west on the tube, she wondered how she should approach Giles, still feeling guilty, yet bold with drink and more than a little horny as she remembered how good their sex together had been.

198

He had taught her so much, and made her appreciate her body in a way she never had before, in particular the full enjoyment of her bottom. It seemed a shame to lose his attention, and his love if he really was in love with her, but it was hard to reconcile that with her desire to give herself to Céleste. Possibly she could compromise because after all, Céleste had no right to full control, only when it suited Sarah.

She knew it was the alcohol making her brave, but it still seemed the right decision. Giles would be her lover, visiting her in her Paris flat for sessions of rude lovemaking, often involving the penetration of her bottom hole. While he was with her there would be no Céleste, but when he was gone Sarah would indulge herself in being made her heroine's plaything, punished and used for the pleasure of her tongue, made to perform for men or even sold on the streets.

When she reached South Kensington she knew what she would do, depending on whether Giles was there or not. She still had the keys, so she would let herself in anyway, as quietly as possible. If he was there she would simply step into his bedroom without a word and begin to undress, allowing him to join her. If he was out she would strip off and climb into his bed. Either way, she would soon be in his arms again or, knowing him, on her knees with his cock up her bottom.

She was smiling as she climbed up to street level, feeling both mischievous and naughty. His curtains were still shut, suggesting that he was in, and she opened the front door as quietly as she could manage, keen to surprise him. The stair was thickly carpeted, allowing her to ascend without a noise, up to the door at the very top. A faint noise from within assured her that he was there, and she slid the key into the lock with extreme care, turning it and easing the door wide.

A low moan sounded from the bedroom and her smile grew broader still as she wondered if she had caught him masturbating, only to vanish as she put her eye to the crack of the door. Giles was there, kneeling upright on the bed, stark naked, his erect cock extending forward to disappear between the full well-turned buttocks of a girl, quite clearly inserted in her anus. She was on all fours, her arms and legs braced to take her buggering, her big breasts swinging gently beneath her chest, her head thrown back in ecstasy, her glorious red hair spread out across her back and hanging down around her face, which was set in an expression of pure bliss as Giles continued to ease his cock in up her rectum.

Sarah stayed as she was, too appalled to speak, her eyes glued to Giles' erect shaft as it slowly disappeared up the girl's willingly offered bottom. Only when the full length was up did she finally react, her emotions raging, but even her sense of betrayal mild beside her shock at the identity of the girl Giles was buggering – Rebecca Compton-Bassett.

Thirteen

A week passed before Sarah felt ready to start inking in the last three episodes of 'Graverobbers'. Giles attempted to contact her several times, but she ignored him, quite unable to come to terms with what he had done, especially as, looking back, it was clear this relationship with his 'sister' had been going since long before she had met him. Most of all, she was glad she had split up with him first, rather than finding out months or even years into a long-term relationship.

The fact of her own infidelity made it easier, and she made a point of thinking about her experiences with Monsieur d'Orsay and the other Frenchmen the first time she masturbated, after four days of shocked abstinence. Even then she found herself unable to concentrate on work, until a phone call from Hugh Bowle to ask how she was getting on forced her to focus.

With three full episodes to do it was going to take at least a week, for which she was grateful, and she was determined to go to Paris the moment she had finished. Sat down at her work bench with her ink, brushes and all the necessary accessories set out, she began her task, stopping only for coffee and the loo until her eyes had begun to hurt and she was forced to stop.

An hour's rest and she had begun again, soon lost in her private Paris as she brought her pencil sketches to life in painstaking detail. It took two hours alone to create Antoine Saint-Coeur, with the need to make him slim yet strong, sensitive yet manly, handsome yet harsh. Only once she was satisfied with the first drawing of him did he seem to come to life, and she used her failed attempts for the faces and bodies of Céleste's legion of rejects, men she was nevertheless going to be privileged to take in her mouth one by one if it was demanded of her.

By the end of the day the first of the three episodes was half finished. She collapsed onto the sofa with a takeaway Chinese thoughtfully provided by Mak, half-asleep even as she ate and listened to him bemoaning the unattainable beauty of a new and unfortunately married colleague at work.

The following day was easier, with no new characters to create and a great deal of background detail to complete, which had always come easily to her. Céleste's apartment grew in form, to occupy the entire upper storey of a block on the Île St. Louis, with the long ironwork balcony directly above the river and looking across to the gardens of Notre-Dame. The furnishings were priceless antiques or modern classics, the walls were hung with impossibly expensive paintings, the glasses the finest crystal and the wines exquisite. Her bedroom was if anything more magnificent still, and all of it in stark contrast to the opposing corners showing Raoul's hate-filled scowl as he was led off to prison and Monsieur d'Orsay's leering pervert face as he contemplated blackmail.

By mid-afternoon the episode was finished, and after a mug of tea and half a packet of biscuits she set to work on the next, the brothel scene and her own grand entrance. It was slower going than the last, the interior of the brothel refusing to come together in her mind until she was forced to break off. A half hour searching the net for Toulouse-Lautrec posters and she was back, creating a piece of gilded baroque extravagance that formed the perfect background for herself as a curvaceous near-naked Parisian tart.

She gave up in the early hours of the morning and slept late the next day. Working on her own humiliation at the hands of Céleste and d'Orsay proved harder still, not for artistic reasons this time, but because every single frame brought her to such a state of arousal that her hands would start to tremble, forcing her either to break off for a coffee or to masturbate. The same problem persisted over the next two days, with Sarah becoming more and more lost in her private world. Hugh Bowle's instructions were forgotten, the full details of herself being urinated on by Céleste inked in with loving care, as were those of Monsieur d'Orsay buggering her and feeding her his dirty cock.

Dawn had begun to lighten the sky when she came to the final frame, but she was determined to finish, putting her heart and soul into the depiction of the two lovers as they stood together looking out over the Seine, and into her own image behind, plump and earthy in contrast to the ethereal elegance of Céleste and Antoine, her cheeky, well-whipped bottom on plain show beneath the skirt of her maid's uniform. By then she was lost completely, in absolute thrall to Céleste as she added one last detail, a patch of light visible through an open door to Céleste's kitchen, and on the floor a bowl piled high with dog food and inscribed with a single word, 'Cocotte'.

Exhausted, Sarah had to force herself to prepare the three completed episodes for the post and send them off, after which she collapsed into bed, too tired even to masturbate. As she drifted towards sleep her head was full of the images she'd been painting, Céleste and d'Orsay and Antoine, Madame Leboeuf from the brothel, her fellow girls and Céleste's suitors, all marching in procession through her brain and on into her dreams, with the Madame taking an ever greater role, until finally the harsh grating voice brought her awake once more.

'Get up, you lazy girl!'

Sarah sat up, bleary-eyed and disoriented, but with a jolt of adrenaline already setting her heart hammering. She was in bed, but not her own bed. The comfortable chaos of her room was gone, replaced by florid crimson and gilt, no longer the room of a young and disorganised artist, but a tart's boudoir. Outside, the dirty red brick of Stepney was also gone, and in its place a high façade of decaying stone and rusting ironwork, with what little sky visible dominated by the massive structure of the Eiffel Tower. In the doorway stood a woman; middle-aged, stern, with a harsh face heavily painted with make-up and dressed to gaudy excess, a woman Sarah knew only too well, having put the finishing touches to her just hours before – Madame Leboeuf.

'What are you gawping at, girl?' the Madame demanded, speaking thickly accented English. 'You're wanted in the salon, this minute. Now get up and get dressed, or do I have to take my stick to your rump?'

'No,' Sarah assured the woman hastily. 'I –'

She went quiet. No words could hope to express her feelings, and yet it was easy to respond to the threat of a beating. Scrambling quickly out of bed, Sarah began to dress, finding that she already knew not only what clothes she had, but which drawers they were in. Madame Leboeuf watched, her face set in impatience as she tapped the short dark cane she held irritably against one booted foot.

Sarah already knew how she would be dressed, as she had imagined a working girl was made to dress as she waited for clients – in a wasp-waisted corset of crimson satin that supported her breasts but did nothing to conceal them and left her bottom looking simply huge, along with seamed stockings held up by suspenders attached to the corset and knee-length velvet boots with heels so high she could barely walk. There was nothing to cover her breasts, her bottom, or her cunt, the only accessories a crimson velvet collar to match her boots and a spray of peacock feather tips for her hair.

She also knew how to prepare herself, just as she had shown girls doing in the background of her drawing, with plenty of make-up and scent, including a touch of rouge to each nipple and a dab of powder between her thighs. Dressed and ready, she felt impossibly lewd, also ridiculous and deeply ashamed of herself, although the last emotion was already fading with a helpless arousal she could do nothing about.

'Downstairs,' Madame Leboeuf ordered the moment Sarah had tied off the second of her boot laces.

Sarah scampered for the door as fast as she could, teetering on her heels with her bottom wobbling behind her to provide a perfect target of the Madame's cane. She was smacked all the way along the corridor, not hard, but enough to make her squeak and set her breasts jiggling as she struggled to move fast enough to escape. Only at the top of an impressive flight of marble stairs did the beating stop.

Below, just as Sarah had expected, the stairs opened out to a grand salon, furnished in the same lavish vulgarity as her room, with chairs and benches upholstered in crimson plush, gilt pillars carved as naked girls supporting the ceiling, huge mirrors and equally huge paintings showing nudes and scenes of debauchery, a deep carpet in the same bold shades, even a painted ceiling showing a full-breasted girl disporting herself with a satyr. There were plenty of people about too; the girls in their finery, corsets and stockings and little jackets, but every one of them bare where it mattered; clients in evening dress or crimson and gold robes provided by the house; a trio of boys in tight britches to serve the drinks, and two massively built, hard-faced Moroccans lounging by the door. Monsieur d'Orsay was also there, looking well pleased with himself as he sipped a pastis, and Céleste, the only decently-clad woman present, her perfect face cool and haughty, showing a touch of amusement as she watched her less fortunate sisters.

Sarah started down the stairs, her stomach churning wildly. She knew what was going to happen to her, in every vivid humiliating detail, and she knew she was quite incapable of resistance. Sure enough, she found herself curtseying automatically as Céleste saw her, and came to stand meekly at the foot of the stairs, with her head bowed, painfully aware of her exposed body, her face hot with blushes for her already hard nipples and the urgent need between her legs.

'*Oui, c'est la fille,*' Céleste remarked to Madame Leboeuf, then addressed Sarah. 'You have come to recognise your true nature, Sarah, yes?'

'Yes,' Sarah admitted.

'As a whore,' Céleste continued. 'Say it, Sarah, tell me what you are.'

'A – a whore, Mademoiselle du Musigny,' Sarah managed. 'I am a whore.'

She was trembling violently all over; a tiny part of her mind was still fighting her fate, but far more of it was not merely willing to submit, but urgent to be paid for and used so that it would become true. Céleste gave a light chuckle, expressing amusement and satisfaction, then spoke to Madame Leboeuf once more.

'Je voudrais l'engager pour plusieurs jours. Ça coûtera combien?'

'Son prix est mille euros par jour, Mademoiselle du Musigny,' the Madame replied, *'mais peut-être je pourrais vous faire une petite remise?'*

'Non, non, pas du tout,' Céleste insisted. *'Deux milles euros, pour deux jours.'*

Sarah had been struggling to understand, but as the awful truth sank in she found her voice.

'No . . . Céleste, please. You are supposed to buy me outright, to be your maid . . . your doggy slave, or anything.'

'Then perhaps you should have made that clear?' Céleste responded with rising amusement.

'But I want to be yours,' Sarah protested. 'I'll be ever so good. I'll do anything you say, anything!'

'What you will do,' Céleste responded, 'is return here to work that is fitting for you, as a whore, which as you admit yourself is what you are. Given that I do not normally move in such circles, it is highly unlikely you will ever see me again.'

'No!' Sarah protested. 'You can't do that, Céleste, you – ow! Ow! Ow!'

Madame Leboeuf's cane had been applied to Sarah's legs three times, and hard, sending her into a little frenzied dance with her hands clutching the backs of her thighs. Céleste smiled and moved to a table, where she began to count out notes to the Madame, both ignoring Sarah as if she did not exist.

'A pretty little show,' Monsieur d'Orsay remarked as he approached. 'Now stay still, and place your hands on your head. Come, come, you must learn to obey, and promptly, unless you wish further decoration on that plump *derrière*?'

'No,' Sarah responded, 'but look, please, Monsieur d'Orsay, I –'

'Uh, uh!' he interrupted. 'No talking. To talk is chief among the faults of woman, so save your inconsequential chatter for your sisters while I enjoy the one thing you have that is worthwhile, your body. Come, come, put your hands on your head, or must I really have you beaten?'

Sarah responded, burning with resentment and confusion as she obeyed his order. He immediately put a hand on her bottom and another to a breast, testing the texture and weight of her flesh, then beginning to stroke and tickle and pinch, until Sarah was squirming with frustration and helpless excitement. Only when Céleste stepped back from the table did he stop, to perform a somewhat mocking bow.

'*D'accord, Monsieur,*' Céleste stated. '*Elle est la vôtre, pour deux jours.*'

'*D'accord,*' Monsieur d'Orsay responded, tugging on his moustache. '*Voulez-vous monter? Je voudrais l'essayer.*'

As he finished speaking he gave Sarah a resounding slap on one bottom cheek, making her squeak and sending her staggering towards the stairs. Céleste hesitated, gave Sarah a brief glance of distaste and followed, unable to do otherwise. Still unable to think clearly, save for apprehension of what was coming to her, Sarah could only allow herself to be taken back upstairs, steered by pats and pinches from d'Orsay's hand to her bottom.

Her room was as she had left it, save that some thoughtful person had made the bed and set out a tray on top of the chest of drawers, a tray bearing a bottle of Champagne in an ice-bucket, two flute glasses with long crimson stems and gold rims, and two improbably large dildoes, both shaped in the fashion of monstrous black cocks. Sarah bit her lip, wishing she had been rather more restrained in her imagination. Monsieur d'Orsay moved to open the Champagne, speaking as he peeled the foil away with a single dextrous twist.

'Pour commencer, une bonne fessée, si vous obligeriez, Céleste.'

Céleste had already sat down on a straight-backed chair, an article Sarah knew existed in every bedroom in the brothel, placed there for the convenient discipline of the girls. Quite unable to resist, she went to drape herself across Céleste's lap, bottom raised in classic spanking position, her head full of consternation and yet grateful that at least she would be spared the humiliating process of having her bottom exposed, even if only because she was already on full show.

A pop signalled the removal of the Champagne cork and a smack the onset of Sarah's spanking. It was hard, and well placed, Céleste working Sarah's bottom with firm matter-of-fact slaps, a spanking given neither as punishment nor for arousal, but purely for the enjoyment of a voyeur. Nevertheless, Sarah experienced all the emotions of a punishment spanking, and the gradual swelling of her sex as she grew warm behind, quickly bringing her close to tears with frustration and pain.

Monsieur d'Orsay watched, sipping Champagne and occasionally moving position to admire either Sarah's bouncing bottom and the rude view between her cheeks and thighs, or the expressions she was making as the smacks fell. Occasionally he would squeeze his crotch, while Sarah could soon smell the natural excitement of her cunt even above the heavy perfume she had been given to wear.

Only when her bottom was a hot throbbing ball behind her did the spanking stop, by which time Monsieur d'Orsay's cock was hard in his trousers. Sarah winced as she glanced at his bulge, wishing she hadn't made it quite so grotesque but knowing she was going to suck it anyway. Part of her already wanted to; she climbed unsteadily from Céleste's lap and crossed to the bed without having to be told.

'Do it on your knees,' d'Orsay instructed her. 'Both holes, but first, let me watch you as Céleste opens your bottom hole.'

'Must I?' Céleste queried.

'I believe you must,' d'Orsay chuckled.

Céleste's face was a frozen mask as she crossed to the bed, on which Sarah had already adopted a crawling position. Monsieur d'Orsay was rubbing his hands with glee and Céleste removed one glove with a fastidious gesture. Sarah winced at the sight of Céleste's long painted nails, and forced herself to speak.

'Could – could you please find something . . . some sort of lubricant?'

'No doubt,' Monsieur d'Orsay responded happily. 'Hmm, you would have thought an establishment such as this would be amply provided with such things.'

'In the top drawer, on the left,' Sarah said, realising that she knew exactly where the anal lubricant was, and how much was in the jar.

Monsieur d'Orsay chuckled and pulled the drawer open, extracting a large jar of some thick paste coloured an unpleasant yellow. Céleste took it with a look of utter disgust and twisted the lid free to dip one elegant finger within. Sarah gave a heartfelt sigh and lifted her bottom a trifle more, making her cheeks spread for easier access to the tight pucker of her anus.

'You have only yourself to blame for this, Sarah,' Céleste pointed out as she wiped a quantity of lubricant between Sarah's open buttocks.

'I know,' Sarah responded, making a face as the cold slimy substance was smeared onto her sensitive skin, a sensation at once disgusting and soothing, especially on her smacked flesh. 'Actually, could you rub a little into my bum, I'm still smarting.'

'Absolutely not,' Céleste answered, and inserted a finger into Sarah's anus.

Sarah gasped as she was penetrated, her ring immediately tightening on Céleste's intruding finger. Beside her, Monsieur d'Orsay had approached the bed, and was fumbling one-handed with his fly, trying to get his cock out and drink Champagne at the same time. Sarah reached out to help, wondering at her instinct to be useful and obedient despite her very real revulsion for the cock she was about to take in her hand.

Out it came, as big and ugly as ever, fully erect, with the bulbous helmet glossy with pressure. Sarah began to tug at it, eager to get her ordeal over with despite knowing she would have to dildo herself and make him come in her mouth before she was done. It was getting hard to resist her feelings too, with Céleste's finger moving slowly in and out of her bottom hole as she was opened and her naked breasts rubbing gently on the bed covers as she masturbated Monsieur d'Orsay.

She gave in, always so much easier than resistance, twisting her neck to take Monsieur d'Orsay in her mouth. Céleste gave a brief mocking laugh and withdrew her finger from Sarah's anus, leaving the hole loose and ready. Sarah sucked for a moment more, then let him free of her mouth and scrambled up the bed to reach for the dildoes. Both were large, thicker than any man's cock, long and black and heavily veined, the monstrous phalli of her darkest fantasies, and yet she knew they would go in.

It was not easy. Squatting on the bed with her bottom thrust out and both Monsieur d'Orsay and Céleste watching, Sarah was obliged to twist and probe at the mouth of her cunt with the bigger of the two dildoes. Her flesh gave only slowly to the pressure, loosening gradually until at last her flesh was stretched out on the full width of the dildo. She began to fuck herself, easing the massive shaft a little deeper each time, and quickly gasping and sighing as she was overcome by the sheer intensity of the experience.

Only when her cunt dildo was wedged in to the hilt did she stop, changing position slightly to hold it in against the bed and flaunt her anus as she picked up the second, fractionally smaller dildo. It looked impossibly large, maybe twice the width of Giles' by no means small penis, and as she put it between her cheeks she was wondering if it really was feasible. The first push hurt, but she forced herself to relax and pretend she was on the loo, adding greatly to her humiliation as she felt her anal ring start to spread.

Again it had quickly begun to hurt, and she was whimpering with reaction as she pulled the dildo back a little and pushed again. Her ring spread a little more, and more still with the next push, opening slowly as she buggered herself, sobbing and gasping as she forced the fat rubber head bit by bit into her straining anus, but still it wouldn't fit.

'Get it in, you little slut,' Céleste said suddenly.

Before Sarah could react the dildo had been shoved firmly up past her reluctant ring and deep into her rectum, wringing a squeal of shock and pain from her lips and leaving her panting and shaking her head, but only for a moment before Monsieur d'Orsay took her by the hair and fed his cock into her mouth.

'Play with yourself then, *cocotte*,' Céleste laughed as Monsieur d'Orsay began to fuck Sarah down her throat.

Sarah was in no condition to obey, choking on d'Orsay's cock and dizzy from the huge dildoes bloating out her cunt and rectum. Only when Céleste planted a stinging slap across Sarah's buttocks did she begin to masturbate herself, as she knew she had to, wriggling on the intruding shafts and clutching at her sex in a desperate effort to get herself off and praying the experience wouldn't leave her anus so slack she would be forced to wear a plug.

To her vast relief Monsieur d'Orsay came quickly, spunking up down her throat and keeping a firm grip in her hair to force her to swallow, then pulling away to wipe his sticky cock in her face. She made to stop masturbating, only to have Céleste take hold of the dildoes again, both of them this time, and begin to work them in and out of Sarah's cunt and rectum. At the knowledge that she was being used by Céleste Sarah gave in completely, sticking her bottom out for more. She was moaning as she rubbed at herself, her eyes closed in ecstasy as her anus and the ring of her cunt pulled in and out on the huge dildoes, and crying out Céleste's name as she came.

'. . . Please, Céleste, yes . . . fuck me . . . use me, make me your slut . . . it's what I am, Céleste . . . please . . .'

She broke off with a choking cry, her orgasm too intense for speech, yet still desperate for Céleste's confirmation of her needs even as she shook and wriggled in climax. Céleste merely laughed, and Sarah was left to slump exhausted on the bed in utter confusion and the deepest misery.

As time moved on she found herself too numb to react, merely following orders as she was told to clean herself up and cream her aching holes. Madame Leboeuf then had her dress in a maid's uniform of black satin with a corseted waist, a low stiffened bodice that left her breasts supported in cups of lace with her nipples showing and a flounced skirt so short it failed to cover her bottom. She kept her seamed stockings and was put in black heels joined by a short chain to force her to take tiny mincing steps, then a collar and lead.

Walking behind Céleste and Monsieur d'Orsay as best she could, she was led through the streets of Paris, an obvious tart, drawing sneers and lustful glances from passers-by as she went. Monsieur d'Orsay lived in the Rue St. Dominique, opposite the church, an address as respectable as his position in life dictated, and yet as Sarah was led to his block and up the stairs it was she who drew the contemptuous disapproving looks and remarks, while he was treated with courtesy. Plainly it was acceptable for a man like him to enjoy a tart, but not to be one.

His apartment was exactly as she had imagined it, restrained and masculine, tasteful and understated, with only a selection of fine erotic prints to hint at his tastes. Sarah was trembling badly as she was led into the large bedroom with the *ensuite* bathroom to one side, and making involuntary little mewling noises through her closed lips. She knew exactly what was going to happen to her, and even Céleste looked nervous for once, speaking to her in a hiss as Monsieur d'Orsay poured himself a Cognac.

'Do not, whine, you little fool. This is your own doing!'

Sarah nodded miserably, opened her mouth to tell Céleste how much she would enjoy at least the first part of what was coming and to plead to be kept, then shut it again as Monsieur d'Orsay stepped back into the room. He was holding a bottle and three glasses, which he put down on his bedside table as he spoke.

'This will, I think, be more pleasurable for all of us with the assistance of a little Cognac, no? It is a *Grande Champagne*, Céleste my dear, a 'thirty-seven. Do help yourselves.'

'It would be a waste to serve the slut anything half so fine,' Céleste responded. 'Do you not have a peasant marc, or perhaps some cheap absinthe?'

'By all means, if you think it appropriate,' Monsieur d'Orsay answered. 'There is the absinthe the woman who does my cleaning drinks, with the green label.'

He made no move to get it, and Céleste left the bedroom. Sarah winced, knowing exactly what was going on, her drink spiked to render her vulnerable and damn Monsieur d'Orsay when the police arrived. Only as she took the glass of milky green liquid from Céleste's hand did she realise that she could play the same trick as had been played on her. After pretending to take a couple of sips she excused herself to visit the loo, tipping the contents of the glass into the bowl before she sat down.

Céleste and d'Orsay were talking outside, her voice cool but compliant, his full of lust as he described what he wanted done, in French too fast and with too many slang terms for Sarah to understand. She didn't have to. The scene was created to her own ideal: a spanking, oral sex with Céleste, being peed all over, then used by Monsieur d'Orsay. Every detail was clear in her head, her desire warring with her shame as usual, and as she dabbed a piece of loo paper to her sex she made a point of rubbing at her clitoris for a moment, determined to overcome her inhibitions as there seemed to be no option but to comply.

'Are you finished, Sarah?' Céleste demanded from the bedroom. 'If I must do this, we had best begin.'

'*Non, non, pas du tout,*' Monsieur d'Orsay began urgently, switching to English as Sarah came out from the bathroom. 'This is not the way. I do not want the false fumblings of whores who perform only for money. I want caresses, sensuality. I want you to make love!'

'I shall do my best, Monsieur d'Orsay,' Céleste responded, 'but you would do well to remember the circumstances of our associate.'

Monsieur d'Orsay shrugged, then spoke again.

'Come, come,' he urged, 'let us put such unpleasant details aside. Set aside your bitter thoughts, or indeed, all thoughts. Let your bodies speak for you, no?'

Céleste's response was a weary shake of her head, but there was unexpected warmth in her voice as she spoke again, already shrugging off the jacket of her smart black skirt suit.

'Come then, Sarah, he is right, is he not? We have no choice in what we do, so we must accept our fate, yes?'

Sarah thought of the police, and yet if there was irony in Céleste's voice it could not be detected. Nodding, she too began to undress, only for Monsieur d'Orsay to throw up his hands in an aggravated gesture.

'No, no, no! What did I say?' he demanded. 'Sensual, sensual! Climb onto the bed, undress each other, kiss and caress as your skin comes bare, as you would were you alone together.'

'It seems we must,' Céleste sighed.

'Yes, yes, you must,' d'Orsay confirmed. '*Alors, Céleste, du Cognac*? Sarah, another absinthe, this time neat, as Alfred Jarry drank it, although I think you need not go quite so far as he did and paint yourself green, no? Perhaps another time.'

He chuckled as he poured a generous measure of absinthe into Sarah's glass, passing it to her where she had climbed onto the bed before seating himself, glass in one hand and the other already working on his fly to flop out his limp penis as Sarah turned to Céleste. To her surprise, Céleste smiled and chinked her glass on Sarah's before taking a sip and setting it carefully down. Sarah imitated the gesture, already hoping against hope that Céleste might be persuaded to change her mind.

'We must undress each other, it seems,' Céleste said, this time allowing a touch of amusement to show in her voice.

Sarah nodded, her hands shaking badly as she reached out for the top button of Céleste's blouse. Just to touch was almost more exciting than she could bear, with the prospect of making love to her heroine so desirable she could barely breathe for her feelings. In contrast Céleste was calm, pinching the catches that held Sarah's corseted uniform close to let them spring open as she let go. Each little shock drove Sarah to distraction and made her trembling worse still as the dress came open across her belly.

With nothing beneath the dress, she was effectively bare as it fell away, her chained heels, stockings and collar her sole garments. To be naked for Céleste felt glorious, although her resentment at the watching Monsieur d'Orsay was rising, and with it came guilt

217

for her own behaviour, stronger than before. As she finally managed to get the third of Céleste's buttons open, revealing the gentle valley of her heroine's cleavage, she had begun to babble.

'I am sorry, Céleste, I am so sorry. Can you forgive me? I don't deserve it, but can you, please? I should be punished, I know, badly ... it's what I deserve, and I have tried ... I even made myself eat dog food, Céleste, just to punish myself ...'

Céleste gave her a look of surprise and not a little disgust, but put her fingers to her lips as she replied.

'Hush, Sarah. Do what we must do.'

Sarah nodded and smiled, forcing herself to concentrate on Céleste's blouse. There was no bra beneath, the small upturned breasts perfectly shaped despite being unfettered, and as Céleste's blouse came open it was more than Sarah could resist not to push her face between them, sobbing as she kissed the milk-smooth skin and, as Céleste cradled her head, bursting into tears.

Monsieur d'Orsay gave a pig-like grunt at Sarah's show of emotion, his hand now working on his cock, which had gradually begun to respond after his earlier orgasm. Fresh resentment and stronger guilt flooded through Sarah as she clung on to Céleste, now nibbling urgently at one neatly formed nipple and whimpering pleas for forgiveness into her heroine's chest until once more she was told to hush.

'Come,' d'Orsay drawled. 'Take her skirt off, Sarah. Let us see how expensive her panties are. Let us see that little bottom.'

'We must,' Céleste whispered, as Sarah hesitated.

'I want to,' Sarah sighed, lifting her face to Céleste's ear. 'I want to so badly, but not in front of that pig, not –'

'Hush!' Céleste urged for the third time. 'Have some more absinthe, you will feel better.'

Sarah broke away to take another swallow of the vivid green drink, draining the glass and leaving a trail of fire down her throat. Again she cuddled up, forcing herself to open the button at the rear of Céleste's skirt, to slip the tiny zip down and ease the garment low. As Céleste came bare Sarah felt the silk and lace of her panties, a sight that provoked another grunt from Monsieur d'Orsay.

'Now her knickers,' he grated. 'Nice and slow. Push your bottom out, Céleste.'

Céleste obeyed immediately, to Sarah's surprise, dipping her back to make her bottom a little round ball in the lacy panties, thrust out directly at Monsieur d'Orsay. Sarah had got Céleste's skirt well down, and took hold of the panties, her mind rebelling against her own action even as she peeled them slowly down to expose her darling's sweet firm cheeks to the grunting sweating voyeur, whose fat clammy cock was now half-stiff in his hand while the other massaged the bulky scrotum he had pulled from his underpants.

With Céleste's skirt and panties down, Sarah paused to refill her glass. She could already feel the absinthe getting to her, pushing the last of her inhibitions down and bringing out her rebellious spirit. Céleste had quickly peeled off her disarranged clothes, leaving her in nothing but the seamed stockings encasing her long and perfectly-formed legs, a sight that sent a shudder through Sarah's body despite the annoying grunts and meaty slapping noises made by Monsieur d'Orsay struggling to bring his cock to full erection.

'Show me your cunts,' he puffed. 'Both of you. Kneeling. And you must lick Céleste from behind, Sarah.'

Céleste hesitated only a moment before rolling onto all fours to lift her bottom, her slim thighs and neat cheeks doing nothing to hide the shaven pouted mound of her sex, nor the tight brown pucker of her anus. Sarah quickly got into the same lewd position, side by side with Céleste, their bottoms lifted for inspection, now biting her lip with aggravation for the way Monsieur d'Orsay was spoiling what should have been the perfect moment.

'A fine pair of tarts, aren't you, no?' he chuckled. 'Look at you, with your bottoms in the air, one no better than the other. Certainly your cunts are equally wet. Now, Sarah, get your tongue in up that hole, from the side, so I can see.'

Sarah responded, cursing him as she moved. Céleste looked infinitely desirable, despite being in such an undignified position, and lust had quickly won out over her rising anger. Coming close she allowed herself to take hold of Céleste's waist and thighs, pushing her head in to kiss the cream-smooth skin of one firm little buttock, the scent of woman now strong in her nose, and the taste in her mouth as she gave in to her needs, burying her face between Céleste's thighs to lick with desperate urgency.

She was licking another woman's sex for the first time in her life, something she had never dared admit she wanted, and not just any woman, but Céleste, with whom she had been in love for so long. Already she wanted to masturbate, Monsieur d'Orsay's crude attention set aside in her urgency, only for his voice to break in on her rising excitement as she found the swollen lips of her sex.

'So that I can see, I said, Sarah. Make her do as I say, Céleste, or you know the consequences.'

Sarah moved without waiting to be told, exchanging the uninhibited ecstasy of freely licking Céleste for the dirty, used sensation of doing the very same for the satisfaction of Monsieur d'Orsay. Now with her head pressed to Céleste's bottom, she extended her tongue, lapping at the fleshy pink folds and the minute glistening bud where they met. It still felt good, there was no denying it, and she began to massage her own sex as she licked.

'That's good,' d'Orsay grated, 'rub your cunt while you do it, my little slut, and now her anus, lick her anus.'

Céleste's body tightened briefly at the order, and Sarah hesitated, her eyes now fixed on the tiny dark brown hole she had been ordered to lick, a dirtier, more submissive act by far, and one she was powerless to resist. Her head moved higher, her tongue poked further out and she was doing it, lapping at the puckered anal ring, pushing in up the central hole, tasting her lover's bottom as she clutched at her own eager cunt, already close to orgasm and, as Céleste sighed in involuntary pleasure, Sarah came.

'That is good,' d'Orsay panted, his cock now hard in his hand. 'Now make her do it, make the proud bitch show she is a woman like any other. Do it!'

Sarah was still coming and ignored him, her tongue pushed deep in up the tight ring of Céleste's anus where she felt it most belonged. Furiously willing d'Orsay to go away, she continued to lick, her face once more buried between the slim bottom cheeks, her tongue pushed in as deep as it would go, and to her delirious joy Céleste had began to whimper and moan. Sarah was still rubbing, and her climax hit a new peak at the response.

With a last tender kiss to Céleste's anus she moved lower, licking her darling's cunt as she masturbated herself to peak after peak after peak. Céleste's moans grew louder, her much-vaunted dignity now gone as she began to wriggle her bottom in Sarah's face and beg to be licked harder. Sarah obliged, her nose now pushed to her lover's wet bottom hole as she lapped, faster and faster, to the sound of ever greater excitement, until at last Céleste came, gasping out her ecstasy under Sarah's tongue and begging for more until at last she went limp.

Sarah rocked back on her heels, panting for breath, dizzy with drink and lack of air. Céleste sank slowly down on the bed, falling sideways to look up at Sarah with half-lidded, happy eyes, only for her expression to change to sudden surprise. Sarah twisted around, expecting to find Monsieur d'Orsay behind her, his erect cock held out for insertion in her cunt or anus, but he wasn't. He was gone.

Fourteen

Monsieur d'Orsay was not merely gone from the room, but from the apartment, a complete puzzle until the sound of an altercation from the street below drew Sarah to the window. Three storeys down, two armed gendarmes were manhandling Monsieur d'Orsay towards a car. He was shouting and expostulating wildly, while his cock and balls still hung from his trousers.

'He is down in the street,' she said, unnecessarily as Céleste had joined her at the window.

Sarah moved back, conscious that she was in nothing but seamed stockings and high heels, as was Céleste. They exchanged glances. Sarah shrugged.

'He could not have taken the stairs,' Céleste said.

'He went,' Sarah said. 'I didn't want him there, and he just went. He must have run down.'

'With his penis showing?' Céleste queried.

Again Sarah shrugged.

'And why would he,' Céleste went on, 'when he was taking such pleasure in our humiliation . . . mine at least.'

'You did come, Céleste,' Sarah answered, still bold with drink, 'and never mind Monsieur d'Orsay. He is gone . . . I made him, I think, because I didn't want him watching.'

'You made him watch!' Céleste exclaimed.

'I know. I'm sorry,' Sarah said. 'I didn't know how I'd feel.'

'How you would feel?' Céleste demanded. 'What of how I would feel? You are my creator, and you parade me in front of perverts like him, for money! You disgust me, Sarah.'

'I . . . I don't even understand!' Sarah wailed.

Céleste gave a sharp intake of breath, then flourished her arm towards the window, a gesture of infinite exasperation.

'This, Sarah,' she said, 'all of it, it is yours, and what do you do? You sell yourself for a few miserable pennies, and me also. We might have lived in the palace of Versailles, you and I, but no, you have me stripping for perverts and debasing myself with the scum of the streets!'

'I – I didn't know!' Sarah answered. 'I'm sorry, Céleste, but I really didn't, and I still don't understand.'

'Do you need to understand?' Céleste asked. 'Do you understand gravity, or infinity?'

'No,' Sarah admitted. 'Céleste, could we start again, do you think? You have punished me, and I have punished myself as well.'

'I punished you because you needed me to,' Céleste responded, 'and as for your disgusting habits with dog food, I would rather not know, although, yes, it is the least you deserve. Frankly, I think you should return to Madame Leboeuf's brothel. It is where you belong.'

'I belong at your feet,' Sarah responded.

Céleste gave a snort of contempt.

'Ah yes, you wish to be my maid, to serve me, until you get drunk, and then . . . then you will have me giving myself to tramps in the street so that you may soothe your pride for what you chose to do in the first place.'

'I won't, I promise,' Sarah answered. 'I'm drunk now, quite drunk, but I'm coming to accept my nature, and you know your own, Céleste. You came, didn't you, just now.'

'How could I not?' Céleste demanded. 'Nobody – no man, because as you well know I have never been with a woman before – nobody has done that to me, not like that.'

'I will,' Sarah promised, 'every night. I'll be your plaything, Céleste. You can do anything to me, all the things you like but dare not admit to, because you are cruel, Céleste, I made you cruel. You can punish me too, you like to punish me, don't you?'

'How can I help it?' Céleste answered.

'You can't,' Sarah told her.

The attic above Céleste's apartment was a bare simply furnished place, suitable for a menial, although far more comfortable than was immediately apparent, and with a perfect north light for drawing. From the windows the rooftops of Sarah's private Paris spread as far as she could see, a constant source of pleasure and of inspiration.

She was seated at her art desk, the same familiar one she had used since college, although a new and expensive model stood to one side, purchased specifically for inking in. The new cartoon was coming on well. Hugh Bowle had given her the go-ahead for the idea, and she was sure he would approve of the results. She had entitled it 'An English Girl Abroad', although she knew that was likely to be changed for something more laddish. The heroine was Becky Wellington, and it followed her exploits as she attempted to seduce one man and one woman from every European country in order to comply with a freak will left by an eccentric and perverted uncle, a simple plot designed to provide exactly what the readers wanted, plenty of breasts and bottoms. For her own amusement Sarah had added the stipulation that a different sex act had to be carried out on each occasion, and that it had to be performed at a recognisable national monument or in some national-istic style. She had already completed the first epi-sode, establishing the plot and showing Becky sucking cock for a London cabbie in the back of his vehicle while parked near Big Ben.

Next would come the seduction of a woman in London, possibly a smart city girl seduced to oral sex in her own office, then Paris, the details of which she had yet to decide on. With each episode covering two countries, a man and a woman for sex and two distinct sex acts, Sarah had calculated that she would need forty-six double page episodes including the first and last needed to open and conclude the plot. The project would take four years to complete, and would keep her amused as it became increasingly difficult to work out national settings for countries like Moldova and Estonia, while the sex acts would need to grow increasingly bizarre.

She was smiling as she laid down her pencil, completely happy with life. It was time to go down-stairs, which meant getting dressed. She padded over to her wardrobe, casting a critical eye over the contents. One of her maid's uniforms would be needed later, but it was hard to choose between one with a skirt so short she would have to endure the humiliation of having her panties or bare bottom showing, or one of the more respectable ones so that she would suffer more if she had to be exposed for spanking.

Before then, she needed something suitable to wear while she was pissed on, which was an even more difficult choice. An expensive gown with silk underwear beneath had a certain appeal, for the thrill of having it ruined, but then she didn't have to pay for it anyway. Tight clothing was perhaps better, so the urine-soaked cloth would cling to her flesh as she masturbated in Céleste's puddle, or possibly woollens to make the biggest possible mess.

None of it quite suited her mood. After a thoroughly businesslike conversation with Hugh Bowle and an hour of sketching she was feeling pleased with herself, the ideal situation from which to be brought down. Yes, that was it, she would wear her smart new skirt suit, which reflected her mood and would allow her to experience the full emotional intensity of being urinated on, while the pale-grey wool would show the wet perfectly.

She chose cotton underwear to go underneath, tight white panties that would cling to her wet skin and a full bra with cotton cups so her nipples would show through. Stay-up stockings and a white blouse added to the image she was building, along with smart black shoes with sensible heels and, last, the knee-length skirt and neatly tailored jacket of the suit. She put her hair up and added a touch of mascara and lipstick, then inspected herself in the mirror. The smart young businesswoman in the reflection definitely did not look as if she wanted to have another woman urinate on her head, which was perfect.

Trotting smartly downstairs, Sarah called for Céleste, who was in the kitchen, reading *Le Figaro* and making a late breakfast of a croissant, coffee and a suspiciously large glass of orange juice. She wore only a short bathrobe, with her elegant legs crossed and extended towards Sarah, who immediately got down on her knees and kissed her lover's foot.

'I don't know what you are grovelling for, Sarah,' Céleste remarked. 'It will make no difference.'

'I know, Mademoiselle du Musigny,' Sarah replied.

Céleste didn't bother to reply, but went back to reading her paper. Sarah stayed as she was, kneeling on the hard tiles of the kitchen floor, her head bowed respectfully, Céleste's foot almost in her face. Five minutes passed, and ten, Céleste ignoring Sarah completely as she finished her breakfast and leafed through the paper. At last Céleste spoke.

'I see they are trying to get around the ban on using non-traditional building materials. You must put a stop to it.'

'Of course, Mademoiselle,' Sarah answered.

Céleste folded the paper and placed it carefully on the breakfast table, turning to look down on Sarah with an amused smile.

'So,' she said, 'you are to be urinated on.'

'Yes, Mademoiselle,' Sarah responded.

'You are a disgusting little tart,' Céleste told her, standing up from the chair. 'What are you?'

'A disgusting little tart.'

'Look up at me.'

Sarah looked up, between Céleste's lean shapely thighs, cocked a trifle apart, to the neatly formed, newly waxed sex, held open to show the pink interior and the tiny hole from which she was about to be given her faceful.

'Open your mouth,' Céleste ordered, and Sarah's mouth came open immediately. 'Good girl. Now, I am going to urinate in your mouth, which I hope will help you to appreciate how far you are below me, yes, to take my waste in your mouth and over your body, Sarah.'

Sarah nodded urgently. A soft whimper escaped her throat, and a tiny ecstatic gasp as Céleste let go, expelling a stream of sparkling pale-yellow piddle full into Sarah's open mouth. Sarah's senses filled with the pungent feminine taste of Céleste's urine, which quickly filled her mouth to bubble out around her lips and pour from her chin, over her suit jacket and her blouse, down her cleavage too, to wet her breasts and belly. She pulled her blouse wide, taking her breasts in her hands and massaging the piss-wet material over the heavy sticky globes as yet more piddle splashed in her mouth and face.

She shut her eyes as Céleste aimed her stream higher, soiling Sarah's hair and sending a rivulet of hot piddle down the back of her collar. Now shivering with pleasure as she squeezed her own breasts and rubbed the piddle into her belly and stocking-clad legs, Sarah already knew she was going to have to come then and there. Quickly she pulled her skirt up, exposing the crotch of her panties, at which Céleste took a step back, to aim the last of her piddle between Sarah's thighs.

Her mouth was still full, and she held on, massaging her soggy panty crotch as her pleasure rose, determined to swallow Céleste's pee only at the very moment of orgasm. Already she was close, her cunt as wet with her own juices as it was with Céleste's urine. She pushed her fingers deep, pressing the wet cotton of her sodden panties into the slippery groove between her sex lips. She was ready to swallow, to fill her belly with the wonderful gift of her lover's pee, when Céleste spoke.

'Not yet, Cocotte. I have a little something extra for you today, then you may come. Now swallow what is in your mouth.'

Sarah obeyed without hesitation, swallowing down her acrid hormonal mouthful as she stopped masturbating. Her whole body was trembling, her need for orgasm close to overpowering, but she held off, waiting obediently as Céleste moved around the kitchen. At length a wet cloth was pressed to her face, cleaning her eyes so that she could open them to look up at Céleste, her robe open at the front to show off her cunt and the turn of her buttocks. Sarah stuck her tongue out in hope.

'Later,' Céleste told her, 'when you are not quite so filthy. For now, you may pleasure yourself, but only once you have eaten. Do not be long. I want you ready in one hour.'

'Yes, Mademoiselle du Musigny,' Sarah answered.

Céleste strode from the room naked, her robe dropped into the puddle of urine as she left.

Sarah looked to the side. On the floor was a plain plastic bowl, labelled with her pet name, Cocotte, and piled high with a lumpy glistening pile of dog food. She winced despite her excitement, but crawled over, unable to resist Céleste's command. Somehow being dressed didn't seem right for eating dog food, and she began to strip off, peeling away her soiled clothing bit by bit, an exquisitely disgusting process that left her trembling harder than before, so that by the time she was down to her wet panties she could no longer contain herself.

Her face went into the dog food, pushed down as she adopted a crawling position, her hand already back between her legs as she started to eat, gobbling down the slimy smelly pulp with rising eagerness. She could feel it going down her throat, while the smell and taste and texture had her close to being sick even as she clutched at her eager cunt with her orgasm rising in her head and dirty thoughts running through her mind.

She stopped, inspired to be ruder still, holding back with an effort as she tensed her bladder and deliberately let go into her panties, the urine spraying out through the thin cotton, all over her hand and between her legs. More trickled down to drip from her belly and over her breasts where they were squashed out on the floor, also wetting her thighs and soaking up into the seat of her panties.

Only when she'd quite finished did she start to eat again, revelling in having wet herself and the state she was now in – sodden with Céleste's urine and her own, face down in a bowl of dog food as she swallowed mouthful after mouthful of the repulsive muck, until her belly was nicely bloated out, when she began to masturbate again, teasing her sex lips through her soggy panties, rubbing more firmly, tugging the piss-sodden cotton tight up between her bulging bottom cheeks, rubbing again, burying her face in what remained of the dog food, clutching at her cunt as she began to lick at the bowl, and coming, in a screaming shuddering orgasm so powerful it brought her to the edge of fainting before she finally collapsed on the filthy tiles of the kitchen floor in exhaustion, still mumbling Céleste's name over and over.

Sarah hung her head as the beautiful young man threw his coat to her and passed on without a second glance, not from shyness or because he made her feel small, but to hide her smile. Around her, the party was in full swing, the apartment crowded almost to capacity. Over fifty of Céleste's suitors were there, handsome young men from Paris and beyond; aristocrats from many of the oldest families in Europe, men of wealth and consequence, the sons of politicians and industrialists, up-and-coming artists and renowned sportsmen, stars of stage and screen. Their behaviour towards Sarah varied from easy condescension through amused contempt to absolute indifference, attitudes that only made her smile. Most of them she had created that very afternoon, every single one was desperately in love with Céleste, and every single one was doomed to failure, even the exquisite Antoine Saint-Coeur. When Céleste chose her lover that night it would not be a man at all. It would be Sarah.

She had chosen her shortest uniform, the one she had been given at Madame Leboeuf's brothel, as to have her bottom and breasts showing provided a constant gentle humiliation embellished with sharper pangs of the same sweet emotion when one or another guest remarked on her unfashionably plump curves. After two hours she was already in a state of rapture, and she knew there would be no release until the early hours of the morning, when Céleste had managed to dispose of the last of the men. Until that time she had to serve, taking coats and passing drinks and, if Céleste thought it appropriate, providing sexual relief for those men unable to contain themselves any longer.

All the guests had now arrived, and Sarah took the last of the coats to her room, tossing it casually on the floor for future reference. Returning downstairs, she made her way to the kitchen. The men were precisely as ineffectual as she would have expected and, while eager to serve Céleste, had very little idea of the practicalities involved. The refrigerator door was open, for one thing, apparently due to somebody's determination to select a bottle of Champagne from the very back and failure to return the others properly.

Sarah quickly rearranged the bottles and selected one, a vintage Krug, which she opened and poured into glasses on a tray, taking one for herself. Céleste had decided that Sarah should drink only in moderation, but she was sure she had come to terms with her sexuality and would not inflict any further humiliations on her lover, so had already allowed herself enough to make her pleasantly tipsy. The Krug was delicious, also cold and refreshing, so Sarah poured herself a second glass and swallowed it down before taking the tray out into the main room of the apartment.

The men paid little or no attention to her, some taking glasses, others not, but very seldom thanking her and then in a distant or superior manner. Most were in little groups, talking among themselves, with a few standing aloof. Céleste moved among them, seeming to glide in her designer gown and shoes, her body clearly naked beneath, providing a constant provocation to the men, many of whom already looked fit to burst.

Sarah's tray was soon exhausted, and she went back to the kitchen to fill it again, this time taking her glasses out to the roof garden, where a number of men stood looking out over the rooftops, apparently lost in contemplation or possibly attempting to project an air of mystery that might entice Céleste to notice them. One even appeared close to tears, exciting Sarah's sympathy as she offered him a glass of Champagne.

'Are you all right?' she asked. 'You look upset. Perhaps I can help?'

She smiled and pushed her chest out a little, eager to indulge herself in the intensely humiliating pleasure of taking him in her mouth or between her breasts while she knew he was fantasising over Céleste. He barely glanced at her, and downed the Champagne at a gulp, then took another glass.

'I could help,' Sarah suggested. 'Mademoiselle du Musigny says I am to assist the guests in any way they please, any way at all.'

'*Allez-vous-en!*' he answered. 'Go away, you fat little horror. To think of you in her place, ugh!'

He shook his head, as if dispelling some unpleasant image.

'As sir wishes,' Sarah said softly, 'but I am available to your command.'

She curtsied and was about to move away when he began to speak again, now with rising emotion and gradually losing control of his language.

'How . . . how can you offer yourself in her place? *Vous . . . vous, la petite boulotte . . .* you little dumpling, you little ape . . . *et vous osez dire . . .* and you dare to think I, a poet and a man of sensitivity, might even think of accepting you in place of her! *C'est comparer le divin avec l'avili, une déesse avec tant de – de* – so much pig's offal . . .'

He broke off with a shriek of dismay, having attempted to strike a dramatic pose with one hand on the rail of the roof garden and missing completely. Sarah leant over the edge, watching as he cartwheeled screaming through the air and hit the Seine with a splash, then long enough to make sure he hadn't actually drowned! Somehow she was not in the mood for quite such intense verbal humiliation, at least not from him.

'Do behave yourself, Sarah,' Céleste remarked as she stepped outside.

'I'm sorry, Mademoiselle du Musigny,' Sarah replied. 'Shall I fetch a whip for myself, or will a spanking be sufficient?'

Céleste peered down into the Seine, where the poet was making heavy weather of swimming for the nearest ladder, then spoke.

'A spanking, I think. Come indoors.'

The sudden firmness in Céleste's voice sent a powerful thrill through Sarah, almost as strong as the one from the threat to spank her. She was already shivering hard as she trailed after Céleste, her head hung low. The tray she placed to one side, scurrying after Céleste towards the straight-backed Louis Quinze chair they had set aside for Sarah's punishments.

Céleste didn't bother to make an announcement, spanking her maid being a task far too trivial to need drawing attention to, while she was automatically the focus of the room in any event. Sarah was simply taken across the knee, her tiny flounced skirt turning up of its own accord to expose the full plump ball of her bottom, which Céleste immediately started to smack.

Sarah couldn't help but sigh as the stinging slaps began to fall, her ecstasy at being punished by Céleste and in front of so many good-looking young men easily pushing aside the pain. In response Céleste began to spank harder, until at last Sarah began to kick and wriggle. Her breasts had flopped free of her bodice and had quickly started to bounce to the rhythm of her spanking, adding an extra touch of shame to her enjoyment as she was punished.

One or two men made remarks, complimenting Céleste on her no-nonsense attitude to domestic discipline, each one sending Sarah a touch higher, and all the while with the relentless smacks landing on her hot bare bottom, until at last she'd begun to wonder if she would come just from spanking alone, only for her soaring arousal to be interrupted by the crash of a door and a cry of masculine pain, then a voice, a quintessentially English voice.

'How about picking on somebody a bit nearer your own size, you stuck-up Froggie bitch?'

Sarah tumbled to the floor, legs akimbo and cunt spread to the world as Céleste gasped in shock. Becky

Wellington stood in the open doorway, her magnificent head of flame-red hair almost touching the lintel, her green eyes ablaze, her impressive chest heaving, her hands placed on her powerful hips. She wore riding boots, jodhpurs, a starched white blouse and a tailored jacket in hunting pink. In her hand was a wicked-looking riding crop.

The scene had frozen, but only for a moment, before Céleste squealed in shock and fear, trying to scramble away as Becky came forward. Not a single man moved to help the object of their adoration, each and every one rooted to the spot and gaping like so many goldfish as Céleste was caught, dragged back to the spanking chair and flipped over Becky's knee with cool and practised skill. Sarah finally managed to react, raising a finger.

'B – Becky –'

'Don't worry, sweetheart,' Becky answered. 'I'll take care of the little minx. Right, Céleste, spankies time! Let's see what your knickers are like today, eh?'

Even as she spoke she had begun to pull Céleste's gown up, to the accompaniment of piercing desperate shrieks and frantic kicking. Becky merely laughed, and when the dress stuck, she bunched her arms and ripped it wide, all the way up the back, tugging it free to leave her victim stark naked save for her designer heels and a pair of black stockings with a seam at the rear.

'No knickers at all, eh?' Becky chortled. 'You dirty French trollop! Oh well, save me the effort of pulling 'em down, I suppose. Right ho, how's this for my Parisian exploit, Sarah sweetie? I'm going to spank the bitch and make her lick me out.'

Sarah's attempt to speak was drowned out as Céleste responded to the news with a long drawn out howl of inexpressible dismay, which abruptly broke

236

to squeaks and gasps as Becky laid in, smacking her hand down on the firm little bum cheeks with all her force. Still the men held back, although in one or two cases shock had given way to prurient interest in Céleste's rear view, with not only the little round bottom on plain show, but her neatly waxed cunt and the dark brown pucker of her anus. Again Sarah managed to find her voice.

'No, Becky . . . Becky don't spank her . . .'

Becky stopped.

'You're right, darling,' she said. 'What she needs is a dose of my riding crop.'

'No, I mean –' Sarah began, but too late.

Becky had already laid in, smacking the broad leather sting on her crop down on Céleste's already pink bottom to draw ear-splitting squeals and a crazy wriggling motion from the helpless Frenchwoman, with her long legs kicking in furious disarray and one fist thumping frenziedly on the carpet.

Sarah pursed her lips, trying to concentrate on making Becky stop it, only to realise that however appalling the sight of Céleste being spanked might be, it was also powerfully arousing, maybe only because of the Champagne she'd drunk, but still . . .

'She likes it,' she said softly. 'She can't help it . . . she's always wanted it . . . see how wet she is . . . she wants to lick Becky too, and so do I.'

'That's you dealt with, you,' Becky announced as she dropped the riding crop. 'Now how about a portion of juicy English cunt?'

Céleste dropped to the floor as she was released, sitting dazed as Becky quickly pushed down her jodhpurs and the panties beneath to bare her full richly-furred sex. As she sat down her thighs were wide open, revealing how excited she was, but no more so than Céleste, whose own normally neat cunt was puffy with excitement and slippery with cream.

'Lick me,' Becky demanded, 'and don't stop until I've come. No, better still, Sarah can lick me, if you'd like to, sweetheart? Céleste, you can do my bumhole.'

As she spoke she had moved a little further forward on the chair, leaving her cheeks sticking out over the edge with her pinkish brown anal star showing between. Céleste had come up into a kneeling position, classically submissive, with her bottom pushed out, and yet there was still horror in her eyes as she focused on Becky's anus.

Again Sarah hesitated, but there was no going back. Crawling forward, she pressed her face to Becky's cunt, licking eagerly as she took a firm grip in Céleste's hair. The response was a little mewling sound, but Sarah knew Céleste wanted to lick. After all, what Sarah wanted was what Céleste wanted, always would be and always had been, only now she understood. Sure enough, Céleste's pointed tongue poked out, to lick between Becky's bottom cheeks, and on her anus.

nexus

The leading publisher of fetish and adult fiction

TELL US WHAT YOU THINK!

Readers' ideas and opinions matter to us. Take a few minutes to fill in the questionnaire below and you'll be entered into a prize draw to win a year's worth of Nexus books (36 titles)

Terms and conditions apply – see end of questionnaire.

1. Sex: Are you male ☐   female ☐   a couple ☐?

2. Age: Under 21 ☐   21–30 ☐   31–40 ☐   41–50 ☐   51–60 ☐   over 60 ☐

3. Where do you buy your Nexus books from?

☐ A chain book shop. If so, which one(s)?

_____

☐ An independent book shop. If so, which one(s)?

_____

☐ A used book shop/charity shop
☐ Online book store. If so, which one(s)?

_____

4. How did you find out about Nexus books?

☐ Browsing in a book shop
☐ A review in a magazine
☐ Online
☐ Recommendation
☐ Other _____

5. In terms of settings, which do you prefer? (Tick as many as you like)

☐ Down to earth and as realistic as possible
☐ Historical settings. If so, which period do you prefer?

_____

☐ Fantasy settings – barbarian worlds
☐ Completely escapist/surreal fantasy

- ☐ Institutional or secret academy
- ☐ Futuristic/sci fi
- ☐ Escapist but still believable
- ☐ Any settings you dislike?

_____

- ☐ Where would you like to see an adult novel set?

_____

6. In terms of storylines, would you prefer:

- ☐ Simple stories that concentrate on adult interests?
- ☐ More plot and character-driven stories with less explicit adult activity?
- ☐ We value your ideas, so give us your opinion of this book:

_____

_____

_____

7. In terms of your adult interests, what do you like to read about? (Tick as many as you like)

- ☐ Traditional corporal punishment (CP)
- ☐ Modern corporal punishment
- ☐ Spanking
- ☐ Restraint/bondage
- ☐ Rope bondage
- ☐ Latex/rubber
- ☐ Leather
- ☐ Female domination and male submission
- ☐ Female domination and female submission
- ☐ Male domination and female submission
- ☐ Willing captivity
- ☐ Uniforms
- ☐ Lingerie/underwear/hosiery/footwear (boots and high heels)
- ☐ Sex rituals
- ☐ Vanilla sex
- ☐ Swinging
- ☐ Cross-dressing/TV
- ☐ Enforced feminisation

☐ Others – tell us what you don't see enough of in adult fiction:

_____

_____

_____

8. Would you prefer books with a more specialised approach to your interests, i.e. a novel specifically about uniforms? If so, which subject(s) would you like to read a Nexus novel about?

_____

_____

_____

9. Would you like to read true stories in Nexus books? For instance, the true story of a submissive woman, or a male slave? Tell us which true revelations you would most like to read about:

_____

_____

_____

10. What do you like best about Nexus books?

_____

_____

11. What do you like least about Nexus books?

_____

_____

12. Which are your favourite titles?

_____

_____

13. Who are your favourite authors?

_____

_____

14. **Which covers do you prefer? Those featuring:**
    (tick as many as you like)

☐ Fetish outfits

☐ More nudity

☐ Two models

☐ Unusual models or settings

☐ Classic erotic photography

☐ More contemporary images and poses

☐ A blank/non-erotic cover

☐ What would your ideal cover look like?

_____

15. **Describe your ideal Nexus novel in the space provided:**

_____

_____

_____

_____

16. **Which celebrity would feature in one of your Nexus-style fantasies?**
    We'll post the best suggestions on our website – anonymously!

_____

THANKS FOR YOUR TIME

Now simply write the title of this book in the space below and cut out the
questionnaire pages. Post to: Nexus, Marketing Dept., Thames Wharf Studios,
Rainville Rd, London W6 9HA

Book title: _____

TERMS AND CONDITIONS

NEXUS NEW BOOKS

To be published in December 2006

SILKEN EMBRACE
Christina Shelly

The Bigger Picture is a radical and powerful organisation of dominant women intent on turning young men into ultra glamorous she-males to become housemaids that serve wealthy women and demanding men. Shelly manages to escape the strict training program and shelters with Mrs Ambrose, a beautiful and glamorous widow who runs a rival academy. But it's not long before the beautiful and severe agents of The Bigger Picture track her down and return her to captivity, where her erotic torments and re-education continue, with an even greater creativity and extremity than ever before.

£6.99   ISBN 0 352 34081 9

WHALEBONE STRICT
Lady Alice McCloud

Petticoats, corsets, frilly knickers, lace, and canes – all part of the Imperial world inhabited by Thrift; a young and naïve foreign office agent sent on special missions on behalf of the empire. In *Whalebone Strict*, Thrift Moncrieff's assignment for the British Imperial Diplomatic Service takes her to the North American colonies, where she is supposed to compromise the position of a politician. In this she is rather more successful than she had planned, leading her ever deeper into difficulties that more often than not lead to the opening of her ankle length corset and elaborate underwear, either for the entertainment of a string of lecherous men, or to have a hand applied to her delectable buttocks.

£6.99   ISBN 0 352 34082 7

IN FOR A PENNY
Penny Birch

Penny Birch is back, as naughty as ever. *In for a Penny* continues the story of her outrageous sex life and also the equally rude behaviour of her friends. From stories of old-fashioned spankings, through strip-wrestling in baked beans, to a girl with unusual breasts, it's all there. Each scene is described in loving detail, with no holding back and a level of realism that comes from a great deal of practical experience.

£6.99   ISBN 0 352 34083 5

If you would like more information about Nexus titles, please visit our website at www.nexus-books.co.uk, or send a large stamped addressed envelope to:
Nexus, Thames Wharf Studios,
Rainville Road, London W6 9HA

nexus

This information is correct at time of printing. For up-to-date information, please visit our website at www.nexus-books.co.uk

All books are priced at £6.99 unless another price is given.

------✂------------------------

Please send me the books I have ticked above.

Name ....

Address ....

....

....

.... Post code ....

Send to: **Virgin Books Cash Sales, Thames Wharf Studios, Rainville Road, London W6 9HA**

US customers: for prices and details of how to order books for delivery by mail, call 888-330-8477.

Please enclose a cheque or postal order, made payable to **Nexus Books Ltd**, to the value of the books you have ordered plus postage and packing costs as follows:

UK and BFPO – £1.00 for the first book, 50p for each subsequent book.

Overseas (including Republic of Ireland) – £2.00 for the first book, £1.00 for each subsequent book.

If you would prefer to pay by VISA, ACCESS/MASTERCARD, AMEX, DINERS CLUB or SWITCH, please write your card number and expiry date here:

....

Please allow up to 28 days for delivery.

Signature ....

Our privacy policy

We will not disclose information you supply us to any other parties. We will not disclose any information which identifies you personally to any person without your express consent.

From time to time we may send out information about Nexus books and special offers. Please tick here if you do *not* wish to receive Nexus information.   ☐

------✂------------------------